"Don't make _____ _____ *than it was,"* Skye warned.

The instant she spoke the hateful words, she wished she could call them back. She saw a hint of anger enter Cash Benedict's green eyes.

"Is that what you think I'm doing?" he asked. "How did *you* see that summer?"

Skye shrugged with feigned casualness. "You were a hired hand. An employee who took unfair advantage."

Cash's turbulent gaze moved over her body with a thoroughness that left her shaken. She felt the color drain from her face.

Damn him! And damn her for still caring....

It was Cash's turn to shrug. "Strange," he said. "Maybe it's you who isn't recalling things correctly." He shook his head. "The way I remember it," he drawled, "I didn't take anything that wasn't offered."

Dear Reader,

Welcome to Silhouette **Special Edition**...welcome to romance. March has six wonderful books in store for you that are guaranteed to become some of your all-time favorites!

Our THAT SPECIAL WOMAN! title for March is *Sisters* by Penny Richards. A dramatic and emotional love story, this book about family and the special relationship between a mother and daughter is one you won't want to miss!

Also in March, it's time to meet another of the irresistible Adams men in the new series by Sherryl Woods, AND BABY MAKES THREE, which continues with *The Rancher and His Unexpected Daughter*. And continuing this month is Pamela Toth's newest miniseries, BUCKLES AND BRONCOS. In *Buchanan's Baby*, a cowboy is hearing wedding bells and the call of fatherhood. Rounding out the month are *For Love of Her Child*, a touching and emotional story from Tracy Sinclair, Diana Whitney's *The Reformer*, the next tale in her THE BLACKTHORN BROTHERHOOD series, and *Playing Daddy* by Lorraine Carroll.

These books are sure to make the month of March an exciting and unforgettable one! I hope you enjoy these books, and all the stories to come!

Sincerely,

Tara Gavin
Senior Editor

Please address questions and book requests to:
Silhouette Reader Service
U.S.: 3010 Walden Ave., P.O. Box 1325, Buffalo, NY 14269
Canadian: P.O. Box 609, Fort Erie, Ont. L2A 5X3

Penny Richards

SISTERS

Published by Silhouette Books
America's Publisher of Contemporary Romance

For Colby Skye, whose toothless, dimpled smile has brightened
my days and my life. I love you.
Special thanks to Judi and Jimmy Reihmann, my Amana connection.
Thanks for showing me your wonderful world of Amana
(I love it!), for making me welcome in your home
and for answering my dozens of questions.
Thanks also to Debbie Rabalais for helping with the details of
Jeb's "accident" and to Louis Marz of the Amana Heritage Society
for his kindness and patience in answering my questions.

 SILHOUETTE BOOKS

ISBN 0-373-24015-5

SISTERS

Copyright © 1996 by Penny Richards

This edition published by arrangement with Harlequin Books S.A.

® and TM are trademarks of Harlequin Books S.A., used under
license. Trademarks indicated with ® are registered in the United States
Patent and Trademark Office, the Canadian Trade Marks Office and in
other countries.

Printed in U.S.A.

Books by Penny Richards

Silhouette Special Edition

The Greatest Gift of All #921
Where Dreams Have Been #949
Sisters #1015

Previously published under the pseudonym Bay Matthews

Silhouette Special Edition

Bittersweet Sacrifice #298
Roses and Regrets #347
Some Warm Hunger #391
Lessons in Loving #420
Amarillo by Morning #464
Summer's Promise #505
Laughter on the Wind #613
Sweet Lies, Satin Sighs #648
Worth Waiting For #825
Hardhearted #859

Silhouette Books

Silhouette Christmas Stories 1989
"A Christmas Carole"

PENNY RICHARDS

is the "real" name of writer Bay Matthews, who has been writing for Silhouette for ten years. Claiming that *everything* interests her, she collects dolls, books and antiques. She has been a cosmetologist, an award-winning artist, and worked briefly as an interior decorator. She loves movies, reading, research, redoing old houses, learning how to do anything new, Jeff Bridges, music by Yanni, poetry by Rod McKuen, flea markets, yard sales and finding a good bargain. She lives in Louisiana, with her husband of more than thirty years, has three children and seven grandchildren, all whom she loves dearly. Always behind, Penny admits to procrastination and working better under pressure. She claims she's trying to simplify her life, but just decided to take up quilting and crocheting.

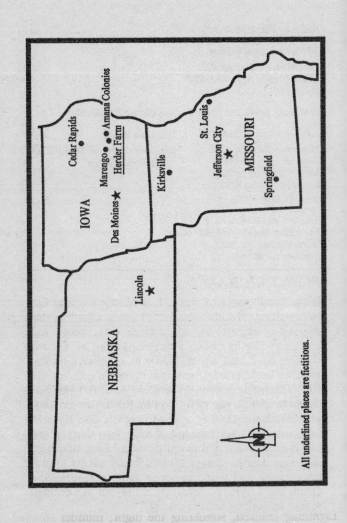

All underlined places are fictitious.

Prologue

1977

He was so wrapped up in his thoughts of her that he mistook the rattling at the door for the wind. It was only when the sound came again that he realized someone was there. He raised himself to one elbow, wondering if something was wrong.

The aperture framed a feminine silhouette. Surprise rendered him speechless, and he drew up the single sheet to cover his nakedness.

It occurred to him that she might be a figment of his fertile imagination, a vision conjured up by his erotic thoughts and the wine he'd had earlier.

The screech of the hinges as the door opened one slow inch at a time warred with the sound of the howling wind. Lightning cracked, sundering the night; thunder snarled

through the heavens. A sudden gust snatched the door free
and sent it crashing against the wall. He fumbled for the
switch of the lamp sitting on a nearby table. Instantly, the
small-wattage bulb suffused the room with a soft glow. Her
gaze locked with his.

Barefoot, she stood before him, wineglasses clutched in
her left hand, the other palm pressed against her heart, as
if it—like his—beat too fast for comfort. The bodice of her
white eyelet sundress tied behind her neck and clung to her
narrow midriff and small waist. The skirt flared out from
her hips and floated around her shapely calves with each
step she took.

A chill wind billowed the curtains at the window. She
shivered. The soft, fine cotton of her dress adhered to her
small breasts so intimately there was little doubt she wore
nothing underneath.

Color enhanced the sweep of her cheekbones. Her lips
gleamed with a vibrant scarlet hue. Soft aqua shadow and
mascara defined the eyes that met his, eyes filled with reckless abandon and—what? Fear?

His own heart beat out a wild rhythm. He was afraid to
dare think what his mind was telling him. He was afraid to
say anything. Speaking might break not only the silence but
the spell binding them, as well. He might awaken to realize
that this was nothing but a dream.

She sat on the edge of the mattress; he froze. With a
smile—a little wry, a little sad—she set both glasses on the
end table and, to his never-ending amazement, reached out
and framed his face with her hands. Then, miraculously, he
felt her lips—undemanding and corn-silk soft—touch his.

The kiss couldn't have lasted more than a second or two,
but it seemed like an eternity. An eternity when his heart
pounded so hard the noise it made inside him was serious
competition to the thunder rolling across the greening fields

of corn. An eternity where his blood surged through his veins like the wind rushing through the open doorway. An eternity he prayed would never end.

She lifted her mouth from his and looked at him with her familiar directness. She trailed her fingertips down his cheeks to his throat. Traced his collarbones. He felt the roughness of the calluses on her hands despite the delicacy of her touch and was seized by a singular, sweet pang of sorrow that had no place in the moment, a sorrow he lacked the experience to understand.

Her hands skimmed downward, over the hair of his chest to his stomach that tightened in response. Cool wind gushed through the open window, carrying the first smattering of cold raindrops, chilling his feverish body. Lightning split the darkness. The scent of ozone and hunger hung in the air.

Thunder rolled through the heavens. The night shuddered, trembled, as he did. He spoke her name, and it was a question. A plea. A benediction.

"Shh," she said with a shake of her head. "Shh..."

This time the kiss was longer. This time he recovered enough to respond briefly before the image of another kiss flickered through his mind. Guilt held him motionless.

Attuned to his withdrawal, she lifted her head to look at him.

How could he tell her he'd kissed her sister this way? That he'd touched her? And how could he tell her that he'd never done what they were about to do?

Her soft smile of understanding was as tender as her touch. She knew.

"Shh," she said again, taking his hand and carrying it to her breast. "Shh."

In a matter of seconds, everything, everyone was forgotten. The storm raging outside might not have been. They kissed—feverishly. They touched—ravenously. She untied her dress. He unzipped it. He'd been right; she wore nothing underneath. Her body was smooth, firm, supple beneath his eager, clumsy hands.

She fit him just right, like a key in a lock. And when he finally rocked against her in a final burst of passion, he thought he might die from the depth of pleasure that exploded inside him.

Later, much later, a palm skimmed over a sweat-dampened flank. "I love you."

"You don't know what love really is."

"I do know! *This* is love."

"This is lust."

"It's the same thing."

A sigh. "It isn't the same thing at all."

A touch. "It's close enough."

A gasp. "Maybe so." Reluctantly. "Maybe so...."

Chapter One

May 22, 1977
Dear Diary,
You won't believe this! Susan has hired positively the best-looking boy in the world to take George Braunfels's place for the summer. His name is Cash Benedict, and he's staying in the garage apartment. He has sort of medium brown hair and green eyes, and eyelashes to make any Maybelline model jealous. He rode up on a bright red Harley-Davidson. He's from Lincoln, Nebraska, and says he's just "bumming around" for the summer. Susan says he's got a chip on his shoulder as big as Texas and that he's green as a gourd, but he looks strong and honest, which counts for a lot in her book. Personally, I think he's dreamy. Susan says she hopes she won't be sorry for hiring him. She's got to be kidding!

The Present

Dark clouds roiled across a bruised and brooding afternoon sky. Cash Benedict plunged his hands into the pockets of his slacks and peered out the courthouse door. A covey of media vultures lay in wait at the base of the wide steps where a dust devil whirled a gum wrapper and fresh grass clippings in a wild pirouette. He sighed. The sensation seekers must be starving for a scrap of news if his divorce generated this much interest.

Thunder growled; the earth moved; the glass in the doors rattled. The imminent arrival of the storm was the perfect conclusion to a day that had been a fitting finale to the past year of his life, a life that held all the stability of the dust devil he'd seen seconds ago.

Claiming she was tired of playing second fiddle to his work, Liz, his wife of fifteen years, had moved out ten months before, taking with her their eleven-year-old daughter, Darby. Cash's sister, Ceil, had gone through a bitter divorce, and Cash Benedict, Sr., had died, following his wife after three short months.

To add to the general misery and stress level, one of the six Benedict magazines that dealt with the life-styles of farming and ranching had shut down two short weeks after the senior Benedict was buried, after being in print for more than thirty years. Just yesterday the corporate attorney had informed him that if something drastic wasn't done fast, Benedict Periodicals ran the risk of losing a second magazine.

Considering the devastating events of the past year, it seemed fitting that, just moments ago, the judge had banged the gavel and ended Cash's marriage, placing the blame squarely on his shoulders.

Cash cast a jaundiced eye at the nasty-looking sky. The way things were going, he'd probably get struck by lightning the minute he started for the car. Daring whatever gods controlled his life, he took a deep breath and pushed through the courthouse doors.

"Mr. Benedict! Mr. Benedict!"

Instantly, Cash was assaulted from all sides by a barrage of questions. Muttering an occasional curse and the ever-popular and highly pointless "No comment," he shouldered his way through the determined journalists, who continued to pummel him with questions.

Across the way, he saw Liz and Darby in the midst of another batch of reporters. Liz's beautiful face wore the same smug look she'd adopted when she'd been awarded a staggering cash settlement and a more than fair share of their community property.

Cash's foul mood deepened. As the old country song went, Liz had gotten the gold mine, and he'd gotten the shaft. His only victory was that the judge had given them joint custody of Darby. His daughter, however, had refused to meet his gaze when the judge announced his decree, which only strengthened Cash's suspicion that Liz had mounted a one-woman campaign to widen the gap between him and his only child.

Though he wasn't proud of it, Cash knew it was his fault that he and Darby weren't close, that, like his father before him, he had given his daughter neither the time nor the attention she deserved. He also knew that bridging the rift between them would take considerable effort on his part. It meant having a serious talk with Liz about her attempts to drive a wedge between him and Darby.

Cash brushed aside another question and focused his gaze on Darby's pale face. Surrounded by the persistent reporters, she looked scared to death and very close to tears. He damned Liz and himself for adding to Darby's pain. Maybe he should play the knight in shining armor and rescue her from the clutches of the cold-hearted media. He could take her to lunch and try to help her get a perspective on the drastic changes the divorce would make in their lives.

And how do you propose to do that? You haven't been able to get much of a perspective yourself.

His lips twisted. The very least he could do was buy Darby a cheeseburger and tell her that despite what her mother might be saying about his inability to love or commit to anything or anyone because of his commitment to Benedict Periodicals, he did love *her*. With all his heart.

"Is it true another of your magazines is in trouble?" a brassy blonde asked, broadsiding him with the well-aimed salvo about his professional life.

Cash's jaw knotted. "Read about it in the *Wall Street Journal*." He pushed past the reporter, intent on reaching Darby.

Detecting his approach, Liz looked up, giving him the full impact of her frigid gaze at the same time as she drew Darby closer in an action that dared him to come nearer.

Cash paused. He wasn't up to another scene, especially in front of a dozen media representatives. He couldn't stand to see his failure displayed for the world to see. He couldn't bear to hear the nagging voice of his conscience that castigated him for putting work before his family. Telling himself he'd done it to secure their future didn't grant him much comfort. He just wanted to forget it, to run to the farthest ends of the earth, even though he'd learned long ago that running never solved anything. The problems were always there when you returned.

Lightning popped; thunder boomed, aggravating the pounding in his head. Without so much as a nod to Liz to acknowledge that she'd won yet another battle, he continued down the steps. He didn't shake the reporters until he slid behind the wheel of his champagne-tinted Lexus, and then probably only because the heavens opened in a sudden deluge.

Safe inside the privacy of the car, Cash switched on the windshield wipers and pulled into the afternoon traffic. The blades swished back and forth in a synchronized frenzy, trying in vain to sweep away the rain flinging itself at the windshield.

Cash hunkered down and crossed his forearms over the top of the steering wheel, peering through the pounding rain as he negotiated the rain-slick streets of Lincoln. He never even realized when he left the city behind, had no idea what direction he was headed. He had no final destination in mind, no estimated time of arrival, no purpose except to put as many miles as possible between himself and the remnants of his shattered life. . . .

A jagged bolt of lightning flashed against the faraway horizon, flung by a mighty, unseen hand. A sullen drumroll of thunder faded into forever. The sound jolted Cash from the numbness that had crept into his brain, into his very soul, as he'd guided the car through the storm-ravaged darkness.

Aware of his surroundings for the first time in hours, he realized with a start that it was almost morning and that he had no earthly idea where he was. The rain had diminished to a light mist, and the eastern sky was that dull, gunmetal gray that precedes the start of a new day. The storm's fury was spent.

So was he. He scrubbed a weary hand down a bristly cheek. After driving through rain—sometimes a blinding rain—for almost twelve hours, he was whipped. Tension

knotted his shoulders. His eyes burned from lack of sleep.
He was past ready to find a motel and crash.

As if on cue, his headlights sliced through the gloom, il-
luminating a state highway sign in the distance. Good Lord!
He was in Missouri.

In a matter of minutes, a sign advising him that he was
entering Kirksville flashed past. A billboard telling him there
was a motel ahead loomed in the glow of the headlights.
Cash drew an exhausted, thankful breath. He was tired.
Tired of the pressure. Tired of the worry. Tired of giving his
life's blood to his father's dream. He'd find a hotel, catch a
few Zs and figure out what he should do when he woke up.

Within five minutes, he was taking a key from a leaden-
eyed night clerk. A few minutes after that he was unlocking
number 225. The room was a clone of a hundred others he'd
stayed in: clean and tasteful, if uninspired. He pulled off his
clothes and crawled between the crisp white sheets, too tired
to shower, too tired to even dream.

When Cash opened his eyes and rolled to his side, the
clock radio on the nightstand told him it was almost noon.
Considering how spent he'd been, he was surprised he
hadn't slept around-the-clock. He called room service to
bring him a pot of coffee, showered and put on the shirt and
slacks of the suit he'd worn to the death of his marriage. It
was a testimony to his state of mind that he'd left town
without so much as a change of clothes. Three cups of coffee later, he switched off the cable news station, dialed
Benedict Periodicals and asked for his sister.

"Cash!" Ceil Rafferty cried, forgoing a salutation.
"Where the devil are you?"

Cash's mouth quirked at the irritation in his sister's voice.
He could picture her pacing the bank of windows that
flooded her office with light, her sleek blond hair coiled in

an elegant, sedate knot at the nape of her neck, her dark brown eyes even darker with worry. Ceil was as smart as the legendary whip, a hard worker and a worrier, and, even though they'd both been adopted by the senior Benedicts and shared no common blood, they couldn't have been more alike if they'd drawn personality traits from the same gene pools.

"And a good morning to you, too, sister dear," he said. "How's it going?"

"How do you think it's going?" Ceil snapped. "Bart has been on the phone a dozen times already this morning, wanting to know where you've gone off to, Gage is insisting I let him have Seth for the month of August and Liz called to tell me in great detail how upset Darby is because you didn't say anything to her after you left the courtroom."

Cash felt his smile fade and his mouth tighten. Though all the things she'd told him were important, his attention focused on Darby's distress...or rather, Liz's version of Darby's distress.

"I did try to see her, but Liz was holding court with the media, and when I tried to get close, she gave me one of those don't-even-think-about-it looks."

"Hey," Ceil said, "don't bite off my head, big brother. I'm just passing on the message."

"Sorry," Cash replied, squeezing his eyes shut and pinching the bridge of his nose.

"Sure." There was a slight pause before Ceil asked, "So, where are you, anyway?"

"Kirksville, Missouri."

"Why on earth are you in Kirksville, Missouri?"

"I have no idea. I guess I was driving on automatic pilot."

"That's dangerous, Cash."

"No lectures, please," Cash said, knowing as he said it that worry lay behind her scolding. "I had a few things on my mind. Let's just call it a moment of insanity. I'll start home in an hour or so."

"Don't."

"Don't what?"

"Don't come home yet. Why don't you take a few days off?" Ceil suggested, surprising him with the generous and very appealing offer.

"We're about to lose a magazine. Now isn't a good time for me to take a vacation."

"Make it a working vacation, then. Drive around and see if there's something we haven't covered in the magazines. Find us some fresh angles and some new and interesting people. Maybe you can come up with something that will save all our hides."

"Aren't you afraid I might never come back?" Cash teased.

"Nah!" Ceil said flippantly. "You're too much a Benedict to desert your responsibilities." When Cash didn't make an immediate reply, she said, "Don't worry about this place. I can handle things here."

"I know that, but you could stand to take a little time off yourself."

"Don't worry about me. If Seth goes with Gage in August, I plan on taking Samantha on a long vacation and leaving you holding the bag. Now stop arguing. I can handle this place."

"What about this deal with Gage?"

A long silence stretched over the phone lines. Cash knew Ceil was mulling over this newest request from the husband she'd divorced soon after she found out he'd been cheating on her.

"He says Seth needs him right now. That boys need their fathers at this age. He's right. I know that, but..." Her voice trailed away. "I can handle it."

Cash heard the pain underlying the decisive statement. Ceil had been cut to the quick by Gage's cheating, but he knew she was right. She could handle Gage and the attorneys and the magazines.

"Okay, then," he said at last. "I'll see you in a few days."

They said their goodbyes and, with a promise to call soon, Cash hung up. After grabbing a club sandwich in the motel's restaurant, he drove to a nearby department store and charged several changes of casual clothes to his credit card. After buying some necessary toiletries he got out his atlas and looked up the town of Kirksville, Missouri. He tapped his finger on the map as remembrance dawned. No wonder this place seemed familiar. He'd come through the area nineteen years ago when he was just nineteen.

A lot had changed since that summer, but a lot was the same, too. He hadn't been driving a Lexus. He'd left Lincoln on his motorcycle, the only thing that truly belonged to him. But he'd been running then, just as he was running now. Running away from a future he didn't want and the certain death of his dreams.

Cash swore at the pain of the old memories and put them out of his mind, the way he always did when they dared to surface. He'd long ago made his peace with his father and accepted the finality of the decision he'd made that August, but every now and then, when the memories rose from the place he'd buried them, he was seized by a sense of having lost something vital to his happiness.

"So don't think about it," he said out loud as he turned the key in the ignition and pulled on to the highway that ran through the town. "It's all water under the bridge."

Cash soon left the city limits of Kirksville behind, but despite his vow not to think of the past, the memories came swirling through his mind.

This time he didn't try to stop them. . . .

He had been barely nineteen that summer, with a year at the University of Nebraska behind him. His grades were good, and he liked college life just fine. The problem was, he liked baseball more. Impressed with his freshman season, a carryover from his impressive high school performance, a scout from the majors had come sniffing around.

"They're gonna offer you a contract," the coach told him. "I can feel it. If they do, you'd be crazy not to go for it."

"But what about getting my education?"

The coach had maintained that people got educations to get good jobs to make money. If Cash played pro ball, he'd be set up for life. He could always go to college when his career in the majors was over. "You're a natural, son. Playing ball is bred into you."

When Cash had approached his father later, Cash senior had hit the ceiling. Playing baseball wasn't a real occupation, and there would be no professional ball players in that family. Cash's future was with Benedict Periodicals.

Cash argued that he didn't want to run Benedict Periodicals. He wanted to play ball. It was in his genes. A gift from his real father.

Cash still remembered the fury on Cash senior's broad face as he'd shouted that *he* was Cash's real father, that being a real father was more than donating sperm. It was taking responsibility for your actions and providing for your family, a role he'd taken on gladly. He'd ended his raging tirade with, "You and your sister *owe* me!"

Strange, Cash thought as the words reverberated through his mind; the anger and pain inspired by Cash senior's statement were as vivid now as they had been when he'd spoken it nineteen years ago. As Cash had grown older, he'd been able to understand his father's position, even though he might not approve of it, but at that moment, all he had been able to see was that his dream was going down the tubes.

Cash remembered telling his dad that he must have misinterpreted the reasons for his and Ceil's adoptions. He thought they'd been chosen because they were loved and wanted, not because Cash senior was looking for a future chairman of the board. He didn't know he was supposed to feel indebted to the Benedicts for adopting him and Ceil over the other kids at the orphanage.

"I may not have fathered you," Cash senior had stated, obviously shaken by Cash's outburst, "but I do love you. Why else do you think I've worked so hard to have something to leave to you and your sister?"

"If that's your version of love, it stinks," Cash shouted. "All you've ever given us are *things*. Did it ever occur to you that we'd rather have had you at home with us than off building your damned magazine empire?"

Cash senior's face paled, and he looked as if he'd been seized by a sudden terrible pain. Cash turned and headed for the door. "And just for the record, I'm signing the contract if they offer it."

"The hell you will."

The coldness of Cash senior's statement halted Cash at the door. His father had demanded that he hand over his car keys and told him in no uncertain terms that he should find a place to move. He wouldn't provide a roof over the head of a selfish ingrate like Cash.

Cash had been shocked but knew that his father meant what he said. Ceil was in Europe with a favorite aunt, and there was no one for him to talk to. More lonely and confused than he could ever recall, he had had no choice but to do as his dad commanded. He had drawn out all his savings, climbed onto his motorcycle and headed out of town, leaving his mother standing on the steps of the Benedict mansion, tears streaming down her cheeks.

The memory of those tears still cut Cash to the quick. He'd gone without a backward glance, with no more of an idea where he was headed than he'd had yesterday when he fled the disaster of his marriage. All he'd known was that he needed to get as far away as possible.

Throughout the last couple of weeks of May, he'd ridden his Harley from town to town, never staying in one place too long, driven by his rage and a feeling of lonely impotence. One day near the end of the month, Cash had crossed the state line between Missouri and Iowa. There was something about the gently rolling hills and the bright green corn stretching from horizon to horizon that gave him a feeling of peace. The air seemed cleaner; the sun beamed more brightly. The farms, with their pristine white houses and rust red barns nestling in the dark green ocean of corn, looked like a photograph that might grace the cover of a Benedict magazine.

Cash knew instantly that he could find contentment there. At a place called Marengo, he'd stopped at several farms to see if anyone needed help. Everyone said the same thing. "Try the Herder place over near Amana."

Through his inquiries, Cash learned that Mrs. Herder had been widowed three or four years before. She and a full-time employee, George Braunfels, had been running the fifty-acre farm, and George had been hurt in a tractor accident a week or so back. Everyone seemed to think that the chance of Mrs. Herder hiring him on for the summer was good.

Situated near the river, between West and South Amana, the fifty-acre Herder farm sat smack-dab in the middle of the twenty-six thousand acres owned by the Amana Society, a religious group that had come to settle the area in 1854.

Cash located it without much trouble. S. Herder was painted in a childish scrawl on the side of the battered mailbox. The farmhouse was a simple white two-story frame with forest green shutters. The only concessions to elegance were the pillars supporting the porch that ran the width of the house and the leaded-glass window lights on either side of the front door.

Cash parked the motorcycle behind the ancient pickup sitting in front of a single-car garage, set his helmet on the seat and headed down the concrete walkway. A plethora of vibrantly hued flowers edged both the sidewalk and the porch. Dozens of beds of different flowers and foliage were scattered throughout the expansive lawn that extended from the house to the copse of trees separating the yard from the river.

As Cash stepped onto the porch, a woman drying her hands on her apron shouldered her way through the screen door.

"What can I do for you?" she asked in a husky contralto.

"I'm looking for Mrs. Herder."

"I'm Susan Herder."

Cash couldn't hide his surprise. "I mean Mrs. Herder, the, uh . . . widow."

The woman's shapely mouth lifted at one corner, and a fine network of lines radiated from the corners of her eyes that were a pale ice blue. "I'm Mrs. Herder . . . the widow."

Cash couldn't hide the stunned expression that crossed his features. He expected the widow Herder to be old and unattractive...widowish looking. This woman was in her early thirties—far from old—and very attractive.

Tall and slender, her form and bearing brought to mind the adjective *willowy,* though he wasn't certain where he'd heard the expression. It looked as if she spent a lot of time in the sun; her fine, shoulder-length hair was so blond it was almost white, and her skin was tanned a golden brown.

Not only was she attractive, there was a look in her eyes Cash found intriguing: an unlikely combination of wry bitterness, shy wariness and a haunting loneliness. It was that loneliness he responded to, that soul-deep sadness that he identified with on some elemental level.

"What did you want to see me about?"

The sound of her voice shattered the silence and ended his scrutiny.

"Uh . . . a job," he said, recovering his voice. He pushed a lock of hair off his forehead, raking his fingers through the traditional, short style he wore at his father's insistence. "I heard your hired hand got hurt and you were looking for some help for the summer."

"I need some help," Susan Herder acknowledged. "Some reliable help. Not some soft kid who doesn't know his way around."

"I catch on fast," he said, her attitude sparking a sudden irritation.

Susan Herder smiled. "Look, I don't want to offend you, but you don't look as if you've done a hard day's work in all your—what? Eighteen years? I don't have the time or the patience to hold anyone's hand."

Anger and embarrassment flushed his face. "I'm nineteen," he snapped, "and if there's one thing I am, it's reliable. I'm smart, and I learn fast. I can handle anything you want from me."

Susan Herder's blue eyes held his for long, silent seconds. Cash refused to look away, refused to give in to the urge to squirm. Finally, she expelled a harsh sigh.

"The job is room and board and fifty dollars a week, paid every Friday evening." She jerked her head toward the driveway. "The room's over the garage. It isn't fancy, but it's clean. I'll do your laundry and clean up once a week, but I expect you to help keep the place decent. There's a hot plate, but you can take your meals with us if you want. Take it or leave it."

"Us?" he queried.

"I beg your pardon?" she said, a blank look on her face.

With a shrug, Cash shifted his weight to one leg and planted his hands on his denim-covered hips. "You said 'us.' Who's 'us'?"

"Me and my sister, and sometimes my father-in-law."

It was Cash's turn to nod. "Fine."

"You'll take it?"

"Yeah."

"I was afraid you would."

Cash thought about asking her what she meant by the ambiguous statement and decided against it. He had the job. There was no sense upsetting the applecart. "When do you want me to start?"

"In the morning," she said. "I'll send Skye out to show you to your room. You can unpack and clean up while I finish supper. We'll eat in about thirty minutes. I hope you like roast."

Cash's stomach rumbled at the thought of something besides fast food. His relief at finding a job helped ease the tension he always felt when he first met someone. He smiled for the first time since he'd stepped onto the porch. "I love roast."

Susan Herder's shoulders straightened imperceptibly, and she drew in a slow, measured breath. "I'll send Skye out," she said, turning away.

"Mrs. Herder."

Halfway through the door she paused and faced him again.

"You won't be sorry," he promised.

That weary, self-deprecating smile made another appearance. "I hope not," she said with a sigh. "I really hope not."

An eighteen wheeler passed the Lexus, spewing dirty water onto the windshield. Memories scattered like a flock of geese before a gun blast, and the sudden urge to go back seized him in a powerful grip. Good Lord, Skye would be a woman by now, almost the same age Susan had been. His pulse quickened at the thought.

He pulled to the side of the road and got out his map. His amused laughter filled the car's interior. He was already headed north, toward Iowa. The state line was just a few miles away. Mentally he traced the route he'd taken when he'd started out the day before. His subconscious had led him down the same path he'd taken years ago, and it looked as if some intuitive force was luring him back toward the Amanas.

Well, why not? Why shouldn't he look the Herder women up? They were . . . friends, weren't they?

They were more than friends, Benedict.

True. Skye was the first girl he'd wanted so badly he'd hurt. Skye was the lush, starry-eyed fourteen-year-old who'd offered herself to him so unashamedly one sultry summer night.

And while Susan might have considered herself nothing but his employer, she was far more than that to him. Susan Herder had been employer, friend, confidante. The thirty-year-old Widow Herder was the woman who would always hold that special place in a young man's heart, the first woman to whom he'd ever whispered the words "I love you."

Chapter Two

June 7, 1977
Cash is working out better than I expected. He doesn't know
much about farming, but he's a quick study, and he doesn't
seem to have a lazy bone in his body. Skye is smitten, as I
knew she'd be. He takes her adoration in stride and is pretty
patient with her questions and her hanging on. Funny how
seeing her in the throes of her first love brings back so many
memories. I remember those feelings, but I can't remember
ever being that young and innocent. I watch them and, God
help me, it makes me feel so lonely. So alone.

"You know what's wrong with you?"

Jeb delivered the question with one corner of his shapely
mouth lifted in what Skye thought of as his snotty sneer.
After finding a condom in the washing machine, she and
Jeb were discussing the wisdom of his ongoing relationship

with Belinda Krammer—if a yelling match could be considered a discussion.

Belinda was a hot little number with a 38D bra size and an IQ to match. The thought of Jeb jeopardizing his whole future for a few minutes of sex was a constant source of conflict between them.

"No, but I'm sure you're going to tell me," Skye said in a weary voice.

"It's been too long since you had good sex."

Skye gasped, and Jeb had the decency to allow a brief look of remorse to flicker in his eyes. "I'm sorry," he muttered. "I didn't mean to get your panties in a wad."

Skye strove to gather her scattered equilibrium. How had she gone so wrong with Jeb? "Let's leave my panties and my sex life out of this," she snapped. "What's more to the point is that if you and Belinda don't cool it, you might end up in a Lamaze class instead of freshman algebra at the university."

"We're careful."

Skye's laughter was as brittle as old parchment. "So are ninety-nine percent of all the people who have kids they didn't plan on, as you should certainly be aware of."

A muscle in Jeb's jaw knotted. "Yeah, yeah." He picked up his motorcycle helmet.

"Where are you going?"

He turned and headed toward the front door. "Out."

Skye grabbed his hard-muscled arm. He impaled her with a fierce gaze. "We're not finished talking about this."

"Oh, yes, we are," he said, pulling free. "Look, I'm eighteen. This is none of your business."

"As long as you live under this roof it is!"

"Well, that's a situation that I can remedy real fast," he said, pushing through the screen door.

The not-so-subtle implication filled her with a familiar panic. All they'd done the past year was argue, and Skye was petrified that he'd resort to moving out instead of trying to solve their differences. "Jeb, wait!"

He turned.

"I love you," she told him in a husky voice. "Don't hate me because I want more for you than a wife and a baby at the age of nineteen. You have a scholarship. A chance to do something with your life besides work at some backbreaking job seven days a week. Don't mess it up. Please."

He didn't answer, but the tension left his features. Without a reply, he turned and clattered down the steps.

Skye went out onto the porch and watched him sling a long leg over the saddle of the red Harley in an achingly familiar gesture. Jeb donned the helmet, started the bike and peeled out down the driveway. Squinting against the glare of the afternoon sun, she watched as he pulled onto Herder Loop, the three-mile half circle that led to the highway. She swallowed hard. Jeb looked so much like his father it was uncanny.

And that, she knew, was part of their problem.

It was midafternoon when Cash turned onto Herder Loop. His mouth felt as if it were filled with cotton, and his palms were damp on the steering wheel. It occurred to him that he might be on a fool's errand.

The doubts fled as the car topped a small rise and the house came into view. He slowed to a crawl, drinking in the sight of the woods, the flowers, the outbuildings. It all looked the same, yet different somehow. The house seemed smaller than he remembered. There were still dozens of flower beds, but someone had added trellises, cement statues and antique iron fencing, creating a pleasing garden montage. The mailbox was in the same spot, but it had been replaced by a new, larger box adorned with hand-painted flowers and vines entwined with flowing calligraphy script that said S. Herder.

Snippets of conversation from the past flitted through his mind. Things he'd almost forgotten; things he'd never forget.

"You won't be sorry."

"I hope not."

"Hi. I'm Skye."

"I'm Cash."

"What kind of name is Cash?"

"What kind of name is Skye?"

"Race you to the river...."

"I love you."

"You don't have any idea what love is."

"I do!"

"You don't know what you're saying."

"Are you sorry?"

"No."

"Neither am I."

Cash's throat tightened as the bittersweet memories swept over him. He gripped the steering wheel. His heart pounded so hard he could hear it thrumming in his ears. It was too late to turn back, but even if he could, he knew he didn't want to. There was too much unfinished business here, too many things he needed to settle in his mind, not the least of which was exactly what his feelings had been back then, and whether or not there was anything for him here now.

He pulled into the driveway in front of the garage apartment. The pickup was missing—no doubt rusting in a scrap heap somewhere. The car sitting in the driveway was about five years old, but looked in good shape.

Cash opened the door and started up the walk to the porch, his keen eye taking in a thousand details while wind chimes tinkled in the silky summer breeze. The house craved for painting. The steps leading to the garage apartment looked in need of repair. The gate that kept the animals out of the vegetable garden swayed drunkenly on one hinge.

He noticed that the calico curtains that once hung at the door and over the window lights had been replaced with delicate lace panels. Two huge ferns hung between the four porch pillars. The porch itself needed some repair.

Cash couldn't escape a feeling that the lace and the ferns and the painting on the mailbox were feeble attempts to alleviate the inevitable encroachment of time. An inexplicable sadness filled him.

The sound of a dog barking in the distance broke the spell binding him. He drew a breath and rapped smartly on the door. Through the airy web of lace, Cash saw a woman step into view. She was tall, blond, lissome. His heart skipped a beat. Susan.

The door swung open, and he found himself staring into questioning brown eyes. For a split second he thought he was looking into Susan's face. Susan, trapped in some sort of time warp... Susan, forever young.

The expression in the woman's eyes mutated, and Cash realized with a start that she wasn't Susan at all. This woman was as tall as Susan, but where Susan's body had possessed a wiry, athletic muscularity—the result of the hard work that went hand in hand with farm chores—this woman's body, while just as slender, had a soft fullness to her breasts and hips that Susan's had lacked. While Susan's hair was a rare platinum blond, this woman's hair was a warm honey tone. Susan's pale blue eyes had held the unlikely combination of earthy innocence; this woman's tobacco brown eyes were guarded, cold.

"Skye?" he queried, dragging his gaze from the clingy ribbed tank top that molded her breasts, obviously bare beneath the soft cotton. Breasts he knew were soft and malleable.

She crossed her arms as if to shield herself from his gaze—or to show a supreme lack of concern. "Well, well, as I live and breathe," she drawled in an exaggerated Southern accent. "If it isn't Cash Benedict."

Whether it was the tenor of her voice or the angry look in her eyes, Cash got the distinct impression that he wasn't exactly welcome, and he couldn't help wondering why.

Go away, Cash! I don't need you here stirring up trouble. Not now.

Skye stared at the face that had haunted her memories since she was fourteen years old. She would have recognized Cash anywhere. He'd filled out, of course, and, as she had, he'd grown older. He was no less handsome—at what, thirty-eight?—than he had been at nineteen. And, darn his hide, he still had the ability to make her heart turn flips. The realization didn't please her at all. She lifted her chin the barest bit.

Why didn't you come before—when we needed you so badly?

"What brings you to our neck of the woods?" she asked with pointed directness. "From the looks of that car you don't need a job."

"No, I don't need a job," he said with a half smile.

"I know! You were in the neighborhood and thought you'd drop by... for old times' sake."

Cash plunged his hands into the pockets of his khakis, obviously taken aback by her sarcasm.

"Actually, that about sums it up. I'm...taking some time off work, and when I found myself in northern Missouri last night and realized that I was this close, I started thinking

about you and Susan and thought how good it would be to
see you both again.''

The words, spoken so casually, ripped open the wounds
his leaving had caused. The pain spurred her ire.

He smiled, a bit self-consciously. ''Maybe it has something to do with getting older and wanting to reconnect with
the people and places that meant the most to me.''

Did either of us mean anything to you, Cash? Did we?

''Don't make the mistake of thinking more of that summer than it really was,'' she warned.

The instant she spoke the hateful words she wished she
could call them back. The last thing she needed was for him
to know how important that summer had been to her. For
the first time since she'd started baiting him, she saw a hint
of anger enter his green eyes.

''Is that what you think I'm doing?'' he asked. ''How did
you see it?''

She shrugged. ''You were an employee who took unfair
advantage.''

Cash's turbulent, arrogant gaze moved over her body
with a thoroughness that left her more shaken than she'd
like to admit.

He shook his head. ''That's strange. Maybe it's you who
isn't remembering things correctly now. The way I remember it, I didn't take anything that wasn't offered.''

Skye felt the color drain from her face. Damn him for reminding her. And damn her for still caring!

''Look, Skye, I didn't come to trade insults with you,''
Cash said, an edge entering his voice. ''It's obvious that you
aren't too pleased to see me, so may I see Susan—if she isn't
too busy?''

Skye felt her nails bite into the flesh of her upper arms.
Clinging tentacles of pain wrapped around her heart. She

felt the sting of tears behind her eyelids. "Susan isn't too busy, Cash," she said in a low, harsh voice. "She's dead."

"Dead?" Cash echoed. His eyes recorded stunned disbelief.

Skye nodded.

"How?"

"Cancer." Skye hid her own anguish with a veneer of bluntness. "Eight years ago."

"I'm sorry."

He choked the words out through a throat clearly knotted with emotion. As much as Skye longed to paint him a villain, there was no denying the pain reflected in his eyes. The genuineness of his distress made her uneasy in a way she didn't understand. And it rekindled her earlier anger.

"I'm sorry, too," she snapped.

Cash shook his head as if he were still trying to comprehend what she'd told him. "She was a wonderful woman," he said in a gruff voice. "I cared a lot for her."

Skye wanted to ask him why, if he'd cared so much for Susan, he hadn't bothered coming back before now. She wanted to ask him why he'd gone away in the first place. But she held her tongue. Speaking her mind would cause more harm than good. She had to play it smart, play it cool, and hope he left town as suddenly as he'd arrived.

Lord, it hurt to see him standing there, a flesh-and-blood reminder of her lost innocence and her introduction to the realities of life and the backlash of a reckless mistake. She was afraid to spend too much time talking to him, afraid that his coming would send her carefully constructed and already shaky world toppling. Nervously, she glanced at the no-nonsense watch strapped around her wrist and then looked past him to the road, scanning the horizon for a flash of red.

"Look, I don't mean to be rude, but I have to go." She half turned to go back inside. "It was nice seeing you," she added, casting him a glance over her shoulder.

"You don't lie very well."

The blunt comment caused her to turn and face him. "I beg your pardon?"

"I don't think you have to go anywhere. I think you're still blaming me for what happened almost twenty years ago." His smile was gentle, wry. "We were kids, Skye. Let it go."

Skye closed her eyes for a brief instant, longing to deny his accusation. But she knew he was right. She opened her eyes and leveled a cool and steady gaze on him. "I do blame you," she told him, unwilling to grant him the forgiveness he wanted. "But I assure you I do have an appointment."

Something flickered in his eyes, an emotion she couldn't pinpoint. Then he smiled, a stilted halfhearted quirking of his lips. "I won't keep you, then."

He crossed the porch to the steps. At the bottom he turned. "It really was nice seeing you again." Offering her another smile, he gave a little wave. "See you 'round like a doughnut hole."

A bittersweet pang of sorrow pierced her. The childish goodbye had been one of her favorites. Skye watched him climb behind the wheel of the expensive car. "I hope not," she murmured. "I truly hope not."

She didn't move from the doorway until the Lexus was out of sight. Then she heaved a relieved sigh, squared her shoulders and went inside. Any other day, she'd have missed Cash because she'd have been at the shop, but she'd taken the afternoon off to take Opa Herder to the doctor.

Skye glanced down at her shaking hands. The tremor frightened her, and so did the realization that Cash's coming had unleashed some powerful memories and equally powerful hurts—not to mention that his being there had the potential to destroy everything she'd worked so hard to build for herself and Jeb.

Thank God Jeb was gone! They'd been having enough trouble. The last thing she needed was for Cash Benedict to come along and stir up more.

Face it, Skye, it isn't just Jeb you're worried about. You're just a little unsettled because, in spite of everything he did to you and Susan, the man still has the power to make your heart go pit-a-pat.

As much as she hated to face the painful irony, it was true. There was no ignoring the way her heart had constricted when she first recognized him standing in the doorway.

He'd changed, yet in many ways, he hadn't. Though a light sprinkling of gray flecked the whiskey-hued hair at his temples and time had called a gathering of fine lines to the corners of his brown-flecked green eyes, those eyes still met hers with familiar directness. The straight blade of his nose was the same, and the shape of his mouth with its narrow upper and full bottom lips triggered a sudden recollection of her young girl's forbidden fantasies.

She had fallen in love with Cash the summer he'd worked for them, loved him with all the purity and strength of her youth. She'd loved him, and he'd betrayed that love.

Susan had hired him on an afternoon in late May, just a few days past Skye's fourteenth birthday. Her hormones had taken her through the threshold of womanhood the previous year, a rite of passage she felt sure gave her new insight and added maturity. She had imagined she sensed loneliness in Cash, the same despondency that sometimes dwelt in her. Later she realized her "insight" was just wishful thinking, but, at the time, she'd believed it as strongly as she'd believed in the tooth fairy when she was six.

As the days passed, her awareness grew. Watching Cash undertake the chores Susan had assigned, seeing the sweat trickle through the hair that grew on his chest, she found herself consumed with the desire to run her hands over that bare, taut flesh to see if it was as smooth as it looked, and if the dark hair that meandered down his flat stomach was soft or wiry.

Her thoughts invariably made her breasts ache and her lower body tingle in an unsettling way. At night, as she lay awake, listening to the drone of mosquitoes and the chirping of crickets outside her bedroom window, she closed her eyes and imagined Cash holding her and kissing her... the way she'd seen in the movies, with his mouth open, as if he were starved for the taste of her. Delicious daydreams. Dangerous fantasies.

She and Susan had shared numerous conversations about the differences between love and sex, and Skye knew that the longings clamoring through her were as forbidden as they were fascinating. And she knew that they were linked to the lust Susan warned her about.

Night after night, Skye tossed and turned in her narrow twin bed, shamed by her risqué thoughts, trying to escape the pictures dancing through her mind: Cash lying beside her, both of them naked in the moonlight while he kissed her... touched her....

Burdened with guilt, she had been unwilling to engage in a lengthy conversation with Susan, who had an uncanny knack for reading her thoughts. Skye was afraid that if she looked into Susan's eyes her sister would be able to see straight into the secret places where she hid all her indecent thoughts. Yet, despite the guilt associated with her shameful musings, she'd known her feelings went deeper than lust. She'd known she loved Cash Benedict with all the fervor of her untried heart.

The night she finally took her courage in hand and dared to tell him of her feelings, Cash had grown red with embarrassment, but there was no doubt her declaration pleased him. He told her she was sweet and leaned over to kiss her. He aimed for her cheek, but she turned her face, and his lips grazed hers.

She'd thrown her arms around his neck and pressed herself against him, craving the closeness she'd dreamed about, wanting to feel his hands on her body. Longing to feel his mouth on hers, she dragged his head down and kissed him again, murmuring over and over that she loved him.

"You don't have any idea what love is," he said, cradling her face in his hands.

"I do!" she contradicted, pressing closer. "I do!"

Finally, reluctantly, she'd felt his arms go around her, and, for a brief and glorious while, she'd thought that he loved her back....

Things between them changed after that. Cash didn't seek her out the way he once had during his off hours. He stayed in his room more, and when their paths crossed, he acted embarrassed. Crushed by his rejection, she'd become quiet, angry, sullen, withdrawing more and more, isolating herself in her room, where she'd listened to the radio and worked on the pressed-flower pictures she created.

Skye wasn't sure when she realized there was something going on between him and Susan.

The change in her sister was gradual, almost imperceptible. Her smile came more often, the look in her eyes was softer, and her gaze often sought out Cash wherever he was working. She even began "fixing up" in the evenings before dinner.

Intuitively sensing what lay behind Susan's sudden interest in her appearance, Skye confronted Susan, who'd laughed away Skye's concerns with her usual sardonic amusement. Cash was a nice boy, she said. Intelligent. Interesting. He made her laugh, and he was certainly better company than George Braunfels, but that's all there was to it.

Susan was convincing, but Skye hadn't bought the denial.

Looking back, she remembered it as the longest, hottest, most miserable summer of her life. How many times had she fallen asleep to the muted sound of voices accompanied by the creaking of the porch swing as Cash and Susan talked late into the night, their undeniable closeness stoking the fires of the deep-rooted resentment of a woman scorned?

Then, on an evening in late August, before the crickets and frogs began to sing the nocturnal lullabys that filled her with such melancholy, Cash had carried his things down from the garage apartment to his Harley. Skye hadn't known he was leaving.

Susan had been silent, stoic. Her ice blue eyes were as barren as the fields before the bright green shoots of corn began to push through the rich ground in the spring.

Cash was leaving, and even though he would take a little piece of her heart, Skye was fiercely glad. Now, perhaps, they could return to the way things were before he came and interrupted the even tenor of their lives. In time, she would forget Cash Benedict and what he had done. And maybe, in time, she could forgive Susan for taking him away from her.

Cash had slung his long leg over the flashy red motorcycle, bade them a solemn goodbye and driven down the driveway, straight into the orange-red shimmer of a summer sunset and, she'd mistakenly believed, out of her life forever....

"Which is exactly where I want him to stay." The sound of her voice dissipated the memories, but it didn't rid her of the realization that despite the passage of time and the heartache he'd caused, she still found Cash extremely attractive. This time, thankfully, she was smart enough not to let her foolish heart lead her astray.

She glanced at the clock and saw that it was time to pick Opa up for his doctor's appointment. Time to put the hateful memories away. They'd be back, though. Cash's return would bring them back in their never-forgotten detail. There was so much to remember, so many things to forget. Things she wasn't certain she'd ever forgive. . . .

What she needed was perspective, Skye thought. As usual when she thought of balance, Skye thought of Harold Herder. Harold, Susan's eighty-three-year-old father-in-law, was the grandfather Skye had never had; indeed, she'd always called him Opa, or grandfather.

In the past, Opa had listened to her problems intently and offered her the soundest advice she was apt to get anywhere, but Opa had been diagnosed with Alzheimer's eighteen months before, and Skye was never certain what shape his mind would be in when she got there. Still, even if he was a bit confused, just seeing him would make her feel better.

She made the trip to the stone house in Marengo in short time. Rapping her knuckles against the wooden door in a perfunctory knock, she stuck her head in the unlocked door without waiting for an answer. Voices came from the living room. She smiled. No doubt Opa was watching the Discovery channel.

"Opa! Are you home?" she called unnecessarily.

A rich chuckle that belied any physical problem was her answer. She followed it to the shabby but immaculate living area where Harold Herder sat in an ancient wooden rocker, his lanky body covered in faded Osh-Kosh overalls and his

slipper-covered feet propped on a splitting red vinyl otto-
man, circa 1950s.

"And who else would be watching the television?" he
asked, his German accent obvious even though he'd been
born and raised in Iowa. He lifted his face for Skye's kiss.

She crossed the room to him, a smile on her face. She
could tell by the twinkle in his eyes that he was having a
good day. For the moment, his memory and thought processes were intact.

"Ugh!" she said, rubbing at his wizened cheek with her
palm. "You need a shave."

Harold caught her hand and gave it a squeeze. "Why? I
don't see any girls but you knocking on my door."

Skye tugged at one corner of his snow white mustache.
"What about Miss Abigail?" she teased, reminding him of
the seventy-nine-year-old widow who lived down the street.

Harold snorted. "Dratted woman's driving me crazy."

"Opa! Be nice. She doesn't have to bring your dinner
every Friday evening."

"I suppose not," he grumbled, "but does she have to
bring it during my favorite program?"

Skye smiled. "Beggars can't be choosers."

"Hmph!" he said again. "I don't know of anyone who'd
be begging for that slop she calls food."

"Oh, really?" Skye asked with a lift of her eyebrows. "I
don't see any of that slop making its way into the garbage
can."

Harold Herder had the grace to look chagrined, but his
faded blue eyes twinkled and his mustache quivered as he
replied, "Beggars can't be choosers."

They shared a moment's mirth before he said, "What are
you doing here?"

"You have a doctor's appointment," Skye reminded him
gently.

Opa looked embarrassed for forgetting. "Oh. Do you have time for a cola before we go?"

"I'm fine, thanks."

"You don't look fine," he observed. "What's wrong?"

"Cash is in town," she said without preamble.

Harold rubbed his arthritic knuckles against the gray stubble on his cheek. "Hmm. What brings him here?"

She shrugged. "He said he was thinking about the past and thought he'd drop by and see us. He didn't know Susan had died."

"What did he say?"

"He was shocked, of course." She shook her head. "He looked ... sad."

"And how did you feel, seeing him again?" he asked, pinning her with a shrewd look.

"How do you think I felt?" Skye asked. "I felt furious. *Damn it!* How dare he come back here after all this time and act as if nothing happened? How dare he!"

Skye felt the threat of tears and heard the quaver in her voice. Knowing she was close to losing her tenuous grip on her emotions, she went to the window and wrapped her arms tightly across her breasts, staring through a haze of moisture at the house across the street.

"You're as scared as you are angry," he observed.

Skye blinked and turned to face the old man. "Scared?"

Harold nodded. "Cash's coming back has the potential to stir up a lot of things, things that could change your future ... and Jeb's."

She closed her eyes momentarily. Opa was right. She was scared. Frightened beyond belief at what Cash's coming could mean to her life and Jeb's.

"You need to tell him about Jeb."

She felt the blood leech from her face. "No!" The denial was an agonized whisper.

"God's brought him back for a reason, and he has a right to know."

"He has no rights!" she cried, the tears she'd struggled so hard to hold back finally escaping to roll down her cheeks. "He gave up his rights when he rode off into the sunset on his fancy motorcycle—the rich, spoiled kid who had his summer fling and left someone else to take care of his mistakes."

"So you consider Jeb a mistake?"

"Yes! No." She shook her head, and her long, honey blond hair brushed the creamy flesh where her neck and shoulders met. "The whole summer was a mistake...for us all."

"Jeb knows about Cash," Harold noted. "Did you ever consider that Cash might have owned up to his mistakes if he'd known about Jeb?"

"If he'd cared enough, he could have found out."

"And you aren't going to tell him?"

The look in Skye's eyes begged him to understand. "Cash took everything away from me once. Jeb is all I have left."

Cash left the Herder farm, his thoughts torn between sorrow over the news of Susan's death and regret over the antagonistic welcome he'd received from Skye. He could only assume she was still angry over what had happened between them that summer. He knew he'd hurt her, just as he knew he'd hurt Susan. Seldom had a day passed that he hadn't damned himself for not being strong enough to resist the temptations set before him back then.

In the end, he'd done the only thing he could do, the thing he'd become adept at doing through the years. He'd run. Run from the mistakes and regrets and from the inevitable repercussions of his actions.

In some form or fashion, he'd been running ever since.

Becoming a workaholic was a form of running, but he hadn't known it until Liz pointed it out. Refusing to have it out with his now ex-wife over the way she was turning their daughter against him was tantamount to running.

Faced with Skye's hostility, it would be easy to run now, to just point the Lexus in a new direction and strike out for parts unknown. But seeing her again left him swamped by a wave of memories and nostalgia. It seemed imperative that he stay, at least for a night. Crucial for him to reacquaint himself with the places he'd frequented that summer... and maybe with the person he'd once been.

Following his heart, Cash turned toward West Amana, intent on driving the thirteen-mile irregular rectangle created by the locations of the seven colonies.

He passed the highway that led to Marengo, a town with between four and five thousand residents, seven miles to the west. Marengo had the closest hospital and the closest law enforcement agency. He drove through West Amana, past Schanz Broom and Basket Shop, past the Old-Fashioned High Amana Store that had been established over a hundred years before.

Cash drove on to Middle. The Amana Refrigeration Plant was in full swing—no surprise there—and the Hahn Bakery was still turning out delicious breads and sweet rolls.

Cash went from village to village, drinking in the familiar sights and the newer additions like a man starved for sustenance. He felt, in a way he couldn't explain, that he had come home, which was ridiculous, since he'd spent only three scant months there.

Main hadn't changed much. Though some of the buildings now housed different businesses than they had nineteen years before, Main Amana's woolen mill, which had once run twenty-four hours a day seven days a week, was still in operation. There was still a plethora of antique stores, and the smokehouse was still curing meats and cheeses for the tourists as well as the locals. The blacksmith's shop was still there, and the Amana Furniture Shop was still crafting some of the most beautiful, durable furniture in the world. A small shop just off Main Street said Herder's. Specializing In Pressed-Flower Art. S. Herder, Proprietor.

It looked as if Skye had made a go of her pressed-flower pictures. He recalled her early efforts—fairies and pixies and ladies in fancy dresses. Even back then, they hadn't been bad. It was easy to see how the delicate creations, dressed in clothing of pressed flowers and grasses with charming watercolor features, would appeal to the tourists that flocked to the colonies throughout the summer months. He wondered if Skye knew how fortunate she was to have been able to pursue her dream and make it work for her. If only everyone could be so fortunate.

Thinking that the houses hadn't changed much, he headed south toward Homestead. Built of weathered cedar or stone, many with walls nearing two feet in thickness to keep out the bitter cold of the Iowa winters, the houses of the colonies were a testimony to the ingenuity and steadfastness of the German settlers who had come from Ebenezer, New York, in 1854 to colonize the Amana area.

Yards were meticulously kept; Cash doubted that weeds dared to grow in the flower gardens. He smiled at the lush grapevines that climbed up the trellises on the sides of nearly every house, a holdover from the thirties when, after the Great Change of 1932, wine making was no longer a communal endeavor and residents were at last allowed to grow grapes for their own use.

Now, several wineries kept the citizens in their favorite spirit, making more than thirty different wines, including *Piestengel*, a sweet libation concocted by an enterprising resident who had begun making wine from rhubarb.

By the time he reached Homestead, thoughts of the good German food had stirred up his appetite, and the hours spent behind the wheel were taking their toll. He knew he'd be smart to drive to the Holiday Inn in Little Amana and get a room for the night.

After he ate a solitary meal in the motel dining room, he bought a newspaper and went back to his room. He didn't even make it through the first page before exhaustion overcame him and he fell asleep with the television blaring and the newspaper clutched in his hands.

He slept, but his sleep was restless, filled with half-formed images: an angry Skye. Susan, looking at a picture of pressed flowers while tears ran down her cheeks. Skye—or was it Susan?—begging him not to go as he drove off into a blazing sunset.

He awakened to the sound of voices in the hallway. The clock radio on the bedside table claimed it was 1:20 a.m. Cash rolled to his side and closed his eyes, willing sleep to return. The memories, enticing, haunting, came instead....

He pictured his body poised over a slender, naked form whose length was fused to his by a film of perspiration. His mouth devoured lips as soft as down, while his hand, trembling with innocence and excitement, caressed tender, willing flesh and his heart rate spiraled with a rising desire.

Hurting with a need too long denied, unable to wait any longer, he sheathed himself inside her. She gasped as if he'd hurt her, and then she was moving with him in the ancient, arcane dance of love.

He felt invincible. Strong. A man, not a boy. Wonderful couldn't begin to describe the feelings coursing through him with every powerful beat of his heart, yet a part of him whispered that what he was doing was insane. Worse, that it was wrong.

"I love you."

"You're too young to know what love is."

"This is love."

"No. Not love. Lust."

"I need you."

"You want me."

"It's the same thing."

A sigh of resignation. A groan of pleasure. A grudging confession. *"Maybe it is."*

Whatever it was, he'd never forgotten. He never would.

According to his upbringing, what he'd done was wrong, and he supposed that a part of him would always cling to that puritanical ethic when it came to sex outside of marriage. On the other hand, he knew that the wrongness was rooted in something that went far deeper than any moralistic teachings from his mother.

Wrong or right, his deepest regret was that he hadn't come back sooner... before Skye had grown into a beautiful, resentful woman... before Susan died.

He pictured Skye as she had been yesterday afternoon, her eyes blazing with anger and dislike. Cash realized with a shock that he was still violently attracted to her. But then, he'd always liked tall, leggy blondes with an attitude.

He sighed in weariness. He wanted to regain some sort of balance in his life. He longed to find some measure of peace with those around him, including Darby and Liz, but his coming here had pointed out what should have been obvious: there was no going on with the future until he had some sort of closure on his past.

He should head back to Lincoln. Ceil needed him, and whether she realized it or not, Darby needed him, too. God knew he needed them. If he was serious about getting his life in order, he should go back home and face not only his past mistakes but the fallout of his failures.

Which presented him with another set of problems. He had a past to try to set right here, too. But how? With Susan dead, there was no way to reconcile his feelings of guilt and sorrow, and Skye had made it abundantly clear that she had no interest in pursuing old relationships or granting absolution of past sins.

Should he heed the inner voice that urged him to see Skye one more time to try to make what peace he could with her? Should he try to explain that he'd never meant to hurt her? How could he make her understand that the summer he'd spent with her and Susan had been the most important summer of his life?

Maybe he couldn't. Maybe Skye would never forgive him. But he had to try. And after he apologized to Skye, he would find out where Susan was buried. He would go to the cemetery and say goodbye and apologize for any pain he might have caused her or her family.

Then, maybe, he could move on.

Chapter Three

August 25, 1977
After a lot of talking, Cash has decided to go back
home. He called his sister, and the offer to play pro-
fessional baseball never materialized. He's really dis-
appointed. I'll miss him when he goes, but it's for the
best. Deep in my heart, I know there's nothing for him
here. He doesn't belong on a farm in the middle of
nowhere—or with me. To ask him to stay would be the
biggest sin of all.

The next day, when Skye unlocked the shop and raised the
old-fashioned roll blind on the front door, the first thing she
saw was the champagne-hued Lexus parked out front. As
she stood staring at the luxurious car, the door swung open
and Cash got out. Their eyes locked; the determination
molding his face forewarned her that he wouldn't be de-

nied. He slammed the car door and headed straight for the shop.

Skye's first inclination was to jerk the blind down and hightail it for the back door, but it was too late. He was a scant two feet away, his hand already reaching for the doorknob.

She drew a steadying breath. Running wasn't her style. She was more accustomed to tackling her problems head-on, and she'd grown used to fighting for her place and her rights in her own quiet way—something she'd learned from Susan. With her heart hammering, she stood aside for Cash to enter.

Instead of speaking, he perused the room slowly, his gaze taking in her collection of baskets, woven by local artisans from native materials. He scrutinized the dried floral displays, and, one by one, he contemplated the pictures she'd done—fairies in pansy dresses dancing beneath a crescent moon; dainty elves in tiny flower caps cobbling shoes while the clock ticked away; antebellum ladies in flower-petal frocks walking beneath fantasy trees whose branches were covered with lilliputian leaves.

As he took stock of the shop, Skye took stock of him, brooding over the breadth of his shoulders, the muscular strength of his arms and the well-remembered shape of his mouth. A random memory of how those arms felt around her and how that hard mouth felt against hers flitted through her mind before she could stop it. Her lips tightened.

Cash turned his decisive gaze to her. "It looks as if you've done well for yourself."

Skye knotted her fingers together. "We get by."

As soon as she said the words, she wished she could call back the telltale "we." Cash didn't seem to notice.

"I should have known you'd make it. You're the kind of woman who goes after what she wants."

The compliment—as backhanded as it was—caught her off guard. If only he knew just how wrong he was. Still, she was pleased. She banished her pleasure to that nebulous place reserved for emotions that were too difficult to deal with. She couldn't let Cash turn her head. Not again.

"I thought you left town," she said pointedly.

"You'd like that, wouldn't you?" he countered, his irritation less obvious, but there nonetheless. "But I'm going to stay until I get a few things straight."

"Look, Cash, this is a business," she said, keeping her tone neutral through sheer force of will. "I have stock to put away. I don't have time for idle chitchat."

Resolve tightened his lips. He reached for his wallet, pulled out a crisp bill, grabbed her hand and closed her fingers around it. "Make time."

As it always had, his touch made her tremble like silky corn tassels in a hot summer wind. She pulled free of the disturbing contact and glanced at the paper clutched in her fingers. A one-hundred-dollar bill.

The frail hope of behaving like a mature, civilized adult vanished. Like the rest of the idle rich she'd had the misfortune to consort with, Cash thought he could buy his way through life. With a screech of rage, she threw the money at him. The rectangle sailed a few innocuous inches and drifted to the floor.

She glared up at him, fury and dismay vying for the upper hand. "Damn you!" she said, her voice low and lethal. "How dare you come back here and think you can buy me!"

The embittered declaration halted Jeb's entrance into the storeroom at the back of the shop. Pursing his lips in a silent whistle, he pocketed the keys to his motorcycle. Skye was mad. Thoroughly. He grinned. Must be that slime ball Lee Ballard. No one else could rile Skye the way Lee could, not even him.

Jeb closed the door quietly, uncertain whether he should stay where he was and eavesdrop, or if he should charge through the swinging, saloon-style door, deck the jerk and save Skye from more lies and excuses. Deciding there was no choice, he started for the front of the shop. It didn't matter that Lee was older and outweighed him by thirty pounds.

"I didn't come to buy you or to fight a battle in a war I didn't even know existed. I came to see two people who once meant a lot to me."

The masculine voice froze Jeb in his tracks. It didn't belong to Lee Ballard. He frowned. Who was this guy who had Skye in such a snit?

"Oh, we meant a lot to you, all right. Is that why you played us one against the other?"

"I didn't do that."

"Like hell! You knew I loved you." Jeb heard the thickness of tears in Skye's voice. "Dear God, I couldn't have made it any plainer, but you just had to add her scalp to your belt, too, didn't you?"

Jeb actually staggered back a step at her announcement. His heart began to race, and his head reeled at the implications of her accusation. He sat down in her chair and rested his elbow on her drafting table, pinching the bridge of his nose tightly as he willed the dizziness to leave.

Instead of answering her question, the man asked, "You knew about me and Susan?"

"Knew?" Skye's laughter reeked of long-guarded bitterness. "Of course I knew. How could I not know?"

Long seconds of silence followed her angry query. Curiosity drove Jeb to his feet, and his shaky legs carried him to the swinging doors.

The man standing next to his aunt Skye was tall and brown haired. Though Jeb was certain he'd never seen the stranger, there was something familiar about him.

"*That's* why you're angry with me," he said, comprehension dawning.

"Give the man a prize," Skye quipped, snapping her fingers in front of his face. "Believe me, Cash, angry can't begin to describe how I feel about you. Try furious. Or enraged. And your leaving is just one in a long list of grievances I have against you."

Cash. Jeb's heart took another sickening nosedive. He turned from the scene unfolding before him and went to the back door to stare out at the building behind the shop through a sheen of tears.

"Wait just a minute. Aren't you forgetting something here? You were fourteen years old. I was barely nineteen. You thought you were in love with me, and—"

"Don't you dare have the audacity to imagine you knew what my feelings were!" Skye's irate voice carried to the back room clearly. "The only feelings you were concerned about that summer were yours—and scratching your particular itch."

"Maybe I was," he admitted. "And it's not something I'm particularly proud of. But it was a long time ago. Time passes. We live and learn. Life goes on."

The annoyance in his voice had been replaced with something that sounded enough like sorrow to draw Jeb back toward the front of the store.

"Oh, you're right about that," Skye said. "Life does go on. You're a taker and a user, Cash Benedict! Not to mention a leaver! You take what you can from people who care for you, and when you've used up all the good, you leave and let someone else deal with the chaos you left behind."

"I never set out to hurt you or Susan. I plead guilty to being young and stupid. I didn't make the best choices. I—" He paused. "I don't have any excuse and no defense for what I did to either of you. All I can say is that I'm sorry."

There was a prolonged silence, but Skye never spoke a word to accept the apology. Then Jeb heard the soft thud of footfalls and the tinkling of the bell on the door as Cash Benedict made his exit.

Cash Benedict.

His father.

Cash parked the car outside the white fence circling the cemetery. He gripped the steering wheel until his knuckles turned white. Damn if he hadn't run away again.

But only from an argument that was going nowhere.

Somehow, the rationalization didn't make him feel any better. He reached into his breast pocket for an antacid tablet. His lips twisted in a rueful smile. At least now he knew why Skye was so angry, so bitter. He'd always known the Herder women were close, but how had Skye found out about his affair with Susan? And who would have thought Skye would still hold a grudge because of his rejection of her?

The question brought a singularly sweet memory of the night Skye had told him she loved him. It had been the last of June, a hot night when they'd gone out to water the horse she used for pleasure riding, a gift from Harold Herder.

He had been taken with Skye from the moment he first met her. She was somewhat introverted, a little shy and an excellent listener. She was also the prettiest, sexiest thing he'd seen in a long time, something she was totally unaware of.

Being with her was both pleasure and agony. Pleasure because he liked listening to her, watching her. And agony because the more he was around her, the more he wanted her. She laughed, and he was captivated. She stretched, the arching of her back pulling the fabric taut over her soft curves, and his body responded in a way that excited and shamed him. He had fallen for her—hard—even though he knew that the five years' difference in their ages made her far too young for him.

He knew she had a crush on him, too, and he'd tried not to encourage her, but her announcement that night had both pleased and astounded him. Embarrassed, he'd told her she was too young to know what love was. Skye insisted she did. Hoping to ease the pain of his rejection and enticed by the delicate floral scent that emanated from her body, he'd leaned over to give her a chaste, brotherly kiss on the cheek. At the last second, she'd turned her head so that his kiss fell on her lips.

He hadn't been prepared for his reaction. In retrospect, he should have known her innocent passion would set him on fire. Not only did he want her badly, he was one of the rare few who'd somehow reached the end of his teen years without ever tasting the forbidden fruits of the flesh. Back then, he'd been certain he was the only nineteen-year-old male virgin in the Midwest.

His arms had gone around her—reluctantly at first—and then, when she'd pressed against him, he'd held her tighter and pressed her against the exterior of the house, crushing her between the wall and his throbbing, aching body....

His lips couldn't get enough of hers. She tasted like Orange Crush and smelled like tea roses. She felt like heaven. His chest burned where her breasts touched. She stood on tiptoe, her femininity pressed against his throbbing, thrusting manhood.

She didn't stop him when his hand, clumsily, almost fearfully, moved between them to her breast, barely covered by a halter top. She froze for an instant, but then her lips moved against his again, and his hungry mouth swallowed her velvety sigh of surrender. He'd wanted to feel her bare flesh against his, to take his fill of what she offered.

"Never be responsible for taking a girl's innocence, Cash."

The words of caution he'd heard a hundred times from his mother stole through his mind with the same effect as the slap of a wet washcloth in the face. Reality returned, and the ache in his loins vanished with a remarkable suddenness. This was insane.

Without being conscious of his actions, he wrenched his mouth from Skye's and, gripping her bare shoulders, he stepped away, putting some distance between their hungry bodies.

"Stop!"

Skye looked up at him, a dazed expression in her eyes, her lips wet from his kisses. "Why?"

"Because…because…you're too young. You don't know what you're doing."

Her tears glistened in the living room lamplight that softened the outside gloom. "I love you, Cash."

"Don't be silly. You're just a kid. You don't know what love is."

Skye looked at him with censure in her eyes, and Cash felt like a bully who'd stolen a child's favorite toy.

"I do!"

"Don't, Skye. Don't do this." The finality in his voice must have penetrated her fog of desire. It definitely kindled her anger.

She doubled up her small fist and hit him in the chest. "Damn you!" she cried in a low, tear-filled voice, hitting him again and again. "I hate you!"

Finally, with a sob of impotent fury, she'd pushed him out of the way and ran inside and up the stairs to her room.

They'd done their utmost to stay out of each other's way the rest of the summer. There were no more teasing conversations, no more races to the river. When they did occupy the same room, the animosity she projected crowded out any hope for calling a truce. Cash felt as if he'd lost one of his best friends, as indeed he had. He missed being with her, and he was sorry to have lost their closeness, but he knew that he'd done the right thing by turning her down. He also knew that to lead her on was to tempt fate.

Later, when he'd succumbed to that temptation with Susan, he had, in typical young stud fashion, all but forgotten about Skye's tender feelings. Obviously, she'd known about the affair all along and hadn't yet forgiven him for it.

Looking back, he could recall several incidents where Susan and Skye had locked horns that summer. He knew now those arguments were rooted in Skye's jealousy and resentment of his relationship with Susan.

Susan.

Cash closed his eyes and leaned his head against the car's headrest, letting another wave of memories wash over him. Though Susan was often sharp-tongued and didn't pull any punches, she was kindhearted, intelligent and had a deep wellspring of caring that extended to everyone she knew, including him.

Gradually, she'd drawn out the details of his life, how he and Ceil had been chosen over all the other babies at the Assembly of God Orphanage, of his dream to play pro ball and how that dream had led to the argument with his father. It was she who'd helped him see Cash Senior's point of view as well as understand that what had transpired between them was a natural happening between adults and teenagers who were spreading their wings.

Cash began to look forward to the time he spent with her, and despite the fact that he was sexually drawn to Skye, he began to spin erotic fantasies about Susan in his head. It never occurred to him that Susan's fantasies might include him.

Or that she would act on those fantasies.

He and Susan had first made love after the Colonies' Independence Day celebration. Patriotism and excitement had run as high as the mercury in the thermometers. He and Susan and Skye had taken the day off from all but the most necessary of chores so that they could join the rest of America in its birthday celebration. After watching the parade, they had joined Harold Herder and some of Jon's other relatives for a picnic and an afternoon of swimming in a pool along the banks of the sluggish North Fork English River.

Skye hung out with her teenage relatives and flirted unmercifully with an older guy named Lee Ballard whom one of her cousins had invited. In her red swimming suit, she was as lush as the grasses growing along the river's edge and as elusive as the butterflies that flitted from flower to flower. Jealously, Cash watched as the group splashed and played in the water.

He might have joined them, if for no other reason than to make sure Skye didn't make a fool of herself, but Susan insisted that he mix with the older crowd. For the first time since he'd come to Iowa, Susan Herder shed her aura of seriousness and showed him a different side of her personality. She laughed and joked and flirted while she frolicked at the river's edge in a plain black one-piece swimming suit.

The afternoon was hell. He could hardly keep his eyes off
either of the Herder women. He was torn between wanting
and anger, and couldn't decide what emotion to assign to
whom. He concluded that maybe God had put women on
earth to keep a man in turmoil. It was a possibility that still
held merit nearly twenty years later.

Exhausted from their swimming, the entire group made
their way back to the farm, where they made another raid
on the fried chicken, potato salad and *Piestengel*. Clouds
continued to roll in, and the atmosphere grew heavier, but
at everyone's insistence, Harold took his fiddle from a worn
case. He was joined by Jon's brothers with their mandolin
and guitar. The teenagers disappeared into the house to listen to rock and roll.

There was polka music and bluegrass and square dancing. Cash remembered the excitement and daring in Susan's eyes as she'd downed another glass of wine and
beckoned for him to join her. He declined, saying he didn't
know how to polka, but the truth was, he didn't want to
make a fool of himself in case Skye and her friends were
watching from inside the house.

That fear vanished the instant he took Susan into his arms
and began to learn the lively dance. It was worth the good-
natured ribbing to see the rare happiness in her pale blue
eyes.

As the edges of the horizon turned dark, Susan called a
halt and snatched Harold's bandanna from his pocket to
wipe her laughing, perspiring face. Sheet lightning flashed
in the West. In the distance, the fireworks displays in Marengo and Amana flashed through the ebony sky in bursts
of light and showers of color that competed with the lightning, while everyone oohed and aahed and indulged in cake
and homemade ice cream.

Even after nineteen years, Cash still remembered that Fourth of July as the most fun he'd ever had...maybe in his entire life. If it hadn't been for his misunderstanding with Skye, the day might have been perfect.

The ice cream finished, the Herders—including Skye, who went to spend the night with a relative—loaded their things, laughing about pushing their luck with the rain. They bade everyone goodbye and drove away, hoping to beat the fast-approaching storm to their homes.

Jagged bolts of lightning split the night-black sky, and thunder rumbled through the stygian darkness as Cash helped Susan carry in the remains of their feast. When he offered to help with the dishes, she refused. Instead, she poured them each more wine that they drank standing in middle of the immaculate, sparsely decorated kitchen.

With the memory of their dance and how she had felt in his arms uppermost in his mind, Cash silently gulped down the last of the sweet white wine. Susan took his glass and set it on the countertop, smiled gently and told him she'd see him in the morning.

Lonelier than he'd been since he left Lincoln, Cash climbed the stairs to his small apartment, pulled out the Hide-A-Bed and stripped down to his briefs. There was no air-conditioning in his room and, even though the approaching storm blew the hot breath of the night through the open windows, the heat was almost intolerable.

He lay with one arm beneath his head, listening to a rock-and-roll station out of Des Moines on the clock radio while the rising wind rattled the screen door and his mind replayed the day in vivid, memorable detail...the Lycra swimsuit hugging Susan's trim body...the smile of mischief on her lips as she taught him the polka....

He cursed and willed the taunting thoughts away.

Unfortunately, those that came instead were just as teasing, just as tormenting: Skye's disdainful looks; the way she pressed her lush body against Lee Ballard's; the way that body felt against his.... Need was an exquisite ache inside him when he heard the rattling at the door.

At first he thought it was the storm. Then he recognized the figure in the doorway as Susan, who came with the offering of more wine. She came in, sat on the bed and, to his never-ending surprise, she kissed him. Unlike the time he'd kissed Skye, there was no voice whispering inside him about taking a woman's innocence. This time the innocence taken had been his. No. Not taken. Given. Gladly...

The sound of a motorcycle halted Cash's reminiscences. He blinked away the lingering traces of the memories. The interior of the parked car had grown hot while he sat there thinking about the past. He wondered how long he'd been there, daydreaming.

He wondered, as he had countless times through the years, how he could have let it happen. Telling himself he was just a drunk kid with a hormone problem didn't assuage his guilt.

Looking back, he knew Susan had been partly right that night. Even though his feelings for her were far more than the lust she claimed and he'd cared for her in ways that transcended the sex they'd shared in the weeks that followed, those feelings hadn't been the love he professed it to be. He hadn't known what real love was. Maybe, as his mother always told Ceil, he had been in love with love, caught up in a young man's fantasy, flattered that Susan had found him desirable.

He was more convinced now of what he'd suspected back then—what had happened between him and Susan was wrong for a lot of reasons. He'd been confused—wanting both Skye and Susan, fascinated with one, caring deeply for the other—angered, enticed and tempted beyond any red-blooded male's endurance.

Perhaps the greatest sin of all was that he'd never really known who he was making love with. Even as he'd found his release in Susan, it was Skye's face he pictured behind his closed eyes. Worse, the greater sin might have been continuing the affair with Susan during the next weeks, when he couldn't place the blame on the wine, when he realized that Skye still held claim to a great part of his heart and his thoughts.

He'd suffered his share of regrets for what had happened between him and Susan, but he didn't regret knowing her. She was a good person, a good woman. He liked and respected her. Admired her. She was a port in his particular storm, his sage adviser. His first mature love; his first lover.

And now she was gone.

Cash let his gaze roam the small cemetery. Sunlight pierced the branches of the pine trees, dappling the stone markers, all aligned in neat rows. Every village had a cemetery, but, contrary to the ways of the "outsider," the deceased members of the Church of True Inspiration were buried in rows in the order that they died, rather than in family plots, next to loved ones. Children were buried in special areas. There were no fancy vaults, no ornate headstones, nothing but a plain white stone marker, an exact replica of the ones next to it, to mark one's passing. Their belief was that no man was better than the next, something, Cash thought, it would behoove all men to realize.

The burial custom might have made locating Susan's grave an ordeal except for the one fact he'd just remembered: Susan had never embraced her husband's beliefs. All outsiders were buried in a place set apart for those who had not seen fit to join themselves to the church.

Cash reached for the small bouquet of flowers he'd pur-
chased from a vendor, and got out of the sweltering car. As
he stepped through the narrow gate, he saw a motorcycle
pull to a stop at a house down the street. The sight of the old
Harley filled him with another surge of nostalgia. It was the
exact model of the bike he'd ridden to Amana that summer, right down to the shiny red paint job.

When Cash had gone back home to Lincoln that August, his father had rewarded him by giving back his car
keys. Knowing how much Susan and Skye had loved riding
on the Harley, Cash had made arrangements for it to be sent
to them, a sort of reminder and a thank-you for everything
knowing them had meant to him. Sending the bike was the
last contact he'd had with the Herder women.

As he watched, wondering what had happened to the
Harley and if either Susan or Skye had made use of it, the
rider, a tall young man wearing a space-age-style helmet got
off the cycle, took off the headgear and raked a hand
through his hair in a gesture that seemed strangely familiar.
He stared at Cash for a moment. Then, cradling the helmet
in the crook of his arm, he started up the sidewalk to a
grayed wooden house.

Sighing beneath the weight of old memories, Cash turned
and made his way to the corner of the cemetery where Susan lay sleeping for all eternity.

It didn't take long to find her resting place. He was glad
to see that while it was the recipient of the morning sun, the
pine branches would shield it from the harsh rays of the afternoon. Susan had loved sunshine, but she had hated
working in it—not that she complained often. Indeed, he'd
seldom heard a word of criticism pass her lips.

He'd asked her once about her accepting attitude and how
she'd grown so wise and gained so much peace, and she'd
told him that whatever good qualities she possessed she'd

learned from her husband, Jon, who was quite possibly the best mortal man ever put on the earth.

"Did you love him?" Cash had asked, in a moment of jealousy.

"With all my heart," she told him with a smile. "But I wasn't in love with him."

Cash didn't understand. "What's the difference?"

Susan's smile grew wicked. "See?" she teased. "I told you that you didn't know anything about love."

"I know enough!"

Her taunting smile vanished. She reached out and touched his lips with her fingertips. "No," she said, "you don't. But one day you will."

"Explain, then," he commanded almost angrily.

"You love your mother and your sister?"

"Of course I do."

"But you aren't *in love* with either of them, are you?"

Comprehension dawned. "No," Cash said. "So if you weren't in love with Jon, why did you marry him?"

"Because he loved me more than enough."

"More than enough for what?"

"More than enough to make up for my stupidity. More than enough to make up for my weaknesses and my short-comings. Enough to give me back my self-worth. Enough to alter his whole life to make a place for me and Skye here on his farm and in his family and in his heart."

Cash imagined he saw a glimmer of tears in her ice blue eyes.

"I did love him. He was the best friend I ever had, and, dear God, I do miss him."

Cash felt another surge of jealousy. Jon Herder sounded like a hard act to follow. "So if you love and miss him so much, why are you sleeping with me?" he asked cruelly.

"Touché," Susan had replied with a brittle laugh. She had swung her leg over his and sat on his lap facing him, twining her arms around his neck. "Because I am weak and imperfect, and it's been so long since a handsome man has held me and made me feel sexy and beautiful and wanted . . . the way you do. . . ."

Cash pushed away the memory. It was almost impossible to believe that the warm, loving woman he'd held in his arms was cold and lifeless beneath the ground where he knelt. He felt the prickling of tears beneath his eyelids as a painful emotion clutched his heart. She should have found someone to love—to be in love with. She should have been happier. He should never have let things go so far.

Skye was right. He should have come back before now. But he hadn't, and now Susan was dead, and there was no going back and making his mistakes right.

He fought back painful emotions and lifted his head. Reaching out, he placed the flowers near the marker. He should never have come back. It hurt too much.

You're wrong, Benedict, and so was Skye. It has nothing to do with your coming back. You should never have left.

Surreptitiously, from the dining room window of his friend's house, Jeb watched the man at the cemetery. Stunned, angry, overwhelmed, he wasn't ready to confront Cash Benedict—his father—just yet. Maybe he never would be. But he was curious about him just the same.

After Cash left the shop earlier, Jeb had slipped out the back door before Skye caught him eavesdropping. She'd worry herself sick if she knew he'd overheard their conversation. He didn't know what he planned to do with the knowledge he'd gained from overhearing them, but he knew he needed to think about it.

He'd ridden around for a while before he decided to follow Cash. Finding the Lexus in the Amanas wasn't hard. From a distance, he'd tailed Cash as he went from one place of business to another, talking to this person and that. Not wanting to rouse his suspicions, Jeb hung back for a good fifteen minutes before paying Jimmy Bogart a visit so he could watch Cash from afar.

There had been a moment of panic when his dad—jeez, it was hard to think of that man, or any man, as his dad— had looked right at him, but Jeb had played it cool, the moment had passed and he'd realized that his fear of being discovered had been unfounded. There was no way Cash Benedict would recognize him, because he had no idea he had a son.

Jeb watched the man who had sired him kneel beside his mother's grave for long, agonizing moments, watched as he brushed at his eyes. Jeb swallowed. Thinking about Susan always made him sad, too. He hardened his heart against the sentiment.

It was a little late for sorrow. A little late for regrets. As Opa said, if you want to dance, you have to pay the fiddler, and Cash Benedict had just begun to pay.

Chapter Four

August 15, 1985

Should I tell him the truth or will it just cause more confusion? Harold says they should both be told, that Jon is dead and can't be touched by it anymore. I know I can't keep this kind of secret forever, but I'm afraid it will make them think less of me. Lord knows they're all I have left that means anything in my life.

Jeb didn't sleep much that night. Instead, he lay awake thinking about the conversation he'd overheard and the scene he'd witnessed at the cemetery.

After Cash Benedict had driven away from the cemetery, Jeb had left Jimmy's and ridden the Harley—his only tie to his father—to Belinda's, too agitated to go back to the shop. Skye would have known something was wrong, and he hadn't been up to a question-and-answer session. He had too many questions of his own, like why had Cash come back after so long? Why hadn't he come before? Had he loved Susan, or had what happened between them been nothing but a summertime fling? Susan had confessed the truth about Cash before she died, but she hadn't given him any details.

Belinda was alone when he got to her house. Both of her parents were at work, and since Jeb didn't have to be on his job at the local Holiday Inn until later in the afternoon, he spent the intervening time trying to forget his problems in Belinda's arms, Belinda's bed.

He and Belinda Krammer had been dating for more than a year, a bone of contention between him and Skye, who feared that he and Belinda would do "something silly," jeopardizing his hope of getting the education Susan had wanted for him. He could care less about college; he wanted to play professional baseball, a prospect that horrified his aunt.

They argued often. Jeb maintained that he had the talent; hadn't his dad had enough talent that the pros had looked at him? Skye retaliated by saying that while a lot of kids had talent, few had what it took to make the cut. On the other hand, his future would be secure if he got a degree.

He and his aunt had quarreled so much over his future that the tension between them was as thick as the lilies growing on Lily Lake between Middle and Main, but so far neither of them had budged an inch. Skye expected him to go to the University of Nebraska at Lincoln in the fall, but all he could think about was getting to a summer baseball camp in St. Louis in August. At least, that had been his main concern until he'd walked into the shop this morning and overheard Skye talking to his father.

His father.

Susan had skirted Jeb's questions about his father all his life, but when he was nine he found his birth certificate and learned that the man who had sired him was named Cash Benedict and that he and Susan were never married.

Susan, who had seldom dated, had always been so practical and solid, so sensible, that it was almost impossible to think of her making love with anyone outside of marriage. Jeb couldn't imagine the woman he'd called Mom going off the deep end and sleeping with some stranger who'd ridden into her life on a motorcycle. Yet if his birth certificate was to be believed, that's exactly what had happened.

When he had questioned Skye about it, she had grown furious and told him not to breathe a word of what he'd found to Susan. Digging it all up would only hurt Susan, and God knew she had been hurt enough for her indiscretion. Jeb hadn't understood what she meant, but he had done as Skye asked. Then, just two short weeks before Susan died, she had called him into her room and told him about Cash.

She had been lonely, she said, tears pooling in her eyes. But she should have known better than to let things go so far. Cash was too young to make a commitment; she was old enough to know better. He hadn't belonged there, but she had loved him in a way no one would ever accept or understand....

The grandfather clock downstairs chimed 2:00 a.m. Jeb rolled to his side. Obviously the love was all on his mom's side. If Cash Benedict had loved her, he would have done something besides send her a damned motorcycle and then forget she was in the same world for almost twenty years.

Why had Benedict come now, when his life was already in turmoil? Jeb wondered. It wasn't as if he didn't have enough on his mind with Belinda's constant pleas to forget college, get married and go to work in her father's business, and Skye pushing him toward college. Now he had to contend with a father he'd never met. A man he didn't think he could ever like or respect.

Jeb jabbed angrily at his pillow, torn between the desire to confront Cash Benedict about his behavior and a desire for him to just leave before anyone else got hurt. He finally fell asleep, still hurting, still angry and very confused.

Skye awakened early after a night of restless sleep. She went outside and got the paper, and then poured herself a cup of coffee, wondering what would happen next. Neither Billy Graham, her daily horoscope nor "Dear Abby" offered any solutions or hope. "Dennis the Menace" and "Calvin and Hobbes" seemed tame. Even the world news couldn't compete with the chaos of her life the past couple of days.

After Cash had left the previous morning, her day had gone downhill fast. She couldn't concentrate on her work, she was snippy with her help and Jeb hadn't shown up to unpack the new framing materials that had come in the day before. Knowing he was probably at Belinda's didn't improve her mood.

Skye fumed, but she didn't try to track him down. Checking up on him would cause another argument, and with Cash Benedict in town, she'd more than filled her quarrel quota for the week.

She had been staring at the front page for several minutes before she realized she had no idea what she'd been reading. All she could think about was her row with Cash and Opa's statement that Cash should be told about Jeb.

Should he? she wondered as she sipped her coffee. If she did tell him, he would want to meet Jeb, and Jeb's emotions were so volatile lately that there was no telling how he would react. Lord knows he was already troubled enough about what to do with his life. Finding out that his father was back had the potential to change everything....

Maybe for the better.

She pushed aside the troublesome thought. Just because Cash had a lot of money and could change Jeb's future with a few legal papers didn't necessarily mean that that future would be better than the one Susan had wanted for him. Hadn't she been told often enough that things you worked for meant more than what was handed to you and that money couldn't buy happiness? Hadn't Cash's coming here that summer proved that beyond a doubt?

Still, Cash had the resources to pay for Jeb's college.

He could also take Jeb away from you.

And that, Skye acknowledged, was her real fear. Susan was gone. Besides Opa, who didn't have too many more years left, Jeb was the only person in the world who truly cared for her. Since Susan's death, Jeb had become more like her son than her nephew. Cash had once taken Susan away from her, and Skye was afraid that the lure of his wealth might do the same with young, impressionable Jeb.

"I thought I smelled coffee."

Skye looked up and saw Jeb standing in the doorway rubbing absently at the hair trailing from his chest down his hard stomach, a pair of denim cutoff shorts hanging low on his lean hips. He wasn't a boy anymore, she thought with dual pangs of surprise and sorrow. He was a man. And he looked painfully like Cash had at that age.

"Why are you awake at such an ungodly hour?" she asked, getting up to pour him a cup of coffee.

"I didn't sleep very well," Jeb said, dragging a chair from under the battered oak table. "I thought I'd go in and unpack those boxes I didn't get to yesterday. I went to Belinda's and forgot."

Skye set the mug of coffee down in front of him. It was as close to an apology as she was likely to get. "I don't think you should be at Belinda's if her parents aren't there. People will talk."

Jeb scooped two heaping spoonfuls of sugar into the steaming brew, stirred it and, leaning back in his chair, regarded her from sleepy green eyes below a shock of unruly black hair. "You know what you need, Skye?"

"Déjà vu. I think we had this conversation the other day, so if you say good sex or a man I'm going to scream," she warned, pinning him with a hard gaze. Her voice took on the sarcastic tone Susan had adopted so well. "Lest you forget, I just came out of a relationship that bruised my fragile ego. I'm not anxious to jump into another."

"Lee Ballard is a jerk. The only thing that qualifies him as a man is what's betw—"

"Jeb Herder, that is quite enough!" Skye warned.

"Okay, okay." He took a sip of his coffee, the gleam in his eyes unrepentant. "What are you doing up so early?"

"I couldn't sleep, either."

Should I say anything or not?

If she didn't and Cash stayed around, the greater the chance became that someone in town would recognize him. All the old gossip would be resurrected, and chances were that Jeb would find out about Cash from someone else.

Skye couldn't remember the last time she'd been forced to make such a hard call. She wanted to scream with frustration. She wanted to throttle Cash Benedict. When it came down to it, she had no choice.

She reached out and covered Jeb's hand with hers. "Jeb..."

His gaze moved from their hands to her face. "Yeah?"

"There's something I...need to tell you." As soon as she said the words, her thought processes seemed to shut down.

She stared into Jeb's curious eyes and struggled to find the words to tell him about Cash. Should she ease into it, or just come straight to the point?

"Cash Benedict is in town."

Skye sucked in a surprised breath. Jeb, not she, had spoken the words.

"How did you find out?" she asked, aghast.

He shrugged his bare shoulders. "I heard the two of you arguing at the shop yesterday morning."

"That's why you didn't show up for work," she said with new understanding.

"Yeah."

"And how do you . . . feel about his coming back?"

Hardness crept into Jeb's eyes. "How do you think I feel?"

A wry smile flickered across Skye's mouth. "Dumb question, huh?"

"You said it." Neither spoke for several seconds. "I followed him," Jeb said at last.

"You did?" Skye asked, surprised.

Jeb nodded. "He talked to some people in town, and then he took some flowers to put on Mom's grave. He was there a long time."

"Do you . . . want to meet him?" Skye asked, her heart filled with trepidation.

"I'd like the opportunity to tell him what a low-life bastard I think he is for leaving Mom, yeah," Jeb said with a nod.

"He didn't know she was expecting you," Skye said in Cash's defense.

"But if he really cared for her, he could have kept in touch. And if he had, she might have told him, and—" His voice broke off. "There's no use rehashing it all. He didn't, so that's that."

Jeb doubled up his fist and tapped his chest at the place over his heart. "What really hurts is that I know how cruel people can be, you know?" His eyes were unnaturally bright, and his voice held an unaccustomed huskiness. "I don't care about me," he said in a touching, gallant gesture, "but Mom... she deserved better."

Skye nodded, afraid to trust her own voice. All these years, ever since Susan had died after having told him the truth, Skye had believed Jeb had come to terms with the fact that he was born out of wedlock. Now it appeared she was wrong.

"I know you're angry," she said at last. "So am I. I've been angry a lot longer than you. But in spite of what he did, I don't believe Cash Benedict is a bad person."

"You're entitled to your opinion."

That said, Jeb stood and went to refill his coffee cup. When he turned, he was smiling, albeit weakly. "Let's forget it. Go take your shower, and let's get that unpacking done."

Skye smiled. He was taking the news about Cash like a trouper. She went to Jeb and hugged him briefly, fiercely. She was a little surprised when he hugged her back. As she went up the stairs it occurred to her that the past fifteen minutes were the first they'd spent in each other's company without arguing in longer than she could remember.

Cash rose early, after a night filled with memories and dreams. After downing a quick cup of coffee, he headed for the Herder farm. He wanted to catch Skye before she left for the shop. He should start back home today, but before he did, it was imperative that he try once more to make what atonement he could for his past mistakes.

He wanted to assure Skye that he'd never set out to hurt her or Susan. If Skye couldn't grant him forgiveness for leaving Susan, he hoped he could at least make her understand why he'd gone.

The sun was just up when he pulled into the driveway, and the golden wash of sunlight spilling over the trees to the east cast the farm's run-down condition into stark relief. If something wasn't done soon to turn the tide of neglect, it wouldn't be many years before the place deteriorated completely.

Cash made his way along the sidewalk where spring flowers dipped and swayed in an early-morning breeze. The front door was open, and he could see clearly into the living room through the screen door. Skye had updated the furnishings, that now leaned strongly toward Victorian. Wind chimes tinkled softly as he rapped sharply on the doorframe.

As he stood there, waiting for Skye, a tall, masculine figure rounded the corner from the kitchen. The sight of the man took Cash aback. Why hadn't he realized there would be a man in Skye's life?

As he watched, the man stopped in his tracks, obviously surprised, too. Then he squared his shoulders and strode across the room with a gait that bespoke a supreme confidence. He was almost to the door before Cash realized that the man was young, still in his teens. His mind calculated a hundred possibilities and settled on the one that made the most sense. He must be Skye's son. After all, she was thirty-three, old enough to have a teenager.

Cash wasn't prepared for the animosity in the young man's green eyes. "Hi. I'm Cash Benedict."

"I know."

The tone was cold. Definitely unfriendly. But there was a note in it that sounded familiar. In fact, everything about the boy reminded him of someone.

"Is Skye here?"

The boy crossed his arms over his wide, bare chest. "She's taking a shower."

Cash nodded. "And you're . . . ?"

"Jeb."

"Do you mind if I come in, Jeb?" Cash asked, his patience with the kid wearing thin.

Instead of answering, Jeb reached out and pushed open the screen. Cash wanted to reach out and knock the chip off the kid's shoulder and see if he was half as tough as he thought he was, but instead, he stepped inside.

The door slammed shut behind him. He glanced around the room, curious about the changes that had been made since the time the farm had been his home. The wallpaper was different, and so was the color scheme. Books, baseball trophies and framed photos shared space on an antique bookcase. A motorcycle helmet lay on a wingback chair. Suddenly Cash realized why Jeb looked so familiar. He turned with a smile.

"You were at the house near the cemetery yesterday."

Jeb shrugged. "Guilty as charged."

"Where on earth did you find such an old bike in such good condition?"

"It was my dad's."

"No kidding!" Cash exclaimed. "I used to have one just like it."

"Small world," Jeb said, hooking his thumbs in the belt loops of his cutoffs.

Cash wondered if he imagined the sarcasm in Jeb's voice and wondered where Skye was. Arguing with her was preferable to trying to converse with this resentful young man. He stifled another sigh. At least the kid was talking—sort of—since he'd mentioned the Harley.

Drawn to a framed snapshot on the mantel, Cash crossed the room.

The young man in the grainy photo sat astride a shiny red Harley-Davidson parked in front of the garage apartment, a helmet tucked under his arm. The kid looked cocky to the point of arrogance, just like the boy standing across the room from him. Cash's heart began to pound painfully.

"That's my old man." Jeb said, his voice caustic with bitterness. "Everyone says I look just like him."

With a sinking heart, Cash turned to meet the challenge in Jeb's eyes. The boy's handsome features were sharp with resentment.

"My aunt Skye said she took that picture the summer of '77. Figure it out, Benedict."

The jeering words lent credence to Cash's nebulous fear. Blood thundered through his veins, pounding in his head until he wanted to cry out at the loudness of the sound. He felt the familiar rise of acid in his throat. He heard a sound and turned toward it automatically.

Skye stood at the bottom of the stairs, wearing a terry-cloth robe, her wet hair wrapped in a towel. If he needed any proof other than what his mind was telling him, it was recorded in the horror on her face.

She gave a little cry and lifted her hands to her lips.

"It's true?" Cash asked, directing his hoarse question to her. "This is my son?"

"Yes." In shock, Skye could summon nothing but a whisper.

She cut her gaze to Jeb, who stood watching his father closely, his features closed and angry... and hurting. Her heart went out to him. Never in her wildest imaginings had she expected Jeb and Cash to come face-to-face before she'd had a chance to prepare them both in some small way. What was Cash doing out here so early in the day, anyway? Her own anger returned tenfold.

"Damn you, yes."

"Dear God!" Cash sank onto the overstuffed sofa.

"Surprised, Cash?" Skye queried, crossing the room on her bare feet. "Babies are a potential risk of sex, you know. Did you ever once think about that possibility while you were using Susan to satisfy your sexual needs, or did you figure she knew how to keep from getting pregnant? Is that why you dumped me and hit on her instead?"

Cash's head came up sharply. Skye saw him cut a cautious look at Jeb, who was watching with unabashed interest. She regretted the impulse that had prompted her to mention her own disillusionment.

Cash uttered a soft curse. "For God's sake, get over it, Skye! Nothing happened between us but some hot kissing." He was speaking to Skye but directed the commentary to Jeb, who stared back, a look of torment in his eyes.

"You were a green fourteen years old," he said, leveling a look at her that imparted the full impact of his disgust. "If you'll remember, you were the one who came on to me. I turned you down, and I hurt your pride. How dare you stand there in your self-imposed righteousness and presume to pass judgment on me and Susan, who, by the way, was the most unselfish, unjudgmental person I've ever known."

Jeb made a strangled noise. Both Skye and Cash turned toward him. His face was red, and the torment in his eyes had grown to agony.

"Get out of here, Jeb," Skye commanded, jerking her turbaned head toward the kitchen.

"No," he choked out in a strangled voice.

"Jeb..."

"Let him stay," Cash countered. "This concerns him as much as it does either of us. More than it concerns you."

Jeb went to stand by the window where he could watch and listen from a distance.

"Susan was an adult," Cash continued, "not a naive kid. She knew what she was getting into, and she knew the risks. I suppose I figured she knew the score."

"And that excuses your behavior?"

"Maybe if you'd be more specific about what you mean, I could answer that better."

Skye threw up her hands in disbelief. "You got Susan pregnant, and then you rode off on your motorcycle and left her to deal with the gossip and the censure. You used her, and you discarded her like a worn-out shirt. Is that specific enough?"

The spasm of anguish that crossed Cash's attractive features tugged at Skye's heart, despite her anger.

"I didn't know she was pregnant when I left," he said. "If I had known, I wouldn't have gone."

Easy words. A predictable response. "Damn you!" she railed. "You never even called her—not once! What happened, Cash? Out of sight, out of mind?"

"I didn't contact Susan because she asked me not to."

"Oh, really?"

"Really." A thoughtful expression entered Cash's eyes. "You know, this cuts both ways."

"What are you getting at?" Skye asked, frowning.

"If you were so upset about my letting Susan deal with the pregnancy and the gossip all by herself, why didn't you call me? You knew where I lived, and you knew how to dial Information."

"Susan asked me not to."

His lips quirked in a humorless smile.

"But I called anyway," she hastened to add.

His smile turned into a scowl that deepened as she went on.

"I called your house several times. I left messages for you and said it was important, but you never called back."

"Assuming you're telling the truth, I never got the messages."

The room grew uncomfortably quiet as the three of them looked from one to the other and back again, searching each other's eyes, trying to read unreadable expressions, doing their best to gauge the truth.

Then, obviously unable to swallow the comment, Jeb turned to Cash. "Liar," he said in a deadly tone. Then, without waiting for a response, he ran out the front door.

"Jeb!" Skye cried, following him onto the porch. He didn't answer. Instead, he headed for the garage. The damage done to his psyche during the past few moments was forgotten beneath a more immediate fear: he was leaving on the motorcycle, and he was wearing nothing but a pair of shorts.

She ran back inside the house, brushed past Cash and snatched Jeb's helmet from the chair. The sound of the Harley's engine wafted into the room on the breath of the morning as she burst back out the door. She reached the edge of the porch in time to see Jeb, astride the Harley, peel out down the driveway, take the corner at a dangerous angle and roar toward the hill.

Skye clutched the helmet to her breast and bit back a sob of fear and frustration. He was angry. Furious. Hurt. And going far too fast for his troubled state of mind. What if he had a wreck? What if he—

"He'll be back."

The sound of Cash's voice sent her spinning around. He had let himself out. His gaze rested on hers, troubled and wary.

"Of course he'll be back," she affirmed angrily. Then, turning her back on him, she stood and watched as the motorcycle topped the hill and disappeared.

"I guess I should go, too."

"I guess you should," she said. "I think you've done enough damage for one day."

"The damage was done a long time ago," he reminded her.

She felt the scalding heat of tears gathering in her eyes as she looked up at him. "Why did you have to come back?" she asked in an anguished voice.

"Because I wanted to see her—and you—again."

Her eyes drifted shut to block out the sight of the pain on his handsome face.

"I know you aren't inclined to believe me, but I did care for you. Enough to push you away, even though I wanted nothing more than to take you up on your offer that night."

A sob shuddered through her.

"I cared for Susan, too. I loved her. And I'm more sorry than you'll ever know that things turned out this way." Without another word, Cash crossed the porch and went down the steps.

Skye felt the tears spill over and slide down her cheeks. She swiped at them with her fingertips. "Cash!"

He turned.

"Were you telling the truth about not getting the messages?"

He nodded. "I swear."

Cash paced his room at the motel, his mind still reeling over the confrontation with Skye and Jeb. He had a son. An eighteen-year-old son. A son who, from all appearances, despised him.

How had this happened? Oh, he knew how it happened, but how had things become so...so...messed up? He'd told the truth when he said Susan had instructed him not to call her or come back.

"Go home," she'd said. "Make your peace with your father. Your future is there, not here."

"I don't want to go back. I love you."

"You think you love me. But believe me, it would never work. There are too many differences between us." She had smiled. "Not to mention too many years."

In the end, he had agreed to her terms. Go home. Don't call. Don't come back. Remember what they'd shared as a wonderful summer dream.

He'd done his best to do just that. He'd missed her, missed the sex they'd shared. He'd missed Skye, too, though he'd refused to let himself dwell on that. He'd wanted to call, had even picked up the phone and dialed the number, but the remembered look on Susan's face had always stopped him—the determined set of her chin, the imperturbable expression in her blue eyes....

He had remembered, though. Not only had he remembered, he would never forget that summer—or her. In fact, every woman in his life had been measured against the yardstick of Susan Herder and come out wanting. Even Liz. The only one who'd come close—probably because they were so much alike—was Skye, and she'd still been too young....

Cash paced to the window and leaned his forehead against the cool glass. "Did you know you were pregnant when I left?" he asked out loud, as if Susan were there to answer him.

Of course she had. That's why she'd been so adamant that there be no more communication between them. It wasn't that she was being selfish by keeping the knowledge of her pregnancy a secret. She was being unselfish by refusing to put him in a position where he would feel obligated to do the right thing and sacrifice what she believed was his bright future just to spare her the burden of shame.

Oh, Susan!

He sighed as another thought crept into his memory. *"Be sure your sins will find you out."* The warning was another favorite of his mother's. Obviously, she was right, even though it might take years for the truth to surface.

Cash went to the bed and stretched out with his hands behind his head. He wondered if Jeb was back yet, if he was all right. It would be a crying shame to find out he had a son, only to lose him in an accident the next instant.

A son. He had a son. Despite the heaviness of his heart, Cash felt an undeniable sense of pleasure. Jeb was right. They did resemble one another. Strongly. And it appeared Jeb was as hardheaded as he was, too.

Cash wondered if Jeb had inherited his skill with numbers. If he had Susan's good heart. He thought about the baseball trophies he'd seen and realized they must be Jeb's. Cash wondered what other sports Jeb liked. There were so many things he wanted to know about the boy he'd fathered, and so little time to find out. He should get back to Lincoln. Ceil needed him.

Ceil. Good Lord! He hadn't thought about the impact the news about Jeb would have on his other life. The first thing he had to do was tell Ceil about Jeb. She could help him get a handle on the situation.

Telling Darby could wait until he went back home. Informing an eleven-year-old girl she had a brother wasn't something to do over the phone—especially when she was already feeling insecure. He found himself smiling again. Darby had always wanted a brother or sister. She'd be pleased.

He'd have to have his lawyer make some changes in his will; Jeb couldn't be left out in the cold. And he couldn't wait to find a bigger place so both Jeb and Darby would have room when they stayed with him.

Whoa! One step at a time, Benedict.

Here he was making plans for Jeb to visit him, and right now the kid hated his guts. He knew Jeb was hurt and angry, but surely in time they could work things out. If the boy would just give him a chance, he'd prove to him he could be a good father.

The way you were to Darby?

A wave of regret washed over Cash. He'd already admitted that he hadn't been the best father, but he intended to change all that. He would go home and get his life in Lincoln straightened out, but first he had to see if it was possible to forge a relationship with Jeb. Surely he hadn't been given this second chance for nothing.

Lifting his arm, Cash glanced at the watch strapped around his wrist. Skye would be gone by now, and there was the possibility that Jeb had returned to the farm. If he had, maybe he could catch him. If he hadn't, Cash knew he could wait....

As soon as Skye could put herself together for the day, she drove straight to her source of strength: Harold Herder. He seemed to be having a good day and, after listening to her version of what had happened between her and Cash and Jeb that morning, asked, "Do you believe he never got the messages?"

"I don't know what to believe," Skye confessed. "I know I was hurt. I know people make mistakes." She thought of Lee Ballard. "Lord knows, I've made my share."

"Then you believe in forgiveness if someone is genuinely sorry for what they've done?"

Skye frowned, uncertain where the conversation was headed. With Opa it was sometimes hard to tell—especially lately. "Of course I do."

"And in spite of what happened back then, do you believe your mother was a good person?" Harold asked.

Skye shrugged with a feeling of dismay and sorrow. Opa was about to go off on one of his tangents. What did Susan and her mother have to do with Jeb and Cash?

"Making a mistake or two along the way doesn't mean you're a lost cause."

Harold rubbed his cheek thoughtfully. "When Jon came home from that vacation of his and said he planned to marry her, I admit I had my doubts, but she proved to be a good and loving wife.

"Your mother made her share of mistakes, mind you—we all do, but she was good for Jon and good to Jon, nonetheless."

"You mean Susan," Skye corrected gently. Obviously, Opa was more confused than she thought.

"Of course I mean Susan!" he said, pinning Skye with a fierce look from beneath his shaggy white eyebrows. "But she kept too many secrets. She was always worried about someone getting hurt. You. Jon. Cash. You have a right to know the truth, the same way Cash and Jeb had the right to know. I always told her that."

"Opa," Skye said, sorrow and confusion darkening her eyes at the way his once-sharp mind was deteriorating. "I don't have the vaguest notion of what you're talking about."

"I'm talking about the truth, girl," he told her in a stern voice. "The whole truth and nothing but the truth."

He gripped the arms of his chair and levered himself to his feet, a clearly painful task.

Skye was beside him in an instant. "What do you want, Opa? I'll get it."

"No. There's something you should see. Something you should have known about your mother a long time ago."

Skye watched him shuffle off toward his bedroom. Her concern about Jeb and Cash was supplanted by worry about Opa. His periods of lucidity were getting shorter and shorter, and the bad days often outnumbered the good.

"I told her she should tell you," he muttered as he disappeared into his room. "I told Jon. They wouldn't listen. Keeping that sort of thing a secret is trouble, I tell you."

Again she wondered what he could possibly have of Susan's and her mother's that he thought would have any bearing on the situation with Jeb and Cash.

When Harold came back, he carried a small box that contained five or six little books. They were diaries, just like the ones she'd filled as a young girl.

He extended the box toward her. "Here you go. Pandora's box."

"My diaries!" she exclaimed. "Where did you get them?"

"They aren't yours, girl. They're your mother's, and I think it's high time you saw what was in them."

Chapter Five

I thought I'd made the right decision about the baby, but it's hard walking down the street knowing everyone knows, knowing what they're thinking about me. I may regret it one day, but I don't think so, even though everyone keeps talking about repercussions somewhere down the line. All I can do is live one day at a time and deal with the fallout when it happens.

Cradling the box against her, Skye flipped through a couple of the small journals and realized instantly that they weren't her mother's diaries at all. That bold, slanting scrawl was undeniably Susan's. Poor Opa, she thought with a sigh. She thanked him for listening, gave him a hug and left him with a kiss and a promise that she'd see him soon.

Tears blurred her vision as she stashed the box of diaries on the front seat of the car. The Alzheimer's was eroding his mind as surely as the constant flow of water eroded the banks of the nearby river.

He'd been bad today, she thought as she drove to the shop, thinking about how little of what he'd said made sense. Mistaking her and Susan and confusing Susan with their mother.... At least he was still able to care for his physical needs. She wondered just how long he'd be able to function alone.

But as worried as she was about Opa, she was more concerned about what to do about the confrontation between her, Jeb and Cash. The scene played through her mind with relentless monotony as she dusted and straightened the shop's merchandise.

She could still see the surprise on Cash's face when he'd asked her the truth about Jeb. She had no doubt that his shock was genuine. Jeb might have been surprised at having Cash show up after so long, but at least he'd had a few years to grow accustomed to the idea of his conception.

After giving herself some time to think about it, Skye was convinced Cash was telling the truth about not receiving word of her phone calls, too. He might have been a rich, spoiled teenager, and he might have grown into a similar-minded adult, but the blank look of total surprise on his face would be hard for even a seasoned actor to pull off.

So what had happened? Had the messages gotten lost, or had someone deliberately kept the calls a secret? Recalling the things Cash had told her about his father, Skye decided that the elder Benedict probably had had no compunction about withholding any information that might tempt Cash to reestablish contact with her and Susan. Still, she thought he could have called anyway.

Tired of trying to rationalize Cash's behavior, Skye started a new picture and turned her thoughts to Jeb. Coming face-to-face with the father he'd never seen had been a shock to him, too. He must be in terrible pain, not to mention confused.

She called the house at lunch—he had never shown up to do the unpacking—but he didn't answer. A quick call to Belinda proved futile, too. She swore she hadn't seen him.

Skye cradled the phone and glanced at the clock again. Maybe he was at the ball field in Middle. He liked to practice his pitching when he was upset. Unfortunately, there was no way to call him there. She prayed that he would come to his senses and show up for work. He couldn't afford to jeopardize his job at the Holiday Inn; he needed to save every penny possible for school in the fall.

The bell on the door jingled, and a customer walked in. Skye pushed aside her worries long enough to give the client her undivided attention. Business was good, but she'd never be rich. She needed to make the sale. Like Jeb, she needed to work. The bills went on, even when the tourist trade tapered off during the winter months.

She'd been saving all she could the past few years to put into Jeb's college fund just in case he didn't get the baseball scholarship they were counting on. Thank God that had come through, even though he was less than thrilled about the prospect of college.

Even with the scholarship, things would be tight. Jeb would need money for his dormitory, lunch tickets and a dozen other things she knew would crop up. Skye knew she couldn't borrow any more against the farm. All that was left of Jon Herder's fifty acres was a run-down house that needed never-ending repairs and five acres of herb and flower gardens. But Skye wouldn't have moved into a new house if someone gave her one. The Herder house was home, and she wasn't about to leave.

Susan had been forced to sell most of the farm to the Amana Society shortly after Jeb was born and the ancient tractor up and died in the middle of planting season. She'd made the decision tearfully, but she simply couldn't keep the farm going any longer.

After paying off the debt at the bank, there hadn't been much money left, and Susan had said they had to save that for a rainy day. To make ends meet, she'd worked as a waitress in various restaurants, a position she'd held until the cancer got so bad she was forced to quit.

The ringing of the phone intruded on Skye's memories. She picked up the replica of an old-fashioned phone that hung on the wall. "Herder's."

"Hey! It's me."

"Jeb!" Relief left Skye feeling weak. "Where are you? Where have you been? Are you all right?" The questions tumbled from her lips on a wave of concern.

"At home, riding around, and I think so."

She heard the hint of humor in Jeb's voice and felt the tension leave her body. "Want to talk?"

"Not now. I'm still sort of punchy, you know? I guess I'd decided I would never set eyes on the guy unless I looked him up, and then, bam! There he is on the front doorstep."

"Would you have looked him up when you got to Lincoln?" Skye queried in a soft voice.

"I honestly don't know."

"He'll be back, and he'll want to try to . . . make amends, or something. I know him well enough to know that."

Jeb sighed. "I figured as much. I know I'm going to have to deal with it, and I will. I just . . . I'm so damn mad right now."

"I know. I've been mad at him for a long time, and there are still a lot of things I'm not sure about, but for what it's worth, I think he's telling the truth about not getting the messages."

"Yeah, well, if he loved Mom the way he claims, he should have called her even though she told him not to."

"That's what I thought," Skye said. The bell at the door chimed again. "Look, honey, I've got a customer," she said. "We'll talk tonight when I get home."

"I'm probably going to stop by Belinda's and tell her what's going on. Maybe she can give me some advice."

Skye's heart constricted at the thought that Jeb preferred getting advice from Belinda instead of her. It was hard to face the fact that he was growing up, growing away from her. She told herself that it was a natural occurrence, that it didn't mean he loved her any less, but it still hurt.

"Don't be too late," she cautioned, forcing her tone toward lightness, not wanting to start another quarrel. Not today, at least.

Jeb must have sensed how she felt. He must have felt the same. "I won't."

Cash returned to the motel just before five—hot, tired and starving. Somehow he'd missed Jeb, even though he suspected the boy had been back home to grab a change of clothes. He'd waited for him, but after a while the sitting got to him and, as he'd looked around, he'd realized that there was a lot that needed doing on the farm. He'd spent the morning taking inventory of what needed fixing and drawing up a list of things needed to implement those repairs.

Then he'd gone into Marengo, bought his supplies and some snacks for lunch and spent the remainder of the day trying to beat back the ravages of time and neglect. He fixed the screen door and the garden gate. He replaced a broken windowpane at the back of the house and replaced a couple of boards on the porch. By late afternoon, he couldn't tell he'd done much. On the other hand, it was the first time in a long while he had felt good about a day's accomplishments.

After showering away the grime from a day of hard labor, Cash dialed Ceil at the office. Even though it was after five, he'd wager she was still there. He'd wanted to call her earlier, but had needed some time and space to try to come to grips with the news about Jeb, before passing it on.

Ceil answered the phone herself.

"Hi, sis."

"Hey!" she said, genuine pleasure in her voice. "You must be having a great time. I thought you'd call before now."

"I've been checking some things out," he hedged.

"Oh? Where are you?"

"At a Holiday Inn in the Amana Colonies."

"That's a great place! Have you come across anything that might give us a new angle for an issue?"

Cash sighed. "Not really. I've been sort of going back to the places I hung out that summer Dad and I had the falling out."

"Caa-ash!" she groaned, drawing his name out to two syllables. "This little vacation wasn't supposed to be a trip down memory lane."

"So sue me," he interrupted, his voice heavy with mockery.

"I don't have the time," Ceil retorted in a sardonic tone. "I'm too busy holding down the fort."

Cash laughed. "I swear I'll make it up to you. What's going on there, anyway?"

"Well, besides Monica Jefferson quitting, plus trying to deal with my headstrong offspring—not to mention a disgruntled ex-husband—I've been going through some of Mom and Dad's old papers. You can't believe some of the stuff they saved!" Ceil said.

"Monica quit?" Cash asked, going straight to the most pressing problem. Actually, he wasn't all that shocked to learn that the art director of *Hearth and Home* was leaving, considering the magazine's unstable footing.

"Mm-hmm. Apparently she's found less stressful and more stable employment. I was hoping you could talk her into giving it a little more time."

"I can't come back right now," Cash told her. "I need a few more days."

"Something's happened," Ceil said in a discerning tone. "Something bad. I can tell from your voice."

"It isn't necessarily bad," Cash hedged. "Just a shock."

"Stop beating around the bush and tell me what's going on," she commanded.

Cash knew there was no sense trying to put Ceil off. She was as stubborn as a dog with a bone. "Do you remember my telling you about Susan and Skye Herder?"

"Yes," Ceil said thoughtfully. "Susan was the woman you worked for that summer and Skye was her sis— Oh, Cash! Don't tell me you looked this woman up and fell for the sister! You just got a divorce. Did you ever hear of a thing called rebound?"

"Did you ever hear of not jumping to conclusions?" he countered.

"I'm sorry." Ceil's tone was properly contrite.

"I did look them up, and I found out that Susan is dead."

"Oh, Cash! I'm so sorry. I know you were fond of her."

"I was more than fond of Susan."

"I know you had a big crush on her, but—"

"We had an affair, sis." The straightforward confession was brusque, tactless and left no room for quibbling.

"I beg your pardon?"

"I had a two-month affair with Susan Herder."

"You mean Skye," she corrected.

"Susan."

"But... you were only nineteen," Ceil argued. "She'd have been—"

"Thirty," Cash said.

"Good Lord." A lengthy silence stretched over the phone lines. "Why are you telling me this now?" Ceil said at last. "I mean, if Susan is dead, why bring it up?"

"I'm telling you because I just found out this morning that Susan and I have a son."

"That isn't funny, brother dear." Shock and disbelief infused his sister's voice.

"I'm not joking. His name is Jeb, and he's eighteen, and yes—I know what you're going to ask next—I'm sure he's mine. Looking at him is like looking into a mirror."

"Oh, Cash," Ceil breathed on a sigh. Then, "Does he know?"

"He does now."

"And?"

"To say that he despises me would be an understatement."

"What are you going to do?"

Cash fumbled in his shirt pocket for an antacid tablet and thumbed a couple from the package. "Damned if I know. But I know I have to do something. I can't pretend it never happened. It's time I started getting my life in some kind of order, and that includes trying to become a good parent to my kids—both my kids."

Skye was waiting on a customer when it occurred to her that Susan's diaries might have entries about her affair with Cash. The thought was both intriguing and loathsome. One part of her wanted to know what had been between them, but another part of her shied away from reading the details of their sexual encounters. After wrestling with the problem for the better part of an hour, Skye decided that the diaries would go into her cedar chest unread. With everything else that was happening in her life, she didn't need to add to her grief.

She was glad when the clock struck five and she could lock up for the day. The afternoon had dragged. Business had slowed to a trickle, and the picture she'd started was a lost cause. It was hard to be creative when her mind was in turmoil.

She got into her car and started home, her thoughts turning to Cash now that she knew Jeb hadn't gone off the deep end. Nervously, motherlike, she wondered what Cash thought of his son. Did he think Jeb was handsome? Did he wonder about his son's likes and dislikes? Would he approve of the way she and Susan had raised Jeb?

Skye shook her head and turned into the driveway. What did she care? What did it matter? Whatever Cash thought, they'd done the best they could.

The first thing Skye noticed when she stepped onto the porch was that the sagging screen door had been fixed. The hinges had been replaced, and a diagonal rod of metal now drew the aging frame taut so it wouldn't drag on the threshold. Nice, she thought with a smile. Jeb must have decided to work out his frustrations by tackling the list of chores she'd made for him a few weeks ago. He was the kind of person who needed to keep busy when he was troubled.

After she finished her dinner—a tuna sandwich, cottage cheese and diet cola—Skye idly flipped through the pages of one of the diaries and realized that she was right. They were Susan's. Then, determined not to go against her promise to herself, she slammed the book shut and tossed it into the cardboard container.

Handling the box as if it held a nest of angry rattlesnakes, she carried it to her bedroom. On her knees, she raised the top of the cedar chest and gathered two or three of the small books. Glancing down, she saw that the one on top was dated the year of Susan's death. Hardly aware of what she was doing, she began to sift through the box.

Skye soon found that the earliest entries were made thirty-eight years ago when Susan lived with their parents, Melanie and Steven Jordan, in Springfield, Illinois. But Susan's youthful writing held no interest. It was the summer of '77 Skye was curious about. It took only a moment to locate the diary, which held three years' worth of entries. Unlike the others, it was locked.

Her curiosity piqued, Skye stared down at the small, faux leather book, wondering what Susan had chronicled inside those locked pages. Were the details of her feelings there, along with her every thought and the tender things she and Cash had said and done to each other?

The thought of reading Susan's most intimate reflections about her affair with Cash left Skye feeling queasy, but deep in her heart she knew that, despite her decision earlier, she was going to read the account—every word.

What was the newest buzzword? Closure? Yes. Maybe if she read about their relationship and saw firsthand what they'd felt for each other, she could put some kind of perspective on her own feelings for Cash and get some kind of closure on the past.

Feeling as if she were about to open a Pandora's box, Skye peeled back the brittle, yellowed cellophane tape that secured a small key to the front. It fit perfectly, and she flipped through the pages in search of the part she wanted.

It soon became apparent that Susan hadn't made daily entries. She would go for weeks, sometimes months without writing a word, and then there would be faithful jottings for an unspecified time. Curiously, Susan hadn't bothered writing down mundane happenings. She seemed to be more committed to putting down her thoughts when she was troubled or when her life was going exceptionally well.

Skye skimmed the daily additions until she got to the place where Susan admitted to being attracted to Cash, which, she wrote, was "stupid, because he's just a kid, and he has eyes for Skye."

A few days later the entry said:

Something happened between him and Skye. I don't know what it is, but he steers clear of her, and she looks at him like she'd like to gouge out his eyes. He's spending more time with me in the evenings now, and even though I know I should discourage it, I don't. When I'm with him I feel pretty and desirable—special, somehow—and God knows I haven't felt that way in so long. . . .

Another day Susan had written:

God help me, I want him. He wants me, too. I can see it in his eyes. When he looks at me and smiles that slow, sexy smile, I feel eighteen again. Eighteen and feminine and desirable in a way I haven't felt since I was fifteen. As wonderful as Jon was, he never made me feel this way—like I want to rip off my clothes and have him take me right there in the field, or wherever we happen to be. Dear God, what's the matter with me? This is so wrong. . . .

There was more of the same; Susan's growing attraction for Cash and the reasons behind it. Cash was the symbol of the youth that was slipping away from her. She loved his determination, his energy, the hundreds of ways he showed her and Skye kindness and concern. Susan hadn't been *in love* since someone named Larry when she was fifteen, and while Cash reminded her of Larry a lot, he also reminded her of Jon in many ways, which was strange because they weren't really alike at all.

Finding Jon when her life had been in turmoil had been like finding a calm, still pool. He had been her center. Their life might not have been exciting, but it had been filled with an abundance of affection and balanced with healthy doses of respect and admiration. Loving Jon was safe. Comfortable.

Contrarily, her flourishing feelings for Cash were like the rushing surge of the river after a spring storm. Dangerously alluring, but with the potential for destruction. As Skye read, she realized that there was no doubt that Susan's inappropriate feelings for Cash troubled her a great deal. Yet there was no doubt where those feelings were leading, either.

Skye found what she was looking for in the entry for July 4, 1977.

It's 2:00 a.m., after the storm. I did it, and while it was wonderful and exciting and made me feel wonderful and exciting, I can't help this wretched feeling of guilt. I have no excuse except that I'm so lonely. Sometimes I think I'll die of loneliness. By most yardsticks, I'm still a young woman, but since Jon died, I feel as if my life has ended, too. I wonder what happened to the wild young girl who went to stay with Aunt Dolores that summer? Who knows? And who, besides me, really cares?

There's nothing for me here, yet I stay, because to think of leaving frightens me so. I stay and get lonelier and more set in my ways and complain in a journal about the inequities of life, and in my loneliness I deliberately seduce young men—well, one, at least.

I guess that's what bothers me the most. Maybe I'd feel differently if Cash had come to me, but no—like a Jezebel, I got fixed up and went to his room. If he'd made the first move, I could feel some sort of righteous indignation, even though I gave in, but he didn't, and all I feel is blame.

To make matters worse, it was his first time. I'm not sure I can forgive myself for that, but even knowing I'm condemning myself, if he comes to me, I know it will happen again and again . . . until he gets tired of me, or until the guilt gets so bad I'm forced to find the backbone to send him away. . . .

In an addition dated almost two months later, Susan said that she'd told Cash to go back to Lincoln and his family. She'd told him to forget her and not to call. There was no future for them, nothing for him there.

With her heart filled with an incredible ache, Skye closed the diary and stared at the darkness outside the lacy covering of her window. She knew what Susan meant about the loneliness. She had been, and still was, a victim of that debilitating condition herself.

Skye also knew that Susan's decision to send Cash away had been the right one, regardless of how much pain his leaving brought. No one in the ultra-traditional rural community around Amana and Marengo would have accepted the relationship between her and Cash. It had been hard enough dealing with the gossip that accompanied Jeb's birth.

As if it were yesterday, Skye recalled the sound of Susan's muffled crying in the days and weeks after Cash left. It was Christmas before she figured out that the tears were about more than Cash's leaving and realized Susan was expecting a baby.

As usual, the speculation about Susan's affair with her summer help ran its course, and by the time Jeb was born the following May something juicier had come along to feed the scandal mill.

Actually, the majority of people from the church who had been close to Jon and Harold had rallied in true Christian spirit, bringing food and gifts and well wishes for the baby's future. Susan might have been an outsider, but she had gained a certain amount of grudging respect during her fourteen years on the Herder farm, and few of Amana's citizens had pointed a finger, knowing too well how easy it was to fall into the devil's snare.

Soon after Jeb's birth, Susan had been forced to sell most of the farm to the Society and had taken a succession of waitress jobs to make ends meet. Skye baby-sat Jeb and other children to earn money for her school clothes and extracurricular activities—not that she'd had much spare time for that. Taking care of children after school and during the summer months didn't leave much time for fun; Susan's mistake had forced Skye to grow up before her time.

Knowing that Cash had slept with Susan and then left her to face the rumormongers fueled an anger in Skye that simmered just below the surface for almost twenty years. Adding what she deemed Cash's coldhearted treatment of Susan to what she considered his callous brush-off of her, Skye went through high school with an inordinate amount of distrust of the opposite sex. In her estimation, there were too many guys like Cash and too few like Jon.

There were several boys who interested her, but she seldom dated anyone more than a few times, refused to go steady and kept her emotions on a tight rein. No male had been able to get past her deep-rooted suspicions until she started dating Lee Ballard.

Lee, father to two young daughters and Amana's most eligible bachelor since his wife's death in an auto accident, was a good-looking blond whose family had lived in Middle since the community was first settled. Skye was twenty-five, and possibly the only twenty-five-year-old virgin in the state the year Susan died, and twenty-nine-year-old Lee suddenly decided that she'd grown up to be "a gorgeous woman."

Unable to entirely banish the very human need for approval, Skye was flattered by his attention. Lee swept her off her feet and into his bed within two months. They were engaged a month later. When she explained to Lee that Jeb was her responsibility since Susan's death, he'd told her to put him in a home; he wasn't ready for the responsibility of another child, especially a rowdy boy who took delight in terrorizing his delicate daughters.

Skye thought she could sway him, but she was wrong. When it became clear that neither of them would budge, Lee broke the engagement. He was married to someone else in less than a year. Unlike Skye, who held definite opinions about how marriage should be, Marjorie Altmann was fresh out of college, still malleable and, like Lee, a descendant of those who'd migrated to Amana. In short, she was far more acceptable to Lee's family.

Total devastation couldn't begin to describe Skye's feelings when she heard of the upcoming nuptials. She was heartbroken. She'd been deceived, deluded, deserted. It took her months to recover even a portion of her equanimity and to realize that Lee had used her, that he'd never really loved her.

Anger and bitterness followed the demise of her hurt. Even though she knew she was at fault, she found herself making excuses for giving in to the despised, but undeniable, demands of her body. Susan's death had left her vulnerable. Vulnerable and lonely. And Lee was the kind of man who could charm anyone with his easygoing banter and that sexy smile.

When the final reckoning came down, she concluded that she'd slept with Lee for two simple reasons: he'd filled a need in her life, and she'd wanted him. How could she blame him for taking what she'd been so willing to give? It had taken her years to get over Lee's rejection of her and Jeb, and then she'd been stupid enough to let him hurt her again....

Lee and Marjorie, who had also given him two children, had divorced almost a year ago, during Jeb's senior year, because of irreconcilable differences. To Skye's shock, Lee had stopped by the shop unexpectedly...just to pass the time.

Though she'd done her best to avoid him the past eight years—no small feat considering Amana's population—she quickly found he hadn't lost his touch. He was still handsome, still charming, still smooth as aged whiskey. Skye's heart still missed a beat when he turned that sexy smile on her, but she refused to give him the satisfaction of knowing, treating him with all the friendliness of a pit viper. Undeterred, he called every evening. Skye vacillated between anger at his gall and an unanticipated and undesirable pleasure at his tenacity.

If anyone had asked her, she would have said Lee Ballard lacked patience. She was wrong. He wore her down like chalk on a sidewalk. Eventually, the calls and visits became dates, where he had confessed that he'd made a mistake by giving in to his parents' wishes and marrying Marjorie.

"That isn't why you broke our engagement," Skye had reminded him that evening nearly nine months ago. "It was Jeb, remember?"

Lee had the grace to look embarrassed. "Touché," he said with a shrug of his elegant shoulders. "I have no excuse. Only a reason."

"And what was that?"

"Taking on the responsibility of a ten-year-old boy was more than I thought I could handle with the girls."

Skye had expected excuses, and his honesty surprised her. She countered with typical directness. "Jeb is still a big part of my life, Lee, so exactly what is it you want?"

He smiled, and those teasing blue eyes twinkled. "You," he said, taking her off guard again. "And Jeb is eighteen now, about to leave home."

She shook her head. "He won't be around to get in the way, is that it?" When he smiled, she asked, "Isn't that a bit selfish?"

Lee leaned across the table. "Is it a sin to want you all to myself?" he asked, those cornflower blue eyes caressing her face with a look that upped the tempo of her heartbeats in spite of herself.

No. It wasn't a sin, and the idea of Lee having her all to himself was sinfully appealing. Since he was the only man she'd ever given herself to, she had no means of comparison, but what she recalled of their brief, passionate encounter made her body tingle with remembered desire.

He reached out and took her hand. "I haven't forgotten how it was, either," he said, reading the look in her eyes. "You were magnificent in bed."

"Lee!" Skye felt her face flame and glanced around to see if anyone overheard his bold statement. She was shocked by his bluntness, but her heart was suffused with a warmth that matched the heat of her face.

She should have known better than to let him lure her into another affair. Her intellect told her she was making a mistake, that she was a fool; her body wouldn't listen. Her last coherent thought before he took her into his bedroom was that she was taking a huge risk with her battered heart.

She rationalized her actions by telling herself Jeb *was* going off to school. The Alzheimer's taking over Opa's mind and body was making him more of a stranger every day. She was thirty-three years old, unmarried, with no prospect of finding love in the future. She was exactly in the same place Susan had no doubt found herself in the summer of '77— alone and lonely and certain that love and life were passing her by.

This time the affair lasted only a month. This time Lee called it off because his parents were afraid that it was too soon to bring another woman into his daughters' lives. They were in the middle of those troubled teenage years, confused and hurt that he would try to replace their mother yet again. As usual, Lee gave over to the elder Ballards' wishes and broke off the relationship—again with profuse apologies.

This time Skye hadn't bothered with the pain. She bypassed the hurt and went straight to bitter anger. She was furious with Lee for letting his children and his parents dictate to him the way he did, and even more furious with herself for being such a fool and falling for his line twice, which was why she'd been so irate when she'd opened the door to see Cash standing there that afternoon.

Like Lee, Cash was a reminder of her failures. Like Lee, Cash was the epitome of the love-'em-and-leave-'em kind of man who seemed to waltz in and out of the Herder women's lives. As Skye had stood there looking at Cash, all the painful memories from that summer had come rushing back and mingled with recollections of her recent romantic fiasco with Lee.

She had felt anything but charitable. Cash had wanted to talk over old times; she'd wanted to rip out his lying tongue and condemn him to an everlasting hell, a feeling that hadn't abated until just now, when she'd read Susan's account of their May-December romance.

Tears filled her eyes as she sat there with the soft breath of the air conditioner washing over her. Skye put the diary in the box with the others. She'd read more later. Right now she was mentally exhausted, emotionally drained.

It was hard picturing Susan as a femme fatale, hard to envision her dressing up and going to any man's room to instigate a night of lovemaking. Yet that's exactly what had happened. Cash had been telling the truth about Susan's request that he not call or come back, too.

Her new insight had cleansed her of the anger she'd harbored in her heart for so many years. How could she blame Cash, when it was obvious that Susan had been the one to initiate their relationship? How could she blame either of them for trying to keep the loneliness at bay by latching on to a warm and willing body, when she was guilty of doing the same thing?

She had been so caught up in her bitterness that she'd forgotten that Cash was barely nineteen when he'd come to work for them. How could she judge his behavior as uncaring and insensitive knowing that his maturity level at nineteen wasn't what it was bound to be at thirty-eight?

Wrath against Cash—against all men—had been a part of her for so long, Skye felt strangely empty without it blazing inside her. Empty and afraid. Cash wasn't finished with her and Jeb yet. Now that he knew the truth, he would want to be a part of Jeb's life; she was sure of that.

Skye pressed her fingertips to her lips to hold back a low sob of despair. How could she find the strength to fight for Jeb without that anger to sustain her?

Chapter Six

Dear Diary,
Right or wrong, I did it. I have no excuse for sleeping
with him—not any that's worth a darn. All I can say
is that he makes me feel special. I was lonely, and—
this is the strange part—I think I'm falling in love with
him, and I thought I was too scarred to ever really love
anyone again. I can't believe I'm writing in my diary,
for crying out loud! I haven't felt the urge to bare my
soul this way in years, but there's no one to talk to,
and maybe confession really is good for the soul.

After a sleepless Friday night, Skye was awakened by a
rhythmic pounding. She opened her eyes to find the saucy
Saturday-morning sun streaming through the lace curtains
at her window. The hands of the bedside clock pointed to

seven forty-five. Groaning, she flung her forearm over her face.

The pounding, which seemed to be coming from the direction of the barn, resumed. Darn Jeb, anyway! she thought, raising herself to her elbows. She appreciated the fact that he was finally getting around to the chores she'd outlined for him, but why didn't he have the decency to wait until she was awake to start raising such a ruckus?

With a deep sigh, Skye climbed down from the antique bed where Jon Herder had been born. Eager to tell Jeb to lay off until she got a cup of coffee in her, she started for the window. She was halfway there when she remembered that Jeb had called late the night before to tell her he was staying over at Dale's because they had ball practice early this morning, and Dale didn't have a ride to the field.

The *bang, bang, bang* of the hammer lured her. What on earth was going on? Had Jeb changed his mind and come home after she fell asleep? She went to the window, where a soft breeze, already seasoned with the promise of heat, rippled the delicate lacework. Placing her palms on the sill, she leaned forward. The sight that met her startled eyes made her knees grow weak. It wasn't Jeb pounding nails into the warped boards of the barn; it was Cash.

Hammer in hand, he was perched on an extension ladder that leaned precariously against the barn's weathered exterior. He was wearing new blue jeans and a short-sleeved cotton shirt that he hadn't bothered to tuck in. The sight of him working on the barn brought back a plethora of memories. Hadn't he replaced barn boards that fateful summer?

Skye thought of the repaired screen door and the new hinges on the garden gate. The listing mailbox had been set in concrete, and the broken pane of glass in the downstairs window had been replaced. She had assumed Jeb was responsible for the restorations, but now it appeared she was as wrong about that as she had been about Cash's reasons for not coming back.

What on earth did he think he was doing? she wondered, grabbing a short satin robe and pulling it on over the silky panties and sleeveless T-shirt she'd worn to bed. And more to the point, *why* was he doing it? Running her hands through her sleep-tangled hair, she headed down the stairs for the back porch.

The sound of the back screen door slamming brought Cash's head around. Skye felt his eyes on her as she approached the ladder and stifled a sudden, ridiculous impulse to tug the short robe down over her thighs.

When she reached the ladder, she planted her hands on her hips and looked up at him. The expression in his eyes was solemn, wary.

"What do you think you're doing?"

He shrugged. "Fixing the barn."

"Like you fixed the gate, the mailbox and the window?"

"Yeah."

"Why?"

"Why?" he echoed. "Because they needed fixing."

"It isn't your place to do repairs anymore," she reminded him.

"Maybe not," he agreed, starting down the ladder, "but I need to do it, and I had some time on my hands while I was waiting."

"You *need* to do it?"

He offered her a self-deprecating smile. "It's crazy, I know, but it's sort of like—" he paused "—it's the least I can do for her, you know?"

Skye compressed her lips to stop their trembling. Strangely enough, she did know what he meant. "And what are you waiting for?"

"Jeb to come home."

A startled breath hung in Skye's throat. She'd known he would want to talk to Jeb, but still... Her sudden anxiety was tempered by the rueful smile that claimed Cash's shapely mouth.

"He must have radar where I'm concerned. I haven't been able to catch him yet."

"He has practice most mornings," Skye told him, stuffing her hands into the pockets of the skimpy robe. "He works from eleven to three. Most evenings he's at his girlfriend's house."

"He has a girlfriend?" Cash asked, negotiating the last step of the ladder and turning to face her.

"Most boys his age do." As soon as she said it, she wished she hadn't. Cash hadn't been much older than Jeb when he'd had the affair with Susan.

Cash's eyes shifted from hers to the house, and she wondered if it was her imagination that his lean cheeks reddened with embarrassment.

"Yeah, I guess they do."

For a moment, they stood awkwardly in the early-morning sunlight, remembering....

Cash cleared his throat and brought his determined gaze back to hers. "Where does he work?" he asked at last.

"The Holiday Inn."

"That's where I'm staying," he said with another smile of regret. "Here I am almost camping out here to see him, and he's been right on my doorstep all along."

Another uncomfortable silence bound them while the memories swirled and danced through their heads. Their eyes met, troubled gazes clashing, then skittering away.

"Truce?"

The unexpected question drew her gaze back to him. She looked down at the hand he extended, torn by indecision and fear.

"If I'd known about Jeb, I'd never have left her. I swear," he said, as if the added explanation might sway her.

Skye considered the possibility that he was saying what she thought she wanted to hear, but she couldn't doubt the earnestness reflected in the deep green pools of his eyes. Still, she didn't speak, didn't offer any word of compromise, for fear of giving him the slightest bit of an edge.

You've got to turn the other cheek, sweetness.

Unexpectedly, Jon's favorite method for righting wrongs sprang into her mind. She felt the sting of tears burning behind her eyelids. Jon was right. Retaliation for wrongs only resulted in more suffering. She knew that Cash had told the truth about his reasons for not coming back. She knew that Susan had instigated their affair, and that Cash had done only what most healthy, sex-minded teenage boys would do. God knew they were all reaping the bitter harvest from the wild seeds that had been so carelessly sown. There was no use deliberately adding to their suffering.

She drew her hand from her pocket and saw that it shook the slightest bit. "Truce," she said in a whisper.

Cash's hand closed around hers. It was as strong and warm as she remembered. Her gaze moved upward. While she stared into his tender eyes, he reached out his free hand and brushed away a stubborn, solitary tear that clung to her lower lashes.

Suddenly, she was assaulted by the memory of his hands caressing her fevered flesh while his body moved against hers in an erotic, primal dance that stoked the heat building inside her. The tips of her breasts grew pebble hard, and her heart shifted into a faster rhythm.

"Skye..."

The sound of his voice snapped the seductive mood chaining them. What in God's name was she doing? Was she fated to make the same mistakes over and over again with the same men? Humiliated, she pulled free.

"Don't!" Shame and anger roughened her voice. "I'm not Susan!"

"No," he said gently. "No one could ever mistake you for Susan."

The unequivocal statement hung there, suspended in the brightness of the morning...intangible in its meaning, taunting in its abstractness.

He smiled suddenly, and a teasing light she remembered entered his eyes. "I don't suppose I could talk you into giving me a cup of coffee while you tell me about my son."

Skye knew he was doing his best to change the dangerous direction their conversation had taken. A smart move, under the circumstances, but she didn't much like the new subject, either. "Sure," she told him. "Come on inside."

While the coffee brewed and a pan of refrigerated cinnamon rolls baked, Skye went upstairs and changed into shorts and a T-shirt, her usual weekend garb. While she brushed her teeth and her hair and added the barest hint of cosmetics, she did her best to conquer her growing anxiety about what Cash planned to do about Jeb.

By the time she went back downstairs, she had her emotions under tight control. She set two mugs of steaming coffee and a plate of cinnamon rolls on the table and seated herself across from Cash.

"I don't want to talk about Susan and what happened here that summer," Cash told her. "We can't go back, and we can't change any of it. If there's one thing I've learned in the past twenty years it's that we make the best decisions we can and we have to live with those decisions—right or wrong."

He was right, Skye thought. That's exactly the way it worked. "Fair enough."

"I want to know what's happened since I left. I want to find out about Jeb... and you."

"Me? Why?"

"Because you're as much a part of that time in my life as Susan was... as Jeb is. You may not believe it, but I've thought as much about you as I have Susan."

The casual admission took her breath. Skye looked into his eyes, searching for the truth. He would never know how much she wanted to believe him, but her experience with Lee told her that to do so would be foolish.

"So what have you been doing the past nineteen years?" he asked. "Besides becoming a successful artist, I mean?"

Her lips lifted in a half smile. "I scratch out a living. I guess that's considered being a success of sorts."

"I saw your work the other day. It's exquisite."

"Thanks," she said, pleased by the compliment.

"I don't guess you married Bobby Balthazer. If I remember correctly, he was calling you twice a day when I left."

Skye felt a hesitant smile tugging at the corners of her mouth. "Oh, yeah, Bobby Balthazer," she said thoughtfully. "That didn't last long, and I've never married."

"You're kidding!" His eyes were wide with surprise.

"No. I was engaged once. Lee Ballard."

"I remember Lee. You flirted with him outrageously that Fourth of July. What happened?"

Skye was surprised he remembered. She'd almost forgotten that day. Probably because seeing Susan flirting with Cash had been so painful.

"It was right after Susan died, and I had Jeb to care for. Lee had a couple of kids and he didn't want to become a father to a ten-year-old boy. I wouldn't put Jeb in a home. He broke the engagement and married someone else a few months later." Skye related the once-heartbreaking events in an even, unemotional tone.

"Poor Skye," Cash said, reaching out and running one long finger across the white knuckles gripping the handle of her mug. "The men in your life haven't done much to promote faith in the opposite sex, have they?"

It was all she could do to keep from pulling her hand free of his disturbing touch. "Jon was the only man I knew I could count on. And there aren't too many Jon Herders around." She let her eyes meet his. "Actually, I figure any woman who's had such rotten luck with men has to be either lacking somehow, or incredibly stupid when it comes to choosing men."

"That's an easy call. It's pretty obvious that you've been choosing stupid men—myself included."

The steady look in his eyes made her heart flip. As much as she wanted him to elaborate, Skye wouldn't touch that one with a ten-foot pole. Instead, she blurted out, "What about you? I assume you went back and took over the family business, married some socialite and had two point five kids."

"You're partly right," Cash admitted. "I did take over the company. I did marry a socialite, but our divorce became final the day before I landed on your doorstep. And I only have one child, an eleven-year-old daughter named Darby."

Skye didn't know if she was more shocked to hear he had married and had an eleven-year-old child or that he was divorced. Though her intellect told her that if he was thirty-eight he probably had a child somewhere, she couldn't visualize him as a father, or divorced. Somehow she always pictured people like Cash living perfect lives—perfect fam-

ilies, perfect homes, no debts, no problems. Certainly no
divorces.

"I'm sorry," she said.

"Yeah. So am I. Liz claimed I was married to my work,
and I have a sneaking suspicion she was right. I didn't give
her or Darby enough of my time and attention. I can see that
now." His lips quirked humorlessly. "What is it they say
about hindsight?"

"Maybe you can work it out," she offered.

He shook his head. "No. Whatever it was we felt for each
other is long gone. I'm ashamed to admit that I don't mind
losing Liz nearly as much as I mind losing Darby."

"Don't they live in Lincoln?"

"Yeah, but Liz is a grudge holder. She's doing her best to
turn Darby against me." His eyes darkened. "But I'll be
damned if I let her."

A fresh wave of panic assailed Skye at the steely determination she saw in his eyes. If Cash turned that conviction toward influencing Jeb, how could she stop him from
taking Jeb away from her?

"Enough of that!" he growled, jarring Skye from her
treacherous thoughts. "I don't want to talk about Liz right
now. Tell me about Jeb. What's he like?"

"Hardheaded," she said without hesitation. "Sensitive.
Smart. Kind, but insensitive sometimes, too, the way kids
can be. He's a lot like you. Or the way I remember you."

For the next hour he peppered her with questions about
Jeb, and she regaled him with tales of his son's boyhood.

"You said he had practice in the mornings. What kind of
practice?"

"Baseball."

For a second, Cash looked as if he'd taken a blow to his
middle. "Baseball?" he echoed, looking a little dazed. "He
plays baseball?"

Skye recalled how important baseball had once been to Cash. "Everyone says he's a natural."

Cash remembered the baseball trophies on the bookcase, and a broad smile bloomed on his handsome face. "Baseball," he murmured. "That's great . . . great!"

"He got a scholarship to the University of Nebraska at Lincoln," she told him, even though the confession was painful. *In for a penny, in for a pound.*

"Lincoln? That's fantastic! It'll give us a chance to get to know one another, and—"

Cash's enthusiasm ended abruptly. He laughed. "Here I go making plans to spend time with Jeb, but right now it doesn't look as if he wants to get to know me, does it?"

"No," Skye said softly.

"Will you talk to him?" Cash asked her suddenly.

"Talk to him?"

"Yeah. Try to help him see that I was just a crazy kid that summer. Try to make him see that what happened between me and Susan could happen to anyone."

"Cash . . ."

"Please," he said. "This is important to me. I feel as if I was led here for a reason. Liz is doing her best to take Darby away from me, and now something has led me here to a child I didn't know I had. It's like I've been given a second chance."

Skye wasn't sure she believed in second chances. After all, she'd been given a second chance with Lee, and it had turned into a colossal disaster.

"He's a Benedict," Cash said. "He has a heritage he should know about. He has a whole other family who'd like to get to know him. A sister. An aunt. Cousins. Talk to him. Help me convince him to come to Lincoln and meet them."

That insidious fear that had been hanging around the fringes of Skye's mind ever since she'd seen Cash on the porch began to creep into her heart.

"He's awfully angry right now," she hedged.

"Consider this begging, if it pleases you, but I want to get to know my son."

Resisting the pleading in Cash's eyes would take a strong person. Maybe someone stronger than Skye believed she was. She thought about what he was saying. He had a sister. Jeb's aunt. He had cousins. It sounded wonderful... for Jeb.

And frightening for her.

On Monday, Jeb was standing on the pitcher's mound when he saw the Lexus pull into a parking space. He watched as his dad got out of the car and walked toward the chain-link fence that circled the ball field. Cash moved in a leisurely fashion, his hands thrust into the pockets of his slacks. Jeb's palms began to sweat, and the scrambled eggs Skye had fixed him for breakfast began to churn in his stomach. *Jeez! Talk about pressure!*

He barely gathered his scattered wits in time to reach out for the catcher's return pitch. It smacked into his worn glove. What the heck was the problem? he wondered, blotting his perspiring face on his shoulder. But even as he asked, Jeb knew exactly what was wrong. Cash Benedict's appearance unnerved him. This was the second day his dad had come to the field, and once Jeb realized he was there, both his pitching and his hitting went to hell in a hand basket—although there had been that powerful line drive he'd hit down third the day before.

Maybe it was his imagination, but that hit had brought what looked like a proud smile to his dad's face. Jeb couldn't deny that the idea of Cash's pride had filled him with an inexplicable pleasure, even though he was furious with himself for caring.

Jeb thrust his mitt under his arm, kneaded the ball and blew out a steadying breath. What the heck was his old man up to, anyway?

To Skye's surprise, Cash had made himself scarce on Sunday, but when she got home on Monday and Tuesday evenings it was clear that he'd picked up where he'd left off on Saturday. The grass was cut, and the vegetable garden had been tilled. The Weed Eater had been put to use around the trees and the patch of tall grass behind the barn. New boards replaced the rotting ones on the steps that led to the garage apartment. Skye couldn't suppress a twinge of guilt, but on the other hand, the work wasn't hurting Cash, and the place really needed it.

She changed into shorts and a baggy T-shirt and fixed a salad for dinner. As she ate, she couldn't help wondering when Cash was going home. She was still contemplating whether or not she should become the mediator between him and Jeb. The tender part of her heart whispered that they had a right to get to know each other, to see if they could build some sort of a relationship. The selfish part of her heart whispered that to give Cash a toehold in her life was to invite more heartache.

She was sitting in the darkened living room still mulling over her options—which were few—when she heard Jeb's motorcycle coming up the driveway. They hadn't had much to say to each other since the confrontation with Cash on Thursday. It was amazing how much Cash's arrival a week before had changed her and Jeb's life.

She heard Jeb's step, heard the click of the light switch. Illumination flooded the room. When he saw her sitting in the wingback chair, he stopped in his tracks.

"What are you doing up?"

"Thinking. What are you doing here? I didn't expect you so early."

"Belinda's grounded for the week."

"Oh." *Thank God for small favors.* "How about splitting a Coke?"

"Sure."

Skye got up and started for the kitchen. Jeb was standing near the bottom of the stairs, and when she reached him she lifted a hand and stroked his cheek with her fingertips, a wistful smile curving her lips.

"You okay?" he asked, frowning.

She nodded. "How about you? I haven't seen much of you around here since..." Her voice trailed away and she flipped on the kitchen light.

"Since my *dad* and I got into it?"

"Yeah."

Jeb slouched in an oak chair. "I'm fine," he said, his tone brusque.

Skye got a cola from the refrigerator and took two glasses from the cabinet.

"He's been coming every day, hasn't he?" Jeb asked as she divided the drink and set his in front of him.

Her eyes met his. "How did you know?"

Jeb grinned, the wry smile so much like Cash's, yet so much like Susan's. "I didn't figure you were the one doing all that repair stuff outside. What's the deal?"

Skye sat across from Jeb. "He says he needs to do it," she said, repeating what Cash had told her. "That it's the least he can do for Susan."

Jeb raised his dark eyebrows in a mocking way. "It's a little late to start trying to earn points, isn't it?"

"I don't think that has anything to do with it," Skye told him honestly.

"Oh," Jeb said with a sage nod and another sardonic smile. "I see. It's one of those things I won't understand until I'm older, right?"

"Right," Skye said with a smile to match his. "And I think he keeps coming by hoping to get a chance to talk to you."

"I don't have anything to say to him," Jeb said, finality lacing his voice. "I think he comes to see you."

The observation took Skye aback. "Me?" she asked, her eyes wide and startled.

"Yeah. Is that so surprising, since you two had a thing going back then, too?"

"We didn't have a thing going," Skye said. "I was fourteen. He was nineteen. I had a major crush on him, and I did throw myself at him one night, but he turned me down. I guess Susan was more to his liking."

"I guess."

They drank their cola in silence for a moment before Jeb asked, "Did you know they were—you know—sleeping together?"

Skye looked up, startled by the question. "I guess it crossed my mind, but I couldn't really imagine it."

"Did you hate her?"

One corner of Skye's mouth curled in a half smile. "Yeah, I did," she confessed. "I hated them both. Susan because I felt she'd stolen Cash away from me, and Cash for coming between me and Susan."

She sighed and her frank gaze met Jeb's. "Susan and I were always so close. I still remember how thankful I was when he left. I kept thinking that our lives would get back to normal, the way things were before he came."

"Did they?"

"Things were never quite the same, but I was young, and Bobby Balthazer started giving me the rush." A twinkle lit her eyes. "Things were better for a while."

"Until you found out she was pregnant?"

Skye nodded. "That caused a lot of hard feelings—not to mention disappointment. I was forced to realize that Susan was as apt to make a mistake as any of us, which was hard for me, because she always seemed so perfect."

"Even I know nobody's perfect," Jeb said.

"Yeah, but Susan always had all the answers, and I never felt as if I measured up, or ever could. When I found out she was pregnant, I lost my own innocence."

"I don't get it."

"Sure you do," Skye told him with a sorrowful smile. "Susan had fallen off her pedestal the way most adults do sooner or later. The way I did when you found out about me and Lee."

An unfamiliar blush darkened Jeb's lean cheeks. He nodded. "I guess I did—do—have a hard time with your telling me not to do what I know you and Lee did."

"I understand that," Skye told him, "and I'm not even going to try and justify my actions. I can't. But there's one difference. I'm twice your age, and I never put my whole future in jeopardy—just my heart."

"Did you love Lee?"

"The first time, I thought I did. The second time I think I was more swayed by the fact that he said he'd made a mistake by not marrying me back when you were ten." She bestowed a rueful smile on Jeb. "Hearing a man admit he's wrong can be a mighty heady experience for a woman. And then, there was the undeniable fact that I'd fallen into the same trap Susan had."

"What trap?" Jeb asked.

"Loneliness. I wanted to believe the things Lee told me. I needed to. I'm thirty-three years old, Jeb, and the chance of my finding some knight to take me away gets slimmer every year. Lee made me feel pretty and special and wanted, and I bought into his line—knowing he'd broken my heart once before—all because I was lonesome and wanted to experience some kind of love before it was too late."

"You make it sound like your life is over," Jeb said, his voice rough with irritation. "That's crazy. And in case you don't know it, you are pretty."

Skye blinked back a sudden rush of tears at the unexpected compliment. "I didn't think you noticed."

"I notice, all right. And so did Cash."

"You're imagining things," Skye said, afraid to count on Jeb's observation.

"Am I?" Jeb said with a lift of his dark eyebrows.

"Yes." She spoke firmly, both disturbed and delighted by the idea that Cash might still find her attractive.

"He's been coming to the ball field in the mornings," Jeb said, changing the subject abruptly.

"Really?"

"What do you think he wants?"

"You're his son. I imagine he wants to watch you, to see if he sees anything of himself in you. That's normal, don't you think?"

Jeb shrugged his wide shoulders.

"He was thrilled when I told him you liked baseball. You know Cash had aspirations to play major league ball when he was your age."

A gleam of interest lighted Jeb's eyes. "I never knew the details. What happened?"

"The offer he expected never materialized."

"Speaking of materializing and baseball, do you think enough money will materialize so we can swing that baseball camp in August?"

Skye gave a remorseful shake of her head. "I don't see how. The shop is doing okay, but I just paid workmen's compensation, and the house and car insurance are coming up. I know how important this is to you, but we've both got to keep our noses to the grindstone if we hope to get enough put by so you won't have to work every spare minute."

"I was afraid you'd say that."

Skye reached out and covered his hand with hers. "You know I'd let you go if there was any way I could swing it, don't you?"

He nodded and squeezed her hand. "Yeah." He offered her a thin smile that spoke of his disappointment. "I'm going to bed," he said, rising. "See you in the morning."

She nodded and watched while he rinsed his glass and put it in the dishwasher.

"Night," she called as he left the room.

"Good night."

She heard the creaking of the stairs and the sound of Jeb's bathroom door closing behind him. With a sigh, Skye rested her elbows on the table and buried her face in her hands. What should she do? Jeb wanted to go to the baseball camp, and she knew that it could only benefit him. As Cash once had, Jeb possessed an abundance of natural talent for the game. And, as with Cash, there had been some tentative interest in signing Jeb to a farm team. If it were up to her, she would probably let him do it, but Susan had been adamant about Jeb getting an education.

So where does that leave you, Skye?

"In the middle," she said aloud. Where she'd always been.

Jeb had taken the news better than she'd expected. Knowing how short the fuse to his temper had been the past year, she'd expected another scene. But Jeb was different since Cash had come to town. Quieter. Easier to get along with.

Skye wondered what it was about Cash's coming that had initiated the small, but significant, changes she saw in Jeb. Was it that seeing Cash gave him some sense of who he was, even though it raised other doubts and questions? Were the problems he was being forced to face helping him to grow up at last?

As much as she hated to admit it, she knew that Jeb could only benefit from an association with his father. Cash was a decent, respectable person. And he was wealthy—Cash could give him the benefit of advantages she could only dream of providing, like the baseball camp, or college. Or both. And, as Cash had pointed out, Jeb had other family that he had a right to get to know, which brought her to the real reason for her reluctance to help bridge the gap between them. She was afraid that this new family with all its exciting potential might take her place in Jeb's heart.

Selfish! Selfish! Selfish! The refrain pulsed through her head, making it throb painfully. Jon would be ashamed of her. She was ashamed of herself. Tears sprang into her eyes, and she heaved another sigh, this one a sigh of capitulation.

She knew Jeb. Despite the problems they'd been having over his liaison with Belinda, he was a loving kid who had a heck of a complex because of his illegitimacy. In time, his anger at Cash would pass and he would come to the realization that the only difference between his situation with Belinda and that between Cash and Susan was age. At some point, he would want to get to know his father.

Skye knew that if she failed to help negotiate a reconciliation just to keep Jeb to herself, she ran the risk of alienating him entirely. Jon had maintained that sharing was always preferable to stinginess, and she knew he'd been right, as usual.

Overcome by a sudden weariness, she got up and put her glass into the dishwasher beside Jeb's. She would call Margie and see if she'd watch the shop tomorrow afternoon, and then she'd call Cash to come out so they could talk. She'd tell him of her decision and ask him exactly what he wanted her to do.

Chapter Seven

Cash agreed to meet Skye at the shop the next day.

"Thanks," he said when he arrived and she told him she'd try to help him with Jeb. "It's nice to know that someone will be keeping my name in front of him when I go."

"Go?" The thought of his leaving took her by surprise, even though she knew his time there was indefinite.

"I have a business to run, magazines to get out," he said, looking as miserable as she felt. "I can't stay forever, as much as I might like to."

Skye didn't comment on the tantalizing statement. She was too busy trying to analyze the sudden, unmistakable depression that swept through her.

"Ceil insisted I take some time off, but I've been gone almost ten days, which is longer than I should have. Darby's birthday is July sixth, and I promised her we'd celebrate together. It's a promise I mean to keep."

Ceil. Darby. His sister and his daughter. Parts of his real life. A life far different from hers and Jeb's.

"I understand," Skye said. And she did. She understood that his business and his daughter were both very important, but it didn't make the thought of his leaving any easier to accept.

"To be honest, I need to get back because we lost one magazine this year and another is in big trouble. It isn't fair for me to leave Ceil holding the bag for so long."

"No," Skye agreed. She drew in a deep breath, wondering at the sudden ache that had settled in the region of her heart. "When are you going?"

"The Fourth is two days away. If you and Jeb are agreeable, I'd like us to spend the day together. I'll leave the next morning."

The request was as unexpected as Cash showing up on her doorstep. "Why do you want to spend the Fourth with us?"

His smile was fleeting. "Old times' sake, I guess."

"What about Jeb? What do you want me to do to help you with Jeb?"

"I hear he's playing ball that evening before the fireworks display."

"Yes."

"I want you to take me to watch my son play ball."

"That's it?" Skye asked, surprised.

"It'll do for starters," Cash told her. "I want to see him play. He's good. I can tell that much already."

"He's seen you at the field watching him practice. It makes him nervous."

Cash smiled again. "Then we won't let him know I'm at the game until it's over."

By the evening of July 3, Skye had all her food prepared for the picnic the following day. She was expecting the

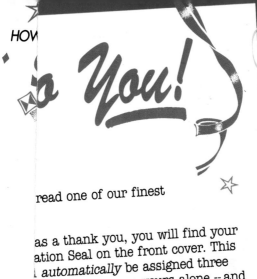

read one of our finest

as a thank you, you will find your
ation Seal on the front cover. This
automatically be assigned three
mbers will become yours alone -- and
sweepstakes prizes. So why not take a
if any one of your three sweepstakes
) Sweepstakes, YOU could be our next

alidation Seal can also instantly
glass for your very own romantic
ur more of the books you love so

Sweepstakes Validation Seal in the
receive -- as our Editor's "Toast to
00,000.00 and much, much, more!

e Canada Luna Macro

" **TODAY**... and, with ABSOLUTELY NO
n our next $1,000,000.00 Sweepstakes
EE GIFTS!

A Toast to You Our Valued Reader!

Herder clan, and didn't want to spend the day in the kitchen while everyone else had fun. Margie would keep Herder's open for half a day and close at noon so that everyone could participate in the festivities.

As Skye predicted, Jeb declined his father's offer of spending the day together. Instead, he planned to go picnicking and swimming with Belinda's family. Skye's only consolation was that Jeb and Belinda would be around people all day and that Belinda's father, a die-hard ball fan, would make sure he was back to the field on time.

The thought of spending an entire day in Cash's company brought mixed emotions. With the new forbearance that had come with the reading of Susan's diary, the day would be a time to renew their old acquaintance without the rancor that had marred Cash's visit so far. It would also bring back the memories of that other Fourth of July.

While the pain itself had faded, Skye remembered well how angry she'd been that day, so soon after Cash's rejection of her and her love. She could hardly bear to look at him and had aligned herself with her Herder relatives and Lee Ballard, letting them act as a buffer while her moods swung from sullen pouting to almost manic vivaciousness as she waited for Cash to join them.

She needn't have wasted her time. Susan kept him nearby, flirting with him unashamedly, even though Jon's relatives gave her terse, concerned looks. That was the day Skye first began to suspect that Susan and Cash's interest in one another was more than that of employer-employee. Their mutual awareness would have been clear to a blind person, and Skye was far from blind.

Watching the two of them together had been the most painful experience of her life. Susan had been gorgeous...daring, as she'd drunk her wine, flirted, teased and enticed Cash to dance with her, letting her body brush

against his temptingly, while she'd smiled and laughed up
into his adoring gaze. Skye couldn't recall feeling so plain
and insipid—before or since.

Now she ground her teeth at the memories, telling herself that dwelling on the heartaches of the past was futile.
She'd gotten past that, hadn't she? Holding the recollections at bay while she was in Cash's company would be an
exercise in control, but Jon had always maintained that
learning control was a character-building experience.

Skye picked up Opa and met Cash in Main. Cash was
friendly, polite and a big help with Harold, who tried to
wander off a time or two during the morning's obser-
vances. Skye wasn't as uncomfortable as she'd feared, and
she had to admit that she was glad for his help. He was good
with the old man, who seemed glad to see him and knew
who he was the instant he set eyes on him.

After a morning in town, she and Cash drove Opa to the
farm for an afternoon of picnicking and outdoor games.
The subtle tension between them was defused somewhat by
the number of Herder relatives that showed up. Though
they'd scattered through the years, those who still lived close
enough brought covered dishes to share with their kinfolk
beneath the trees, a Herder Fourth of July tradition that was
as old as Skye's memory.

The Herder clan's treatment of Cash was stilted, reserved, polite. As so often happens among families, Susan's sins had been whitewashed, and she'd been forgiven
for her transgression years before—if not during her life,
then certainly at the time she was laid to rest beneath the
pines. Cash was a different matter altogether. He had lured
one of theirs down the path of iniquity and had used and
forsaken her, something they weren't likely to forget, even
though they might claim they'd forgiven.

As Skye had in the summer of '77, Cash kept himself apart, whiling away the somnolent afternoon hours beneath the trees playing chess with Opa, who, though he sometimes couldn't remember what day it was, seemed to be as sharp as ever when it came to the challenging board game.

At six o'clock, she and Cash drove to the ball field to watch Jeb's game. Sitting next to Cash in the bleachers, Skye realized that, in spite of the slight tension between them, it had been a good day, only slightly marred by the bittersweet memories.

Unaccountably saddened by the fact that he was leaving the next day, she glanced at Cash from the corner of her eyes. His rapt gaze was focused on Jeb, who was standing at home plate, tapping the dirt from his shoes with his Louisville Slugger.

She stifled a small pang of hurt and smiled wryly to herself when she realized that he didn't even know she was on the same planet. What had she expected? For Cash to suddenly announce that he'd made a mistake all those years ago? That it wasn't Susan who'd interested him after all? That it was Skye he truly loved?

Before she managed to banish the frivolous musings, a new, thought-provoking question popped into her mind: Why was she even thinking about herself in connection with Cash after all these years?

Because you still find him attractive. Because in spite of all the heartache and disillusionment Lee Ballard dished out, you're still looking for love—or at least a reasonable facsimile.

Love. Skye sneaked another peek at Cash. Why in heaven's name would she even think the word *love* in connection with Cash Benedict? Fourteen-year-old girls didn't fall in love. They had crushes. They had the hots for boys. And a thirty-three-year-old woman couldn't possibly love a man who'd rejected her and then fathered a child with her sister—could she?

No, Skye thought, she couldn't. Shouldn't.

What she felt for Cash was simply the same attraction she'd had at fourteen, the same attraction she'd felt a few times for other men. He was just a handsome man who made her heart skip a beat whenever he came into a room, and she was a healthy, lonely woman with long-neglected, ongoing desires that Lee Ballard hadn't begun to satisfy.

Oh, Lee had been fine in bed the short time they'd been together. But fulfilling her sexual needs was a far cry from fulfilling the needs of her heart and her soul. It took understanding for that. It took two hearts that spoke the same language, hearts that *listened*. It took sacrifice and commitment, traits Lee had a hard time understanding.

What makes you think Cash can commit?

He had left Susan, and that was a hard, cold fact. But as both he and the diary had reminded her, he was just nineteen and had had no idea that she carried his child.

There was the sorrow she'd seen in his eyes as he told her about his recent divorce and the rift between him and his daughter. Whether or not his marriage had been happy or successful, he had been committed to it, and its dissolution had been an eye-opener as well as a blow to his self-esteem. Cash might have been a negligent husband and father in the past, but Skye would bet a week's profits that it wasn't a mistake he'd make again.

Which doesn't answer the question, which is what, exactly, do you feel for the man?

She had no ready answer. Her track record with men was lousy at best. She was afraid to trust her instincts, and more afraid to trust her heart. Both had led her astray before, and as battered as her heart was, she didn't think she could survive another wrong move.

The best thing she could do was get through the rest of the day with as few tense moments as possible, bid Cash goodbye and let him and Jeb work out their problems once Jeb went to Lincoln to school. It sounded like a good idea. She hoped it worked.

To Cash's delight, Jeb's team won the game. He couldn't help the pride that filled him almost to bursting as he heard the people around him refer to Jeb as the next Bill Zuber. Bill, who was born in Middle Amana in 1913, had possessed a fastball that had led him to a professional career with four major league teams.

If only Jeb were so lucky, Cash thought, grinning from ear to ear. He wished he could stand and announce to the world that Jeb was his son. But he couldn't say it, not yet, anyway, so he had to content himself with rehashing every swing of Jeb's superior batting and every perfectly thrown pitch all the way back to the car. Skye accepted his praise of Jeb's skills with an amused smile, but Cash saw the pride in her eyes, too. Even Opa seemed to understand that Jeb had really accomplished something.

Hating to see the end of his last day drawing near, Cash talked Skye into going to Colony Cone for a sundae before they took Harold back home.

Once Harold was ready for bed and ensconced in front of the television, Cash and Skye drove back to the farm in silence. The porch light was on, and a shaft of illumination streamed across the darkness of the yard from Jeb's room. He must have beaten them home.

Good, Cash thought. He'd been trying to corner the kid for the better part of a week. Maybe now he'd have a chance to at least offer Jeb the opportunity to spend some time together when he came to Lincoln. He probably wouldn't accept, but they would both know that Cash had made an attempt to bridge the gulf separating them.

He pulled to a stop in front of the garage and turned off the ignition while Skye unfastened her seat belt. Cash leaned over to open her door with his right hand, and instantly his senses were awash in a light scent that hinted of roses and moss and femininity. Just as quickly, he became aware of the close confines of the front seat and the way his heart began to race. He was aware, too, of the way his arm pressed against the soft fullness of her breasts.

It occurred to him on an intense wave of need that he hadn't held a woman in months, a fact that had escaped him until this moment, this woman. He clenched his jaw and yanked on the door handle. The almost silent click snapped the palpable tension stretching between them.

"Would you like to come in for some coffee ... or something?" Skye asked.

The breathless, somehow sexy quality of her voice betrayed her nervousness and sent Cash's libido spiraling. He turned his head fractionally, meeting her gaze over his shoulder. His face was mere inches from hers. Her eyes were wide and watchful. Cash fought the urge to slide his arms around her, press her into the car's luxurious seats and take her...the way he'd longed to take her that night so long ago when she'd offered herself to him so sweetly, so innocently.

The need, long repressed and buried beneath two decades of guilt, was a burning ache inside him. He'd hurt her once, and they were just beginning to establish a working relationship in regard to Jeb, maybe even a cautious friendship. Now wasn't the time to indulge in his longtime fantasy. Kissing her would undo everything.

He stifled a sigh of regret and straightened. "Coffee sounds good."

She opened the door, flooding the interior of the car with light. "I'll go start it. Make yourself at home."

"I'll be a minute," he said. "I think I'll walk around outside for a while."

Confusion dimmed the light in her eyes. "Sure." She got out of the car, shut the door quietly and started across the dew-damp yard.

"Skye," he called softly through the open window.

She turned.

"Is the garage apartment unlocked?"

She nodded. "Yes."

"Do you mind if I have a look around? For old times' sake?"

"Be my guest."

Cash watched her until she disappeared into the house. Then he got out of the car, leaned his hip against the door and stared up at the small room he'd called home nearly twenty years earlier. The room where he and Susan had first made love.

Strangely, it wasn't memories of Susan that had filled his mind today; it was memories of Skye. He'd observed her gentleness with Harold and seen how efficiently she had kept the picnic running. She had a knack for making everyone feel welcome and needed, and it came to him on a gentle realization that she'd grown into a beautiful, capable and caring person. So much like Susan. So different.

He wondered, as he had a hundred times, what would have happened if Skye had been a little older and he'd made love with her instead of Susan. There was no clear-cut answer to the question. There never had been; never would be. Right or wrong, choices were made and lived with—or lived down, as Susan had learned and he was learning. There was no turning back the clock. No changing history. No predicting the future. What had been, was. *Che serà, serà.*

With a heavy heart Cash started toward the apartment. As he neared the steps he noticed a faint glow from the screen door and heard the soft, clear notes of Kenny G's "Songbird" drifting through the still night air.

Jeb must be up there, instead of in his room. The garage apartment was a good place to disappear to. Thinking that it might be better that he talk to Jeb out here, away from Skye, Cash climbed the steps and pushed through the door. He stopped just inside the doorway, rooted to the floor by the sight in front of him.

Jeb was on the sofa, his body half covering a feminine form, both bathed in the soft glow of candlelight. All Cash could see was one bare leg and an arm, both twined around Jeb's shirtless body. Jeb and the unknown girl were kissing hungrily, their feasting accompanied by soft groans and sighs.

A feeling of déjà vu seized Cash. It might have been him and Susan. For a moment, he imagined he heard Susan's soft voice whispering to him. For a moment, it was as if history were repeating itself.

But it wasn't Susan's voice; it was someone else's. And it wasn't him; it was Jeb about to repeat history, about to make a mistake that could alter his entire life.

"What in the hell do you think you're doing?" The sound of the biting question overrode the moans and the music. The depth of the anger he heard in that voice shocked even him.

The girl gave a startled shriek, and Jeb leapt up so fast it would have been comical if it weren't so pathetic. The girl, whose short skirt was pushed up around her waist, jerked her blouse together and began fastening it, watching Cash with wide, terrified eyes that swam with tears.

"What the hell are you doing here?" Jeb cried in a venomous voice.

"I asked first," Cash said. "But I guess it's pretty obvious what's going on."

"You'd know," Jeb said.

"Yeah, I would." Cash pinned the girl with a hard look. "Get dressed and get out of here."

She clamped her teeth over her bottom lip and nodded as she tucked in her blouse and felt around on the floor for her sandals with her bare feet.

Jeb took a step toward him, fury in the set of his jaw and the loose fists curled at his sides. "Just because you were my sperm donor doesn't mean you can come up here and tell me what to do."

"Shut up, Jeb," Cash warned.

The girl slipped her feet into her shoes, and, with a final glance at Jeb, scurried toward the door. The sound of her shoes clattering on the steps faded into the night. Stillness, broken only by the saxophone's wail, gathered in the small room, filling every crevice and thundering in Cash's ears as he stood glaring at the son who'd made him so proud just an hour before.

"Are you out of your mind?" he asked at last.

"No," Jeb said, "but I'm not too sure you aren't."

Cash took a step forward and stopped, shut his eyes and counted to ten. When he opened them again, Jeb was still glaring at him. "Drop the bad-boy act," Cash commanded. "I'm not impressed."

This time it was Jeb who made the move, muttering a curse and coming at Cash with raised fists.

"Come on, boy," Cash said with a jerk of his chin as he raised his own fists. "You need taking down a notch or two."

Jeb paused, the muscle in his cheek working as he glowered at Cash and mulled over the challenge. Finally he lowered his hands. Cash did the same.

"You're playing with fire," Cash said in a quiet voice. "You know it, and I surely do."

Jeb didn't respond.

"I know what you're thinking, that it's none of my business. Well, you're wrong. I may be late coming to the job, but I'm your father, and I'm going to tell you what I think, whether you like it or not."

"Well, I sure as hell don't!"

"Well, that's too damn bad," Cash said. "Because I'm talking and you're going to listen. You're a fantastic ball player, Jeb. You've got more natural talent than I had at your age. Skye says you have a chance at the pros. Don't throw away a promising future for a quick roll in the hay with some hot babe."

"Belinda's not—"

Cash held up a silencing hand. "I'm not saying anything against that girl. I'm saying it about any girl. It's a dangerous game you're playing, son, and you damn well know it."

Jeb didn't say anything for several seconds, but he finally asked, "Is that what Mom was to you? A hot babe? A quick roll in the hay?"

"No," Cash said with a shake of his head. "Susan was my best friend, my confidante, my mentor. She helped me through a rough patch in my life, and I respected her very much. What happened between us was just...the situation we found ourselves in. I was young, mixed up, angry. She was lonely. We each saw something in the other we needed, even wanted. And we took it, even though it was wrong."

"What could a grown woman like Mom have seen in a nineteen-year-old kid?" Jeb asked.

"Her youth slipping away," Cash said without hesitation. "A chance to feel young and desirable again, if for only a little while."

"And what did you see in her?"

Cash thought about that for a few long seconds. It was a question he'd considered for years, and one he'd never really had an answer for. It was only now, at this moment, that he saw the truth more clearly than he'd ever seen it before.

Skye.

The name—confession, benediction, excuse—popped into Cash's mind as Jeb's gaze probed his, seeking truth, looking for any sign of a lie, and finding no apology for the professed sins of the past. The sound of someone coming up the stairs saved Cash from voicing the truth and drew both men's attention to the doorway, where Skye stood looking flushed and harried and upset.

"What's going on?" she demanded, looking from Jeb to Cash. "Belinda is out in the yard crying her eyes out. She said you told her to get out."

"I did."

Skye's gaze moved from him to Jeb and back. "Why?"

"Ask Jeb."

Jeb bent and picked up his shirt from the floor. He drew it on slowly, his eyes never leaving hers.

"Oh, Jeb!" Skye cried, shaking her head in despair. "Haven't you heard anything I've said?"

He buttoned his shirt and thrust the tail into his jeans. "I heard. And Cash, here, just read me his version of the riot act."

"I read it. The question is, were you listening?"

"Yeah," Jeb said. "I was listening. Now, if you're finished with me, I'll take Belinda home."

Sick of Jeb's attitude, disgusted with himself, Cash gave a careless wave of his hand. "Go."

Jeb crossed the room and disappeared through the screen door. Neither Skye nor Cash spoke until they heard the roar of the Harley. She brought her gaze to his, and the grief reflected there was almost more than he could bear.

"I'm sorry," she said, her voice hardly more than a whisper.

"Sorry? For what?"

"For Jeb's attitude. For...your catching him up here with Belinda...like that. I've talked to him until I'm blue in the face, but I..."

She threaded her fingers through her hair and scraped it away from her face in a gesture that betrayed her desperation. "I've done the best I can with him, but obviously I've done a bad job. I—"

"Stop it!" Cash chided. "Stop blaming yourself for his actions. He's almost a full-grown man. You're not responsible for his decisions or his mistakes."

Cash saw the glimmer of tears in her eyes and took two steps closer. Reaching out, he used his thumb to brush away the moisture in a caress as achingly gentle as the saxophone's soft sobbing. Her hands fell to her sides.

"Don't blame yourself," he said again, trailing his fingertips over the curve of her ear to the back of her neck. "You've done a great job."

Her lips trembled. "He's smart-mouthed."

Cash exerted the slightest pressure, forcing her to take a step nearer to him. "Most kids his age are."

"He's oversexed, and—"

Cash drew her a step closer. And another. "Most guys his age are."

"He's... Wh-what are you doing?" she asked as he framed her face between his palms.

Cash didn't answer. Instead, he lowered his mouth to hers in a soft kiss. Skye was perfectly still, stunned into immobility. Her wide mouth was soft and pliant as he shaped it with his, urging her to part her lips for him, begging her to accept what he longed to give her.

With a sigh, she opened her mouth. She tipped back her head and stepped closer, flowing into his embrace. He felt her arms go around his waist, felt her body press against his, searing him with a burning, blazing heat.

The kiss deepened; her nails dug into his back. Cash was hungrier than even he would have believed. Hungry not just for a woman, but this woman. Relentlessly, his hands moved over her back, seeking to memorize each curve before sliding down, over the swell of her hips to her curvaceous bottom. Employing a gentle, caressing motion, he coaxed her into the V of his legs and the heat building there, knowing as he crushed her closer that it would never be close enough.

He slid a hand between them up over the fullness of her breasts. A low whimper of need emanated from deep in her throat, and then, as if the sound brought her back to reality, she stiffened in his embrace.

Confused by her sudden withdrawal, Cash raised his head and looked at her... the troubled, passion-glazed eyes, the mouth wet from his kisses. "What is it?" he asked, his voice low and husky with desire.

She moved her hands to his waist and pushed away, holding her arms wide. "Take a good look at me, Cash!" she cried in a voice that bordered on desperation. "I'm not Susan."

"Damn it, I know you're not Susan!" he said in a low, angry voice. He grabbed her shoulders, refusing to let her put any significant distance between them. "I know you aren't Susan," he said again softly.

Her brown eyes were dark with pain. "And I'm not easy like Susan."

Cash gave her a single sharp shake. "You, of all people, should know Susan wasn't easy."

"No?"

"No," he said unequivocally. "She was a beautiful, vibrant, intelligent woman. When Jon died she was more or less alone. So was I. Haven't you ever been so lonely you craved the touch of another human?"

Skye's teeth clamped down on her bottom lip, and tears filled her eyes. It was answer enough. Cash ran his palms from her shoulders to her elbows and back again.

"Susan made a mistake, the way we all have." His eyes were filled with an incredible tenderness and the barest hope of a smile. "Or have you managed to reach the age of thirty-plus with a perfect record?"

"No," she whispered, shaking her head.

"I didn't think so. Making errors in judgment is okay, if we learn from them. It certainly doesn't make anyone easy or bad."

"I hope not." She laughed shakily.

Cash feathered his thumb along her bottom lip and sighed. "If you want to hear me say I'm sorry, I have to disappoint you. I can't bring myself to apologize for doing something I've wanted to do ever since the day I got here."

"I don't expect you to apologize."

"Are you going to be okay?"

"I will be when Jeb gets home," she said with a sniff.

"Do you want me to go look for him?"

"No," she said with a shake of her head. "He might be late, but he'll come back."

"I didn't have a free-for-all in mind when I came up here. I wanted to ask Jeb to have lunch with me before he went to work tomorrow afternoon. I planned to leave afterward."

"Can't you stay longer?"

He thought he saw a hint of red creep into her cheeks. She lowered her eyelashes, but not before Cash spied the forlorn look in her eyes.

"Nothing seems . . . finished somehow."

"You're right," he said. "It isn't finished. Not by a long shot. But Darby's birthday is the sixth, and I promised her we'd spend the day together. I've broken so many promises in the past that I have to make good on this one."

"I understand."

Cash fought the urge to take her in his arms again. He didn't know what was happening to him—sexual attraction or the prelude to love—but the thought of leaving her was more than he felt he could bear. "I'll try to be back in a couple of weeks, if that's okay."

She nodded. "If you like, I'll talk to Jeb when he gets home tonight," she offered. "I'll see to it that he goes to lunch with you."

"I'm very attracted to you," he said, almost as if he hadn't heard her, as if they were talking about them instead of Jeb.

The unexpected comment brought back her blush. "You're attracted to a memory," she said, shaking her head sadly. "You're on the rebound. You came here looking for your old flame, maybe to rekindle it. Susan isn't here, but I am. We look alike. We're alike in a lot of ways. It's easy to see how you'd get us mixed up in your mind and project all your memories and feelings onto me."

A considering light glittered in Cash's eyes. "You may be partly right. Maybe I want you so much because I am on the rebound." He ignored her startled gasp. "But let me clarify one thing. I projected my feelings for one woman onto another once in my life, but it wasn't just now, with you."

Chapter Eight

Skye heard the Lexus leaving. She went to the window of her bedroom and peered through the slats in the miniblinds until the taillights disappeared down the road. Tears sprang into her eyes, and she pressed her fingertips to her lips that still throbbed from Cash's kisses. With a moan, she squeezed her eyes shut and leaned her head against the smooth, cool surface of the window trim.

He was leaving. She'd known it would come to this, so why did it hurt so much? She heard the sound of the breeze rustling the shrubs outside her open window while the rhythmic whispers of her heart canted, *You love him...love him...love him.*

She brushed aside the idea impatiently. How could she even think she loved a man who had been her sister's lover, who had probably loved her sister?

He never claimed to love Susan.

No, but he had admitted to caring for her, to respecting her. Skye thought better of him for that. The past couple of days, she'd come to realize that even though there were plenty of solid reasons to keep Cash at arm's length, she had run out of reasons to hate him.

Skye sighed and turned away from the window. Had he been telling the truth just now when he said he wanted her? She closed her eyes and lost herself in the memory of his kisses, kisses that demanded a response she couldn't help giving. Oh, yes. He was telling the truth. Her breasts ached with the seductive memory of how his body felt pressed against hers. Hard. Intimate. Proof positive of his wanting.

She sank into the bed and covered her face with her forearm, thinking about the look on his face when he'd said things weren't finished yet. Did he mean that things weren't finished between them, that he wanted her to be a part of his life, too? Were his feelings deeper than wanting, or were they just remnants of a long-ago summer love? And why did she persist in the notion that he was different from Lee Ballard?

He is different. Far different. She knew that as surely as she knew Jon Herder had been a good and decent man. Deep in her heart, she'd always known the truth, but she'd let her jealousy and her love and fierce protectiveness of Susan blind her to it.

Skye also knew Cash had made mistakes in his life—with his wife, his daughter and even with Jeb. She knew, too, that he wanted to make those wrongs right. Wanted it badly. He was man enough to own up to his errors, and that, in itself, was an admirable trait. Obviously, there was much to admire about Cash Benedict besides the fact that he was very attractive, hardworking and dedicated. Much to admire. Much to love.

Now all she had to do was to convince Jeb that his father wasn't the blackguard he saw him as. And the only way she could think to do that was to let him read the diaries.

True to her word, Skye saw to it that Jeb met Cash for lunch at the Pizza Factory and Grill. Cash didn't know how she managed it, and he didn't care. All that mattered was that he had approximately an hour to convince his son that he wasn't a villain and that he sincerely wanted them to forge some sort of relationship.

Having little experience with boys, Cash figured the best thing to do was find a common meeting ground and go from there. And the only common ground he could think of was baseball.

"You played a great game yesterday," he said after they'd ordered their pizza.

"Thanks."

"You've got a great arm and a powerful swing."

"Thanks."

Okay, Cash thought, regarding Jeb's bent head with irritation, so neither of them was a scintillating conversationalist, but he was trying. "Skye says there's been some interest from a pro scout."

Jeb stirred his cola with the straw. "Some."

Cash exhaled irritably. "Look, I know you don't want to be here, but you are, and I intend to say what I want to say to you whether you like it or not. We can either sit here and stare at each other while we eat, or we can try to have an adult conversation. Now, what'll it be?"

Jeb glared at him, and jabbed the straw into the crushed ice in his drink. The muscle in his jaw tightened. "I guess I'll try to behave like an adult, even though that isn't necessarily an admirable way to act."

"Point taken," Cash said, holding his son's indignant gaze. He counted to ten and felt in his breast pocket for an antacid tablet. "You'd rather go to college, huh?"

Jeb looked righteously indignant. "Who told you that?"

"No one," Cash said. "I just assumed as much, since you don't seem too interested in talking baseball."

"There's no use talking about something that's almost finished."

"So you do like baseball."

"I love it," Jeb said, his face a study in wistfulness. "But according to Skye, playing pro ball is just a pipe dream."

Cash thought back to the time his own father had said the same thing. He remembered how much it had hurt to see his fragile wishes start to slip and fall. "She knows how you feel, then?"

"Sure she does, but she says I have to go to college. Mom wanted it, so it's as good as done."

"I understand their thinking. I imagine Susan saw your getting an education as a way for you to make something of yourself."

"I guess," Jeb said, shrugging his wide shoulders. He looked at Cash. "I don't want to talk about this, okay? It makes me crazy."

"Sure." Cash acquiesced. They sipped their drinks in silence for a moment before he said, "The same thing happened to me."

Jeb looked up.

"I had interest from a pro scout after my freshman year of college. I told my dad—my adoptive dad—that I'd rather play ball than finish school. He wouldn't listen to how I felt. He wouldn't hear any of my arguments. We had a big fight, and he took away my money and my car. That's how I wound up here that summer."

"You were adopted?"

Cash nodded. "Me and my sister, Ceil, both. You aren't the only kid ever conceived outside of marriage."

"I never thought I was," Jeb said, his irritation on the rise again.

"At least your mother cared enough for you, and maybe even me, that she wanted to keep you. I wasn't so lucky."

Jeb didn't reply for a few seconds. "Did you ever try to find out who your biological parents are?"

"I went so far as to find out their names and where they live. My dad was a minor league ball player and my mother was a dance instructor. They never married, of course, and I never got up the courage to face them."

"What about your sister?"

Cash smiled. "My sister—your aunt Cecilia, better known as Ceil—looked up her parents and found out that her mother was dead. Her dad didn't want anything to do with her. It hurt. All I can say is that it was his loss."

The waitress arrived with their pizza, and for a few moments there was silence while Jeb devoured a slice. He reached for another piece and said, "Tell me about that summer."

Though Cash expected Jeb's curiosity, he was unprepared for Jeb to see his weaknesses. But he'd do whatever it took to win his son's good favor. "What do you want to know?"

"About you and Mom. About you and Skye."

Cash picked up another slice of pizza and put it on his plate while he gathered his thoughts. What could he say to Jeb to make him understand things he wasn't sure he understood himself?

"I guess the most important thing about that summer is that I was barely nineteen and away from my family for the first time. My dad had all but kicked me out. Susan and

Skye and Opa Herder made me feel like part of their family.

"I didn't know anything about farming, but they taught me, and I learned just how stubborn and self-reliant two women alone can be."

"How old was Skye?"

"Fourteen."

"Why didn't you fall for her instead of Mom?"

"I did."

The admission drew a startled look from Jeb.

"I was crazy about her. I spent every free minute with her and dreamed about her every night."

Seeing the query in Jeb's eyes, Cash continued. "She had a crush on me, too. Things almost got out of hand one night, but I remembered my mom cautioning me about not taking a girl's innocence."

Jeb's gaze slid away from Cash's.

"Anyway, I told Skye she was too young, and I guess I hurt her pretty badly. She wouldn't talk to me, wouldn't spend any time with me. Then along came the Fourth of July, and there was this big celebration. Skye was ignoring me and flirting with Lee Ballard—"

"Lee Ballard! That slime was around even then?" Jeb asked.

"He was around," Cash said with a slow nod. "Susan was drinking *Piestengel* and flirting like crazy. I'd never seen her that way. She was always so upright, so play by the rules...."

He sighed and stared at a spot across the room, but his gaze was focused inward, on the past. "I have to be honest. I'd thought about being with Susan, too, especially after things went bad between me and Skye. Susan and I spent a lot of time together, just talking."

Cash's lips curved in a reminiscent smile. "She had a way of making me feel I was the only thing on the planet that held any interest for her. She was pretty, and to me she seemed worldly, even though I know now that she was more innocent than anyone would imagine."

Jeb was taking it all in, a rapt expression on his face. "Anyway," Cash said, "that night before the fireworks display, Susan insisted that she teach me to polka. We danced and drank more wine, and I felt pretty macho and cocky because she was paying so much attention to me.

"After everyone left I went up to my room over the garage. I thought about Susan's actions, but decided that all she intended to do was leave me hot and bothered. And I thought about Skye. How she'd ignored me and played up to Ballard all day. And I thought about how she'd looked in her red swimsuit, and I—" his voice trailed away and he blew out a shaky breath "—I imagined making love to her. A storm had been brewing all day, and when I heard the noise at the door, I thought it was the wind."

"It was Mom."

"Yeah," Cash said with a nod. "It was Susan. All dressed up and bringing more wine. She never wore dresses, but she was wearing one then. She'd put on makeup and perfume, and..."

"She seduced you." The statement was flat, emotionless.

"I guess you could say that, but I can't put all the blame on her. I was willing. More than willing. My hormones were in revolt, and I thought I was the only nineteen-year-old virgin in the Heartland."

"You made love with Mom, but you wanted it to be Skye."

The calm observation caught Cash off guard. In a matter of minutes Jeb had figured out what Cash had only recently realized.

He met Jeb's steady, disconcerting gaze and nodded again. "I didn't realize that until yesterday, after I found you and Belinda together. I wanted it to be Skye that first time, but after that, I forgot Skye. All that mattered was that Susan made me feel like a man."

Cash felt his own cheeks grow hot, but he knew he had to be as honest with Jeb as he could be. "I'm not proud of it. I'm not proud of any of it. My only excuse is that I was young and hot-blooded, and inconsiderate of anyone's feelings but my own."

"Mom could have ended it after the first time, but she didn't," Jeb observed. "So she was getting something from it, too."

"Maybe." Cash picked up his glass and took a swallow of his cola. "You know the rest. I realize now that she was pregnant when she sent me away." He forced aside a sudden, piercing sorrow, and his eyes found Jeb's once more. "If I'd known, I would never have left," he said. "If I'd found out, I'd have come back. I want you to believe that."

Jeb's gaze searched his while the jukebox played some rap song and the noise of the other customers' conversations buzzed around them. Finally, apparently satisfied with what he saw there, he nodded and then said, "Tell me about your sister."

"Ceil?" Surprised by the unexpected question, Cash began babbling. "Ceil is stone-cold gorgeous. She has a daughter, Samantha, who's about...sixteen now. And a son, Seth, who's thirteen. Ceil's just gotten a divorce this past year, but she's still crazy about the guy."

"I have cousins," Jeb said, a thoughtful gleam in his eyes. "And a sister."

"What?"

Cash nodded and reached into his back pocket to pull out his wallet. "Her name is Darby. Here," he said, thrusting the picture across the table. "That's Sam and Seth and Ceil." He flipped a plastic-coated photo over, revealing a picture of a pretty, dimpled eleven-year-old with dark hair, green eyes and a mouthful of braces.

"And that," Cash said proudly, "is Darby."

All in all, Cash felt his time with Jeb had been productive. While he couldn't say that he and Jeb were bosom buddies, he felt he had answered a lot of questions to Jeb's satisfaction and that they had worked through the worst of his animosity.

"I'm going to do my best to come back in a couple of weeks," Cash told Jeb as they exited the dimness of the pizza parlor and stepped into the bright afternoon sunshine.

"Fine."

Cash reached into his pocket, drew out a money clip and peeled off five crisp one-hundred-dollar bills. "Here. Use this to go to that ball camp you told me about."

Bewilderment mingled with anger in Jeb's eyes. "You can't buy me. I don't want your money!"

The corner of Cash's mouth lifted in a wry smile. "I'm not trying to buy you. You're a Benedict. This money is as much yours as it is mine."

Jeb shook his head and swallowed hard, but he looked longingly at the money in Cash's hand. "You don't have to do this for me."

"I'm not doing it for you," Cash told him. "I'm doing it for me. I want you to be the best damned ball player to ever come out of the state."

"That's what I want to be," Jeb said.

"Then take it. Consider it a graduation gift if it makes you feel better."

Reluctantly, Jeb reached for the money. "What will I tell Skye?"

"I'll take care of Skye."

"Do you mean that?" Jeb asked, stuffing the money into the front pocket of his jeans.

Cash saw the expression in Jeb's eyes. He was talking about far more than Cash explaining to Skye that he'd given Jeb money for the baseball camp. He was talking about a lifetime.

"I'm through letting people down," Cash told Jeb. "I promise I'll take care of Skye if she'll let me."

Jeb ducked his head once in understanding and extended his hand. Though Cash would have liked to take his son in a bear hug, he resisted the impulse and clasped the outstretched hand instead. They stood awkwardly until Cash said, "You'd better go. You're going to be late for work."

"Yeah."

Cash watched as Jeb swung his leg over the Harley, donned the helmet, kicked the engine to life and, with a single jaunty wave, pulled out onto the street. He watched until Jeb disappeared from sight, then, with a lump in his throat and a heavy heart, he drove to Skye's shop to say goodbye.

"You did what!" Skye cried when he told her what he'd done.

"I gave Jeb the money for the baseball camp," Cash repeated.

"We'll never be able to pay you back!"

"I don't want you to pay me back."

Skye sighed and stomped across the shop to straighten a picture hanging on a far wall. How dare Cash go behind her back like this! "You had no right, Cash," she muttered. "I feel like a charity case or something."

Cash swore softly and followed her. He took her by the shoulders, turning her around to face him. When she averted her face, he grasped her chin and tilted it upward until their eyes met.

"You aren't a charity case, and I don't want you feeling that way out of some distorted sense of misplaced pride. Jeb's my son—I have every right to give him money. I not only owe him this, I want to do it. It's an honor."

"An honor?"

"Yes," Cash said solemnly. "Look, I know he needs money for school, and I want you to know right now that I intend to help with that, so stop worrying. You worry too much. You're too young to be so burdened."

"I think I was born worrying, and some days I feel as if I've never been young," she admitted.

"I know you've had a rough time of it these past twenty years, and especially since Susan died, but all that's about to change. I intend to see to it that things are easier for you and Jeb from now on—"

"But, I—" she interrupted.

"And if you say one word about charity, I'll just have to kiss you to shut you up."

Skye gasped at the gently voiced threat. The look in Cash's eyes was teasing, tender, the way she remembered it from the past.

"You said it yesterday," he told her, stroking her jawline with his fingertips. "It isn't finished yet. You know as well as I do that there's something between us. Maybe we were too young and stupid to recognize it for what it was before. Maybe it wasn't anything but a couple of kids' crazy hormonal urges. But my hormones are still urging, and so are yours—aren't they?"

"Yes," she admitted on a soft sigh. To deny it would be to deny her very existence.

"Admitting there's a problem is the first step to recovery," Cash quipped. "Who knows? Maybe sex is all there is to it. But I think we owe it to ourselves to see if there's the possibility that it's more."

Skye opened her mouth to say something about Susan, but he stopped her with a finger against her lips.

He knew what she was about to say. The sorrow in his eyes was indisputable. "I can't change what happened, no matter how much I might want to. But if it's any consolation to you, I want you to know that I wanted it to be you."

Cash headed the Lexus toward Nebraska, images flashing through his brain like silent frames of an old movie. The facade of cool disinterest that hid Jeb's anger. His reluctant acceptance of the truth about the past. The intense expression on his face when he said he wanted to play ball. Jeb and Belinda making out on the couch.

Damn! How could Jeb be so stupid, so careless, knowing that he himself was a product of an ill-fated love affair? And how could he deliberately hurt Skye this way?

Skye. What was he going to do about the persistent, crazy notion that he might want not only Jeb but Skye in his life on a permanent basis? He had enough to worry about with Jeb and Darby, yet he couldn't forget the feel of Skye in his arms, her mouth warm and open beneath his. Even though she responded to his kisses with all the hunger and fervor any man could want, she still believed he had confused her with Susan.

He didn't want the added complication of a woman in his life, especially not a woman whose sister he'd had a child with. His life was already a shambles with his recent divorce, the ailing magazine and his problems with Darby.

The last thing he needed was a rebellious, bullheaded son who considered him just a notch above pond scum, and a stubborn, hardheaded woman to give him grief. On the other hand, maybe that was exactly what he needed.

When Cash walked through the door the town house seemed emptier than it had been when he'd left almost two weeks before. He resisted the impulse to call Skye and let her know that he'd made the trip all right and that he already missed her and Jeb and the farm. Instead, he called his favorite florist and sent her a dozen red roses. Then he dialed his former home to let Darby know he was back and that their date for the following day was still on.

Liz answered. He wanted to hang up, to try back later when she wasn't there, but he was finished with running. He intended to fight for his place in Darby's life, just as he intended to fight for his magazine and for Jeb and Skye.

"Hello, Liz," Cash said.

"So you did come back," Liz said, the familiar sarcasm firmly in place.

"Of course I came back. I haven't forgotten that Darby and I are supposed to celebrate her birthday tomorrow."

Cash heard Liz's exasperated sigh through the phone lines. "I'm sorry, Cash, but there's been a change of plans. Darby is spending the day with Don and me."

Even with disappointment sweeping through him, Cash couldn't help noticing the cat-that-ate-the-canary satisfaction he heard in his ex-wife's voice. "What happened?"

"What happened?" Liz echoed. "You took off to God knows where, and you didn't once call Darby to tell her where you were, what you were doing, or if you planned on being back in time. What was the poor child supposed to think? She's been an absolute basket case worrying about it, so Don and I decided to give her a party rather than have her birthday ruined."

Cash gritted his teeth to keep from saying something he knew he'd regret. "I promised her I'd be here," he said evenly.

"Well, it would be the first time you kept a promise."

Sadly, Cash acknowledged that Liz's frosty statement wasn't far from the truth. "Look, I admit I'm not without blame in anything that's happened, but I'm not the villain you're so anxious to paint me, either."

"Villain? I don't know what you're talking about."

"Sure you do. When I walked over to say something to you and Darby the day the divorce was granted, you let me know real fast that I'd better not—"

"I—"

"No! Don't try to deny it. You know exactly what I'm talking about. Then you had the gall to call Ceil and tell her I hadn't even tried to speak to Darby. You're messing with her mind, Liz," Cash said in a terse voice, "and I won't have it."

"You won't have it?"

"You heard me. I love my daughter, and she loves me, even though we may not have the closest relationship in the world. You're making a big mistake by underestimating Darby's intelligence."

"What does that have to do with anything?"

"She may not be able to pick up on it immediately, but Darby knows gold from dross. You need to stop and consider that what you're doing can backfire on you if you aren't very careful."

"Meaning?"

"Meaning that sooner or later Darby will figure out what you're trying to do and she's going to resent it—and you. You just might find yourself on the outside looking in."

* * *

When Ceil heard that Cash was home she invited him to her house to have dinner with her and Samantha and Seth. Ceil wanted to catch him up on what had been going on with the magazines while he was gone, and to look him in the eye to make certain he was all right with the changes that going to Iowa had wrought in his life.

Cash was only too glad to accept. The emptiness of the town house only magnified the ongoing battle raging inside his head: what to do about his tentative feelings for Skye and how he should go about incorporating Jeb into the family and the future he had in Lincoln.

Sixteen-year-old Samantha met Cash at the door and, after an exuberant hug and kiss, left him in the kitchen where Ceil—dressed in a pair of disreputable shorts and one of Seth's T-shirts—was busy doing something to chicken breasts that involved wax paper and a wooden mallet.

"Taking out your frustrations on another helpless victim, I see," Cash said, rounding the chopping block to kiss his sister's cheek.

Ceil nodded. "Better this poor bird than a dozen people I could name."

"Myself included, I'm sure," Cash said, going to the huge oak-covered refrigerator where Ceil kept a supply of sturdy mugs in the freezer. He plucked a leaf of mint from the pot on the windowsill, crushed it between his fingers and dropped it into the frosty mug, drowning it with the sweet tea she kept made up all the time.

"Yeah, but you're way down the list."

"Thank God. I have enough people who want a piece of my hide."

Ceil laughed.

Finished with her pounding of the chicken, Ceil layered Swiss cheese and ham over the breasts and started rolling them up, securing them with toothpicks.

"Chicken cordon bleu, I presume?" Cash asked, seating himself on a nearby bar stool.

"Uh-huh." Ceil stopped what she was doing for a moment and stared at him from beneath a thatch of thick, dark eyelashes that looked incongruous with her natural blond hair. "You look a little down in the mouth. Are you okay?"

"I'm fine. I called Darby to let her know we were still on for tomorrow, and Liz informed me that she and Don had decided to throw Darby a party, since they weren't sure I'd be back."

"That's not surprising."

"No." Cash took a swallow of his tea. "Mmm, good," he told her. "What's happening with the magazine?" he asked, deliberately changing the subject.

"Monica refuses to stay. Bart had another meeting with Liz and her attorney. She's thinking about resigning and getting out of the business altogether, which would give us free rein to make some major changes and maybe salvage the whole shebang."

"For a hefty price, of course." Cash added.

Ceil raised her eyebrows and shrugged. "It might be worth it not to have to look at her smiling—smugly smiling—face every day."

"Good point." Cash rested his elbows on the ceramic-tiled bar and scrubbed his face in his hands. "I'm really sick of all this. It was never what I wanted to do, and it seems like the longer I go, the less enthusiasm I can get up for it."

"You're very good at what you do," Ceil reminded him, dipping the rolled chicken into beaten egg and bread crumbs.

Cash's lips twisted into a semblance of a smile. "Yeah."

"I hear a big qualifier coming on."

"I don't know what's wrong with me. I feel edgy, dissatisfied with my whole life."

"We've all been there, Cash," Ceil said in an understanding voice. "It'll pass."

"I hope you're right. I think the trip made it worse. I think that in twenty years I'll look back and call this the summer of my discontent."

"What happened?" Ceil divided her attention between Cash and the chicken that was browning in a skillet.

"You mean besides finding out I have a son and that I think I still have feelings for Skye?"

Ceil cast him a look from beneath her eyelashes. "You do?"

"I think so, but it's too soon to know what those feelings really are."

"Which means you don't want to talk about it. So tell me about your discontent," Ceil prodded.

"It's a little thing, really. While I was in Amana I saw that Skye had opened up a shop where she sells things made in the colonies as well as the original pictures she does with watercolors and pressed flowers. She isn't getting rich, but she's happy with what she's accomplished." He saw a strange look cross Ceil's face, heard her utter a soft curse. "What?"

Ceil's gaze shifted from his. She blew out a troubled breath, then found his eyes with hers again. "I found something while I was going through those old papers of Mom and Dad's. I don't think you're going to like it."

"Don't tell me!" Cash said, certain that nothing could compare to what he'd learned in Iowa. "My real parents are Joe DiMaggio and Marilyn Monroe."

"You wish," Ceil said with a low, girlish giggle. Cash realized it had been too long since she'd been happy enough to really laugh. She sobered as abruptly. "Watch the chicken," she commanded. "I'll be right back."

Frowning, Cash went to the stove to keep an eye on the browning pieces of meat. Ceil returned to the kitchen, a yellowed envelope extended toward him.

"What's this?"

"The future you could have had."

The ambiguous statement, along with the return address that bore a St. Louis Cardinals logo, sent Cash's stomach into a slow roll. He reached automatically for his antacid tablets and found that his pocket was empty. The letter was from Joseph Mahoney, the scout who'd come to the university in '77. It was an offer for Cash to play for the Arkansas Travelers, a farm team of the Cards.

Conflicting emotions warred inside him. Elation battled with hopelessness. Joy strove with anger. The Cards had wanted him. He had been good enough after all. His father had betrayed him. He wanted to cry for the life he might have had, but he didn't. Instead, he raised tortured eyes to Ceil's. Hers held empathy and regret.

"I was in Europe when you and dad had the fight," she reminded him. "The letter must have come while we were both gone. Dad or Mom intercepted it and ignored it. If this Mahoney guy tried to write or call, it would be easy enough for them to say you weren't interested, that you'd decided you needed to get your education."

Cash crushed the missive in his fist. "Damn him," he choked out through the thickness in his throat.

"Yes," Ceil agreed. "Damn him. He wanted complete control, Cash. We both know that. Unfortunately for him, he picked two rebel kids to bring home from the orphanage."

"Yeah, I'm a rebel, all right," Cash said, his disgust with himself apparent. "When push came to shove, I folded like a taco and came back to do exactly what he wanted me to."

He turned away, and Ceil whipped around in front of him and stopped him by taking his forearms in a strong grip. "If you'd known about the offer, you'd have hung tough," she said, her nails digging into his flesh. "But you didn't know.

"Susan told you to leave. Faced with limited options, you did what any smart nineteen-year-old kid would do. You came home and made peace with the father who loved you—and he did, Cash, even though he tried to control you. You came home and you accepted the legacy he wanted you to have. No one can fault you for that."

"Things would have been different if I'd known."

"Of course they would have. If you'd played ball, you'd still have left Iowa, so you still might not have discovered Jeb's existence before now. You probably wouldn't have met Liz, and without Liz there would be no Darby."

Ceil's eyes filled with tears. "Since Gage and I split up, I've come to believe one thing. God is in control. Things happen for reasons we can't always understand. Maybe one day we will."

Chapter Nine

Cash went back to work at Benedict Periodicals the next day. He immersed himself in the everyday structure of the magazine publishing business, so that he wouldn't have a lot of time to think about the bombshell Ceil had dropped into his lap the night before.

He told himself that what had happened was ancient history, that he was a grown man and should be able to forgive and forget. But forgiving was hard when all he wanted to do was have the chance to face Cash Senior and tell him how he felt. Fortunately, time passed at its usual breakneck pace, and he was left with little time to brood over the fact that his father had cheated him out of his dream to play ball.

The evening of the second day Cash was back at work, he took Darby to her favorite Italian restaurant in honor of her twelfth birthday. Prior to their dinner engagement, they'd gone on a shopping spree where he bought her a pair of new in-line skates, a ruby ring—her birthstone—and a funky

outfit she'd seen and wanted that Cash had serious doubts
about Liz letting her wear. They planned to end the evening
by going to see the latest Brad Pitt movie.

Cash did his best to keep up a stream of chitchat while
they ate their lasagna, but Darby's answers were, for the
most part, monosyllabic. No, nothing much was happening; yes, her piece for the upcoming recital was coming
along nicely; yes, she'd had a good birthday party, and yes,
she got some good presents from Liz and Don.

Cash knew he might not be the best father in the world,
but he'd learned something about people the past few years,
and he knew that Darby was far too quiet and reserved for
a girl her age. She should be more animated...happier. She
should be concerned about whether or not some boy in her
class thought she was cute instead of whether or not her dad
intended to show up for her birthday.

Darby was lonely, too. Liz saw to it that she was so involved with various lessons that there was little chance for
Darby to develop friends her own age. She was more like a
miniature, emotionally stunted adult than a child. His heart
ached because it had taken him too much time and a divorce to realize where he and Liz had gone wrong.

"I'm sorry, baby," he said, breaking a growing silence.

"For what?" Darby asked, looking up at him from beneath too-long bangs.

"For not being the kind of father you deserve."

Darby shifted uncomfortably. "It's okay."

"No," he said, "it's not okay. When people bring a child
into the world, they owe it to that child to be the best parent they can be." He tried to smile, knew he failed misera-
bly. "I failed all the way around there, just the way I failed
your mom."

Darby put down her fork. "Did you and Mom ever love
each other?"

The out-of-left-field question took Cash off guard, but after a moment's consideration he saw its validity. "Sure we did."

"What happened?" Darby asked, leaning toward him, her grass green eyes filled with earnest entreaty.

Cash considered that a moment. "Love is sort of like a plant," he said finally. "If it's watered and fertilized and cared for, it grows and flourishes. If it isn't tended, it withers and dies. I was so busy taking care of business that I didn't have much time for tending my marriage and my family. Your mom and I just sort of... grew apart, and, after a while, whatever love she felt for me died."

Darby looked as if she might burst into tears.

"I'm very sorry for letting that happen, Darb, but even though your mother and I don't love each other anymore, nothing in this world could ever make me stop loving you. Please believe that."

Darby nodded.

"Things can't change between us overnight," he told her, "but I want you to know that I'm interested in what's happening in your life. I want to be a part of your life from here on out, and I want you to be a part of mine. I want you to be able to come to me with your problems and know that I'll listen and that I care."

"Mom says you're too busy with the magazines to have time for me."

Stifling the urge to strangle Liz, Cash nodded. "Managing Benedict Periodicals is a lot of work for everyone. And, as you may or may not know, we recently lost one of our magazines. There's a chance we might lose another. I worked very hard to try and save it, but if I learned one thing from the divorce, it's that losing my daughter isn't worth any magazine—or all of them." Cash cleared his throat of a sudden thickness. "I love you, Darby. So much."

Darby's braces flashed briefly as she smiled through the threat of her own tears. "I love you, too, Daddy."

"I want you to promise me something."

"What?"

"That we'll talk. That you'll tell me if we have a problem or you think I'm shutting you out."

"Okay."

Cash held out his hand across the table. "Shake on it?"

Darby put her hand in his and they sealed their new pact. Satisfied, she picked up her fork and began eating again.

"Where did you go on your trip?" she asked, surprising him by making a sincere effort at instigating a conversation.

"Iowa."

She wrinkled her nose. "Why Iowa?"

"Because I spent some time there a long time ago."

"You must not have had a good time," she observed.

"Why do you say that?"

"You're frowning."

Cash's assessment of his daughter had been right. She was not only intelligent, she was intuitive. In fact, she picked up on emotional states far too easily. He wondered if he should tell her about what had happened to him while he was away, or if learning about Jeb would be too much too soon after the divorce.

As usual when he was faced with decisions that required quick answers, Cash relied on his gut intuition. Even if Darby got angry over the news, everything inside him warned that if they were ever to have a satisfactory, healthy relationship, that relationship needed to be founded on the mutual respect that came hand in hand with honesty.

"What is it?" Darby asked when Cash made no response for several seconds.

"I have something to tell you that I don't want to tell you because things are so up in the air. But if you and I are going to deal with each other in a straightforward way, it's only fair that you be told."

"What is it?" she asked, her eyes reflecting her confusion.

"When I went to Iowa, I found out that I have another child." Darby's eyes grew wide. "A son."

"You cheated on Mom?" she asked, stunned, and stunning him with the depth of her understanding. "You had *sex* with someone else! Is that where you went all those times you told Mom you were going out of town on business?" Her eyes glittered with angry tears. "Were you going to see your *son?*"

Cash recognized Darby's insecurity and jealousy for what it was. It was no secret that he'd often vocalized his wish for a brother for Darby. Neither was it any secret that Liz had adamantly refused to have another child.

"No. I had no idea Jeb even existed until two weeks ago, and I've never been unfaithful to your mother," Cash assured her. "Jeb is eighteen. This . . . affair happened before I ever met your mom."

"How could you?" Darby challenged, moisture pooling in her eyes. "You're always telling me not to cave in under peer pressure, that the time is coming when a boy will want to touch me and not to let him!"

"That's still good advice."

"Isn't your attitude a little hypocritical?"

"Maybe so," Cash agreed, seeing their hard-fought-for truce swiftly passing into nonexistence. "I'm not condoning my actions, Darby. I can't. But I was just nineteen myself, and very mixed up. If it's any consolation, Jeb isn't any happier about having me come in and upset his life than you are about finding out about him."

"What's *he* got to be mad about?"

"He thinks I abandoned his mother, that I never wanted him. But I didn't know she was pregnant, or I'd never have left."

"If you'd stayed in Iowa, you wouldn't have met Mom and you wouldn't have had me, which might have suited you more."

"No," Cash said in a gentle voice, "it wouldn't have suited me at all. You've been a great joy in my life, and not having you would be a great loss."

Darby looked skeptical.

"What you want me to do is choose which one of you I'd rather have, and that isn't fair. I couldn't possibly choose, and I shouldn't have to, because there's enough love to go around. Finding out about Jeb doesn't change my love for you."

Cash paused. "Think about this. What you're asking me to do is sort of like your mom wanting you to choose between her and me. I don't think that's fair to you, because I think you love us both."

Darby's eyebrows drew together. Cash could almost see the wheels in her mind turning. He decided to press his small advantage. "Because you love us both and we both love you, we should both be a part of your life. The same goes for Jeb. Having him in my life isn't going to make any difference in our relationship. It's how you and I deal with each other that controls that."

"You're going to bring him here?" Darby asked, incredulity supplanting her anger.

"He got a scholarship to come here to go to college. Since he'll be here, I'd like very much for him to get to know the rest of his family."

"I don't want to get to know him," Darby said flatly.

Cash knew he couldn't expect her to make a complete turnaround in a matter of minutes. All he could do was hope that she would think about what he'd said and come to the right conclusions.

"Would you like to hear what happened?" he asked, "or have you already tried and convicted me?"

Darby lifted her chin in a haughty gesture. "Suit yourself."

She sounded so much like Liz he wanted to shake her. Instead, Cash gave her an unemotional, condensed version of what had happened and finished by saying, "This is hard on all of us. I know that all the hurt and resentment you and Jeb are feeling now is my fault. The only thing I can tell you is that if you don't want to wake up some day with your kids resenting you and doubting your love, be smarter than I was."

The expression on Cash's face was steady, solemn. "I don't know what will happen with all this, Darby. All I know is that losing either of you would break my heart."

Cash took Darby home after the movie, promising he'd call in a few days to see about the exact time of her upcoming violin recital. Properly trained in all the social graces, Darby rather stiltedly thanked him for her birthday gifts and told him she'd enjoyed the day and the movie.

Truth be known, she was so upset about what her dad had told her, she'd hardly been able to follow the plot of the movie. She had a half brother named Jeb who was eighteen years old and lived in Amana, Iowa! Her dad had *slept with* some woman named Susan Herder. It was too horrible to even think about!

As soon as she got home, Darby told her mom she was tired and went straight to her room where she could indulge

in her depression without being under the unnerving scrutiny of her mom's eagle eye.

Darby curled up into a ball on her frilly bed. Her dad had
the son he'd always wanted. To lose that son would break
his heart. She squeezed her eyes shut to hold back the tears,
but it didn't work. A ragged sob tore its way up her throat,
and she gave in to her misery, sure her own heart was
breaking.

Cash hadn't called in the three days he'd been gone, but
he'd sent Skye long-stemmed red roses, a bottle of pricey
rose-scented perfume and a box of expensive chocolates that
Jeb had made a serious dent in. Jeb's fear that once he and
Skye were out of Cash's sight they'd be out of his mind was,
so far, unfounded.

Jeb would have died before admitting it to anyone, but he
felt a little sad at knowing Cash was gone. It wasn't that he'd
gotten attached to him or anything, but the man had made
an impact on his life, no doubt about it.

At any given moment, Jeb would find himself indulging
in daydreams where he was a pro pitcher...or a suave ex-
ecutive, heir to a magazine empire—pretty heady illusions
for a kid who'd grown up surrounded by cornfields. He also
gave a lot of thought to his little sister, Darby, and his aunt
Ceil and her two kids, wondering what they were like, if they
would accept him. Wondering if it would be worth the effort to find out. Knowing he'd always regret it if he didn't
try.

Skye missed Cash, too. It was evident in the way she stood
staring out the window, in the forlorn look in her brown eyes
and in the wistful way she sighed for no reason. She might
not be as willing as Cash to admit her feelings, but it was
obvious to Jeb she felt something for the man who'd fathered him.

Jeb felt something for Cash, too—he just wasn't sure what it was yet. He had accepted the possibility that Cash wasn't the low-down, dirty scum he'd thought him and was faced with the possibility that Cash was exactly what he claimed: a grown man who'd made a mistake as a teenager. A mistake he longed to set as right as he could.

Jeb was intrigued by Cash and the things he'd told him about his other family in Lincoln, but he was afraid to expect too much. That way he wouldn't be hurt if things didn't work out. He decided to adopt a wait-and-see attitude. If there was one thing he'd learned in his eighteen years, it was that even though some things couldn't be changed, they worked themselves out if left alone.

Jeb was thinking about that the night after Darby's birthday—he'd hardly thought of anything else the past few days. Bushed from a day of trimming hedges and sidewalks, he'd come straight home from work. The phone rang as he stepped through the front door—probably Belinda wondering where the heck he was. Guided by the lamp Skye always left on for him, he raced through the living room to the phone, hoping to get it before it woke Skye.

He grabbed it midway through the second ring. "Hello."

"Is this the Herder residence?"

Jeb frowned. The voice belonged to a young girl. "Yeah."

"May I speak to Jeb Herder, please?"

Jeb's frown deepened. "This is Jeb Herder."

There was a significant pause before the girl spoke again. "This is Darby Benedict...."

Darby Benedict? Darby Benedict was . . .

"Cash Benedict's daughter."

So the call was from Cash Benedict's daughter, Jeb thought, not his sister. His heart took a nosedive. He had a sneaking suspicion that this call wasn't about scheduling a happy family reunion. "Yeah?" he said again, his voice carefully neutral.

"My dad told me about you."

There was no disguising the animosity in the young voice. "He told me about you, too," Jeb said warily.

"I guess you're wondering why I called."

"It crossed my mind, yeah."

"I called to tell you that Cash is *my* father," Darby said, her voice bristling with anger. "He was married to my mother, and your mother was nothing but a—a tramp!"

For a couple of seconds, Jeb was stunned to speechlessness. Then coherent thought returned, and with it full-fledged anger and words of retaliation. "My mother was not a tramp. She was a good person who at least had some class, which your mother obviously doesn't, or you'd have better manners than to call other people's parents names when you don't know what the hell you're talking about!"

Jeb heard Darby's heavy breathing over the phone lines.

"I want you to stay out of his life and leave him alone."

"You spoiled little brat!" Jeb said. Darby started to speak again, but he cut her off. "For your information, I don't need a kid telling me what to do or not to do. But I will tell you this—all I want is to be left alone. I did just fine for eighteen years without the illustrious Cash Benedict for a father, and I sure as hell don't need him now. Is that clear?"

"I'd say we understand each other very well," the small, quavering voice replied.

"Good," Jeb said, but he doubted if Darby heard, because the line suddenly buzzed in his ear. The little snot had hung up on him! Angrier than he'd been since the day he and Cash had confronted each other in this same room, Jeb slammed down the receiver. Just who in the hell did Darby Benedict think she was, anyway? he wondered as he stomped up the stairs.

Breathing heavily, he stormed into his bedroom, stripped off his shirt, wadded it into a loose ball and flung it across the room. He ground his teeth while ugly words spun through his head. His throat felt tight, and his eyes burned, but he refused to admit, even to himself, that Darby's phone call had punctured the blissful reunion scenario that had been playing through his mind with increasing regularity.

He wouldn't admit that her rejection hurt him to the quick.

"Who were you talking to?" Liz asked, poking her head into Darby's room just as she slammed down the receiver.

Darby jumped. "No one important."

Liz pushed the door open wider and stepped into the elegantly appointed room, one that would do any decorator proud but lacked the stamp of Darby's personality.

"I know something's bothering you."

In dismay, Darby watched her mother cross the room and sit beside her on the bed. She knew from experience that Liz wouldn't leave until she was satisfied that she'd pried out the information she sought.

"You haven't been yourself since your father brought you home. Did he say something to upset you? Something about me?"

"He didn't say anything about you," Darby replied, gazing into her mother's beautiful face, her green eyes swimming with tears. "He never says bad things about you."

"Then what is it?"

Darby choked back a sob. "Daddy said that while he was in Iowa he had an affair and now he has a son named Jeb."

"What!" Liz shrieked, leaping up from the bed. "That sorry, no-good, pseudo-pious—" She whirled and pinned Darby with a look of fury. "I can't believe he cheated on me all these years on top of everything else! A baby, for God's sake!"

"Jeb isn't a baby, and he didn't cheat on you!" Darby said through the tears that were falling faster and faster.

"You just said he had an affair!"

Darby nodded. "It happened before he met you. He was just nineteen, and he and Grandpa Benedict had a fight, and Jeb is eighteen, but I told him to stay away from my dad!"

"Wait a minute!" Liz held up a hand to stop the incoherent jumble of words spilling from Darby's lips. "Stop crying and start at the beginning. You're not making any sense."

She handed Darby a tissue and put an arm around her shaking shoulders. It was several moments before Darby calmed down enough to talk without punctuating every other word with a hearty sob. She told her mother the story as best she could, relating the events as she remembered Cash telling her.

When she finished, the anger in her mother's eyes had faded, replaced with a thoughtful expression. "So Cash has a son named Jeb, and he's going to bring him here to Lincoln so the two of you can get to know each other, is that right?"

Darby nodded. "But I told Jeb to stay away, not to come here."

"Good girl," Liz said, her face lighting up with a smile. "I'm going to talk to your father and make sure he knows exactly how you feel. Exactly how I feel."

Skye had gone upstairs just moments before she heard Jeb come in. She heard the phone ring and knew he'd get it. When it rang at this time of the night it was always for Jeb, and usually Belinda.

Exhausted, but knowing she wouldn't go to sleep for hours, Skye had brought a couple of the diaries upstairs with her. Now that she'd read the account of Susan and Cash's summer romance, she'd decided to go back to the beginning. Back to Susan's teenage years.

The entries were written with the flowing, rounded handwriting that most high school girls seem to adopt, and were filled with the usual angst-ridden thoughts of any normal fifteen-year-old girl.

Evidently headstrong and "different," Susan had given her parents a row to hoe, as Jon would say. Unable to cope with her wild ways, Melanie and Steven Jordan had sent Susan to stay with Melanie's sister, Dolores, in St. Louis. Dolores, a social worker, was used to dealing with rebellious teenagers.

Susan was philosophical about the move. She liked St. Louis, and she liked Aunt Dolores, who understood something her parents didn't: different didn't necessarily mean bad. Skye skimmed several semiboring pages about their discussions, and how much Susan liked living with her aunt.

Skye's interest picked up when Susan began writing about Larry Martin. According to the diary, Larry had come to the café where Susan worked as a waitress, and their attraction to each other had been instant and intense. It was, Susan wrote amid drawings of arrow-pierced hearts, love at first sight.

Susan had filled pages with trivia of her dates with Larry and her escalating sexual longings. Considering the detailed accounts of Susan's feelings, Skye was only marginally surprised when Susan made the confession that she and Larry had "gone all the way."

Things appeared to go well for several months, until the fated happened and Susan got pregnant. Skye read the entry with a sense of fatality. The accompanying response was typical of the situation. Susan was desolate, and both sets of parents were furious, not only at Susan, but at her aunt for not keeping a closer eye on her. Aunt Dolores was pragmatic. There were worse tragedies in life. From Larry came the promise that they would be married, even if it meant postponing college.

Skye put the diary facedown in her lap and frowned at her reflection in the vanity mirror across the room. What had happened to the baby? Had their parents talked Susan into giving it up for adoption? Had she lost it? What had become of the child that would have been her niece or nephew? Filled with a deep curiosity, she read on.

The tone of the next few pages was more upbeat. Susan and Larry had found an apartment. They were gathering furniture, cookware and knickknacks from all their relatives. There was a lapse of two weeks between entries, and then Skye encountered page upon page of writing where the ink ran together so badly in some places that the words were almost indecipherable. Even so, three words stood out.

Larry is dead.

Skye gasped at the blunt statement, realizing belatedly that the ink was smeared from Susan's tears. Skye read as fast as she could, fascinated by this unknown portion of Susan's life and anxious to find out what had happened next.

The story was tragic. Just days before the wedding, Larry had been leaving the café when his pickup was broadsided by an eighteen wheeler whose driver was hopped up on pills. Susan, who had been standing at the window to wave goodbye, had seen the whole thing. She had, naturally, gone to pieces and had to be sedated.

Spellbound by the tale unfolding in the yellowed pages of the diary, Skye read Susan's account of the funeral and how the Jordans and Martins had urged her to give up the baby for adoption.

Susan had balked, even though she knew being a teenage mother would be hard. She wanted to keep Larry's baby, the only thing she had left of their love. Her parents were upset and ashamed about the scandal, but she refused to budge. To their consternation, she wanted to live with her aunt and went back to her job at the café, saying she needed to keep busy or she'd go crazy.

The record of Susan's pregnancy was sketchy. The number of entries didn't pick up noticeably until she mentioned a customer who had started coming to the café: Jon Herder.

At mention of Jon, Skye sat up straighter. There was a week-long account of sixteen-year-old Susan's meeting and strange friendship with thirty-seven-year-old Jon. Her first observations were about Jon and his background....

Wednesday
He's really nice. And good-looking, too. He's tall and blond, and he lives in Iowa. He has a fifty-acre farm near the Iowa River, not far from Marengo. That's about eight miles from the Amana Colonies—where they make Amana appliances—the place Jon says was settled by a religious group from Germany back in the eighteen hundreds. Jon says the church—which was a communal society and became a corporation during the thirties—owns twenty-six thousand acres of farmland. They gave everyone the chance to buy the places where they lived when they incorporated, but Jon's family joined the church much later, and that's why they own more land than most members.

His farm sounds pretty and peaceful. I told Jon that after standing on my feet all day listening to the woes of every person who passes through, it might be nice to just go somewhere like that and get away from every-thing....

Thursday
I couldn't believe it when Jon came back today. I spent my whole break talking to him. He told me that his wife died about ten years ago with diabetes. They never had any children. The doctors said she shouldn't, and Jon had the mumps or something when he was a boy, so they were a perfect pair. Maybe I shouldn't have said anything, but I told him that I wasn't married. Of course, now that I'm almost seven months pregnant, it's pretty obvious what happened. I told him about Larry, and he was very sympathetic. He said everyone is entitled to at least one mistake.

Friday
Jon asked if he could take me to dinner at that new steak place. I told him I didn't want to embarrass him, my being pregnant and all. He said that wouldn't be possible. Who would know we weren't married? I didn't go, but I wanted to.

Susan had made an entry every day that week. It was plain to see that she missed Jon when he went back to Amana. He helped fill the emptiness in her life left by Larry's death. A week later, Susan said Jon phoned her and told her he had a great idea. He wanted to marry her.

I told him no, of course, but it was tempting. I told him I didn't love him, and he said that was okay, because he needed to love someone, and he'd decided I was that person. He said I needed love, and he had enough for us both. Well, that was sweet, but I told him that it wouldn't be fair for him. He looked real sad and said it wasn't love that was stopping me, it was because he was too old. I told him that it was more like I was too young, that he deserved the very best....

Over the next month and a half Jon Herder waged a battle to win Susan's hand, both by phone and letter. His arguments were strong. He loved her. Even though she didn't love him, he could give her security and a name for her baby. Farm life was hard, he said, but he'd do his best to make it a good life. He wanted, at some point, to have a physical relationship with Susan, but he was willing to wait until she was ready. He believed that marriage should be until a couple was parted by death.

Aunt Dolores chose the better part of valor and stayed out of this one, but Skye could see that Susan was flattered by Jon's attentions. Of course, Melanie and Steven were mortified. Why, Jon Herder was only two years younger than Steven!

As the date of the baby's birth drew near, the entries in the journal once again became few and far between. Then, after an absence of a month, Susan had written, *I had a baby girl ten days ago, on May 25.*

Skye's heart lurched to a stop; the rest of the page blurred before her eyes. Blood beat in her ears in time with the ticking of the clock sitting beside her bed. Heat suffused her face, and she was seized with a sudden dizziness.

May 25. Her birthday.

Bits and pieces of her conversation with Opa Herder drifted back into her churning thoughts. Opa talking about Susan being secretive, about Skye needing to know the truth and saying the diaries belonged to her mother. Her eyes filled with tears that began to flow down her cheeks.

"Oh, Opa," Skye whispered into the silence of the room. "I thought it was the Alzheimer's talking. I thought you were confused, but you knew exactly what you were saying, didn't you?"

Susan wasn't her sister. Susan was her *mother.*

Dear God! Skye thought, doing her best to come to grips with the lie that was her life. How had she been so gullible as to swallow the story about her being Melanie's "change of life" baby? With the big gap between their ages, how could she not have suspected the truth?

Why should you have doubted?

Why, indeed? To her knowledge, both Susan and Jon were as honest as they came. And in her own defense, Skye knew of at least two people who had children with age differences the same as hers and Susan's.

Skye's mind roiled with questions, the most pressing being why Susan had chosen to pass her off as her sister instead of her own child. She wiped the tears from her face with a corner of the sheet and opened the journal again with trembling hands, knowing that some of the answers would be found inside.

Aunt Dolores took me to the hospital. Mama and Daddy got there just in time. Jon came the next day, after calling to check on me. I can't believe he drove all that way just to see me. He really is a wonderful man. I wish Daddy could be so understanding. Uh-oh. The baby's crying, so I have to go till later. Oh, I almost forgot. I named her April Skye.

If there had been any lingering doubts in Skye's mind, the last sentence erased them. She pressed her trembling lips together and turned the page determinedly.

Again, the additions were sketchy. Notations about her first smile, her first teeth—all the usual baby things that Susan said were also in her baby book.

Then, ten months after Skye's birth, Susan wrote a lackluster account of the boating accident that had killed her parents. The incident was related in an impersonal style, almost as if Susan were writing it for the newspaper.

Her reactions were something else.

She wrote about her guilt for not being a better daughter and expressed grief that she hadn't been closer to her parents. She was genuinely sorry that she hadn't tried harder to bridge the gap in their relationship and that she'd run away to her aunt's instead of trying to work things out.

Skye was stunned to read that Jon had attended the funeral. Afterward, he'd once again asked Susan to marry him. Susan was torn between her new insight to life and the desire to take him up on his offer.

I know how important Jon's religion is to him, and I told him I didn't want the townsfolk to think that he had married a whore. He's far too good a man to have to carry that burden. I've learned that running away is a lot easier than sticking something out, and I'm never running away from my problems again. Jon says marrying him wouldn't be running away. It would be starting over.

There was no account of what finally swayed Susan, but within a month Susan had packed her own and her baby's meager belongings and let Jon move them to his farm.

Her mind churning, Skye turned down a corner of the page to mark her place. If this was true, and obviously it was, Susan had gotten pregnant not once but twice! Skye rubbed at her throbbing forehead with her fingertips. Why hadn't Susan ever told her? she wondered. She'd told Jeb about Cash. He would have to be told about this, too, of course.

Jeb! Skye's stomach lurched at the thought that leapt into her mind. According to the diary, Jeb would be her brother, not her nephew. Dear heaven, how could she tell him this, especially now, when he was just coming to terms with his relationship with Cash?

Another, more startling thought wrung a sharp cry of anguish from Skye. She thought of Cash touching Susan. Kissing her. Making love to her.

Making love, not to her sister, Susan, but to her *mother*.

Chapter Ten

Sleep was impossible as Skye lay awake thinking about Susan's lifelong lie that they were sisters and fighting the growing anger she felt because Susan had kept the truth a secret.

Why? Skye thought again. Why hadn't she been told the truth about her father as she'd grown into adulthood? Didn't she deserve that truth, as well as the right to work through whatever negative feelings it might bring her?

She couldn't help thinking about how different things would have been if she'd known the facts about her conception and birth earlier. She'd had no cousins, no blood relatives except Aunt Dolores, who'd died when she was eight. And, while Opa had been a wonderful substitute, she might have liked the chance to get to know her paternal grandparents.

Alone except for Susan, Skye had felt empty somehow, as if a part of her were missing. If she'd known she had

family somewhere, how much more grounded she might
have felt. How much more secure in herself and who she
was....

By keeping her self-imposed silence, Susan had denied her
the opportunity to find out about her father's family, the
same opportunity Cash was offering Jeb. Skye couldn't help
taking exception to the fact that she'd been given no choice.

The unexpected news did make one thing clear. As
frightening as it was, she knew she had to put her own selfish feelings aside and encourage Jeb to at least see what the
Benedicts offered. He deserved the chance that had been
denied her, the chance to make his own decisions about
whether or not he wanted to be a part of the Benedict family.

Forget it. The past is past.

God knew she was trying, and she'd been making some
headway until this came along. There was no ignoring the
fact that this new information made a difference in Skye's
blossoming relationship with Cash, and maybe that was
what hurt the most. It was one thing for her to come to some
sort of acceptance and understanding about Cash having an
affair with her sister, and quite another for him to have slept
with her mother.

The alarm clock buzzed, and Skye reached out to shut it
off. She rubbed her burning eyes and threw back the sheet
to start a new day. Jeb would have to be told about this new
wrinkle in their lives. No matter how he reacted to the news,
he had a right to know. She was finished with lies and secrets.

Skye thought she was down in the mouth until she took a
good look at Jeb, who came stumbling sleepily into the living room, a disgruntled look on his face, his eyes red-
rimmed from lack of sleep.

Ever since the day Cash and Jeb had lunched together, Jeb's attitude had improved considerably. Skye kept waiting for him to revert to type, and maybe he was about to.

"What's the matter with you?" she asked.

"Nothing," Jeb said grumpily, getting a mug from the cabinet and pouring himself a cup of coffee.

"Liar."

Jeb smiled, a grim arcing of his lips that gave him an older, world-weary look. "You're too sharp for me," he said.

Skye pointed at him with the wooden spoon she was using to stir the scrambled eggs. "And don't you forget it."

Jeb slumped in an oak chair and heaved an exaggerated sigh. "If you have to know, Darby called me last night."

"Darby?" Skye asked with a frown. "You mean—?"

"Darby Benedict. My half sister." Jeb smiled. "Better shut your mouth, Skye. Flies'll get in there."

Skye's mouth snapped shut. "What did she want?"

"She told me to stay away from Cash, that he was her father, that my mom was a tramp...that kind of stuff."

Jeb related the information in a careful, neutral tone, but Skye saw the pain in his eyes. It was the same pain she felt. Pain rooted in the inevitable inequity linked to Cash and Susan's behavior, inequity that spilled over into the lives of their loved ones. Pain that might never go completely away.

"And what did you tell her?" Skye asked, dividing the eggs onto two plates.

"I told her no problem." He lifted his indignant gaze to Skye's. "Hell, I've lived all my life without a father. I don't need one now."

Skye disagreed. Every child should be lucky enough to have parents. Skye thought about Larry Martin, the biological father she'd never known. And she thought about Jon, who'd been the very best father a child could have.

She set the plate heaped with eggs, bacon and toast in front of Jeb and handed him a paper napkin. "You're wrong, honey. Having any family who cares for you is a plus."

"Maybe."

"Don't let this undo the little bit of progress you and Cash have made," she cautioned. "Darby's jealousy is natural. I felt the same thing when I realized there was something going on between Cash and Susan."

"You did?"

Skye nodded. "I felt as if Susan had taken him away from me. On the other hand, Susan and I were always close, so I felt as if Cash had taken *her* away from me, too. It didn't make a whole lot of sense. All I know is that I felt passed over and left out. That's a scary feeling at any age."

"I see what you're getting at," Jeb said, a thoughtful expression in his eyes.

"If Cash lets Darby know that loving you doesn't negate his love for her, she'll get over her insecurities." Seeing the incredulous look that crossed Jeb's face, Skye asked, "What's wrong?"

Jeb shrugged, aiming for nonchalance and falling far short, somewhere around uncertainty. "You said something about Cash loving me."

Skye's smile was as gentle as the morning sunshine. "Of course he loves you," she told him, suddenly confident that what she said was true. "Why do you think he hung around here so long, trying to find some way to reach you?"

"I guess I was so busy resenting him I never thought about it," Jeb replied.

"Well, maybe you will now." She sat down across from him. "The way I see it, your problem is different from Darby's, but no less troublesome."

"And what exactly is my problem?" Jeb asked with a lift of his dark eyebrows.

"Cash wants to incorporate you into his family. You need to decide whether or not you want to be part of the Benedict family, and that very much includes the meddlesome Darby."

Jeb rubbed his bottom lip thoughtfully. "To tell you the truth, the meddlesome Darby intrigues me." He grinned at Skye. "It might be interesting to get to know a kid who's got the guts to call up a stranger and warn them off."

"You've always been a big admirer of spunk," Skye said with a wistful smile. "I'll bet you and Darby will get along like a house on fire. You owe it to yourself to give them a chance, Jeb."

"Why does that make you look so sad?" Jeb asked.

"Because I'm like Darby. You were mine first, and I'm as afraid of losing you as she is of losing Cash."

Skye was in the back room of her shop, thinking about her earlier conversation with Jeb while she glued pale pink rose petals to a fairy skirt. After she'd confessed her feelings and fears to Jeb, he'd come around the table and drawn her into a big bear hug, assuring her that he'd always love her, that no Benedict would—or could—ever take her place in his heart; she was more like his mother than his aunt.

Clasped in his familiar embrace, Skye had opened her mouth to tell him that she'd just learned that they were brother and sister, but the words had died on her tongue. She knew that the longer the secret was kept, the harder it would be to divulge, but still she'd hesitated, telling herself that Jeb had problems enough for now.

If she were honest, she knew that she was hesitating not for Jeb, but for herself. She needed time to come to grips with this new image of Susan: Susan the secretive liar.

In Skye's mind, Susan had been above reproach. She was thinking that coming to terms with the fact that Susan had borne two children out of wedlock would take some getting used to when the phone rang.

Margie smiled over the saloon doors. "It's for you." She winked. "A man."

"Thanks, Margie." Skye picked up the extension. "Skye Herder."

"Hi."

"Cash!" Skye's mouth went dry; her heart faltered and then picked up a more rapid pace. She hated the weakness that made her so susceptible to him, hated whatever it was about him that made her so defenseless, especially now when she was in such inner turmoil. "I didn't expect you to call."

"Why not? I thought I made my feelings pretty clear when I left."

Skye forced a laugh. "My luck with men hasn't been the best. I figured you were no different. You know—out of sight, out of mind."

"Did you get my presents?" he asked.

"I got them."

"Then you know that I thought about you at least once a day."

"I guess you did," she conceded.

"I can promise you two things, Skye Herder," Cash said. "First, it may take time, but I'm going to prove to you that I am different. Second, your luck is about to change."

The determined tenderness in his voice brought tears to her eyes and a quaver to her voice. "I wish I could believe that."

"Do you?"

"Yes." It was a whisper, a caress.

"Believe. It's a promise."

Skye couldn't speak for several seconds.

Cash's voice was husky when he finally said, "I miss you. I miss the farm and the puttering around."

She was too afraid of being hurt to make herself say that she missed him, too. "You miss the puttering around," she said with a light laugh. "You must be crazy."

"You could be right," he said. "Crazy about you."

Tension, as taut as a watch too tightly wound, sprang up between them. Skye felt a delicious but frightening sensation...as if she were standing at the edge of a precipice, her heart in her throat, anticipating the thrill of free-falling through the myriad emotions that accompanied the first rush of love, yet so afraid that Cash would disappear as Lee had done, so afraid the fall would lead to more pain and the death of her latest, and possibly last, dream.

The sound of Cash's voice shattered the silence and stole her breath. "I think I'm falling in love with you."

"Don't!" Skye replied quickly, almost angrily. "It's too soon. We don't even know each other."

"I know all I need to know," Cash told her. "I have great recall, and I remember a hundred things about you to love."

"You remember the fourteen-year-old me," she said, "but neither of us is the same person we were back then. You might not like the grown-up Skye."

"*I* don't much like the grown-up me," Cash told her, "but I'm doing my darnedest to change him into someone worth liking...loving. I'm trying to establish a real relationship with my daughter and become more accessible to my other family, and even Liz."

"Liz?"

"Why not? I figure if we couldn't have a successful marriage, maybe we can at least have a successful divorce. I'm tired of all the bickering and the constant friction. I want to heal the rift between me and my kids and go on from there."

"Then you certainly don't need to add to your problems with Darby by telling her you think you're in love."

"What does that have to do with anything?"

"Darby called here last night."

"Called?" Cash's voice was infused with incredulity. "What on earth did she want?"

"She warned Jeb to stay away from you."

Cash swore. "What did Jeb think of that?"

"In a typical Jeb reaction, he told her not to worry, that he didn't need you after all this time."

Cash swore again. "I'll talk to her. It won't happen again, I promise."

"No! Don't say anything," Skye begged. "You'll embarrass her. Jeb and I talked about it. I told him she's just feeling insecure about you right now and that once she realizes that you don't love her any less just because Jeb is part of your life, she'll be fine. I think he understands."

"I'm glad he does," Cash groused. "I'm not sure I do. What does Darby's phone call have to do with my feelings for you?"

"Your *professed* feelings for me," Skye amended. "For argument's sake, let's just say you are in love—"

"I'm pretty sure I am," he interjected.

"Cash!" she cried softly. "Just listen. If Darby resents Jeb coming into her life so much she called and told him to keep away from you, it's pretty safe to assume that she'll resent another woman—no matter who that woman is."

The way Lee's girls resented me.

Skye wondered how strong an influence Darby's opinion of a woman in her father's life would be if it came down to Cash making a choice between the child he'd fathered and the woman he loved.

"You have a point," he admitted with a sigh. "This parenting thing gets pretty hairy at times. I'm not sure I'm cut out for it."

"Susan always said if a child knows you love them no matter what, everything will sort itself out."

"I hope she's right."

Neither spoke for a few seconds. Finally Cash said, "I'm not sure I'm going to be able to make it back as soon as I hoped."

Skye's heart plummeted. "That's okay."

"No," he said, "it isn't. I miss you, and I want to see Jeb play ball, and I never did get all those boards replaced on the barn, but this magazine thing is making us all crazy, and we have to stay on top of it if we hope to pull off a miracle."

"I understand."

"I'll make it up to you," he said. "I promise."

"Please don't send any more chocolates!" she cried in mock horror, hoping to turn the too-serious conversation toward a less personal topic.

Cash laughed and took the hint. "Can I call you tomorrow?"

His voice was low, tender, caressing. Skye imagined that voice murmuring love words in her ear, whispering them against her throat and lips. A shiver of longing tripped down her spine. "If you like."

"I do."

Margie called out from the front of the store, letting Skye know that one of her favorite customers was waiting for her. "I have to go," she said.

"Talk to you tomorrow, then."

"Yes," Skye said. "Goodbye." She heard Cash's goodbye and recradled the receiver. She wiped her trembling, perspiring hands on the paint-smeared smock that covered her clothes, wondering what on earth she was thinking by letting Cash Benedict get a toehold in her life.

Regretfully, Cash hung up the telephone. He'd thought talking with Skye would lift his spirits; instead, he was more depressed than ever. Not only did she still refuse to acknowledge the attraction she felt for him, she was doing her darnedest to convince him that his fascination for her was, at best, a fleeting sentiment based on youthful emotions.

As if that weren't enough, he had to worry about, and somehow deal with, Darby's phone call to Jeb. And all this while he coped with a malicious ex-wife and tried to put back together a failing magazine!

There were times—like now—when he was tempted to tell Bart he wanted to chuck the whole thing and just shut down the presses, but he had an obligation to his shareholders to do what he could to try to salvage *Hearth and Home* while still maintaining a strong marketplace for the other magazines.

Obligation. It was something he knew well. Obligation was that intangible goad that kept him in Lincoln when he longed to go back to Iowa and try to straighten out that part of his life. Obligation was the impelling prod that made him put business before his personal life. His sense of obligation—to Cash Senior and Benedict Periodicals—was the single most significant reason for the breakup of his marriage and the rift between him and Darby. And now, by postponing his return to Iowa, he was doing it again with Skye and Jeb, despite his vows not to. He only hoped they understood and that this time the results would be different than they had been in the past.

When Darby's dad left her at the door that afternoon, she wanted to crawl into a hole and pull it in on top of herself.

Even though he hadn't yelled—yelling was her mom's style, not his—he had made it very clear to her that he was disappointed with her for calling Jeb.

Anger and yelling she could have taken. Disappointment was something else. Disappointing anyone, especially her dad, always made her feel like such a failure. This time she felt worse than a failure. She felt small. Selfish. Ashamed.

Cash had explained that her telephone call had been cruel. Not only had Jeb been denied a father all these years, his mother had died when he was ten. Although Darby and her mother had their ups and downs, she couldn't imagine not having her mom as part of her life. She couldn't imagine life without her dad, either, and she was afraid that if she didn't change her attitude about Jeb that's exactly what was going to happen. Her dad said he wouldn't choose between them, but common sense told her that if she kept acting like a spoiled brat, he would probably like Jeb best.

"It looks like you'd better get used to having a brother in your life, Darby," she said to the reflection of the young girl regarding her from the shining depths of the mirror. "And liking it."

Could she get to liking it? Maybe, she admitted grudgingly. Cash had shown her a picture of Jeb on his motorcycle that Skye Herder had given him, and Darby had to admit her brother was a hunk and a half. Actually, he looked pretty cool, and if she were honest—and her dad insisted they be honest about their feelings and fears from here on out—she had to admit that she'd often thought it might be nice to have a big brother to sort of look up to and take care of her.

Leslie Parker had a big brother, and all the girls thought he was so great, so handsome. Jeb was better looking than Kevin Parker, and her dad said Jeb was a fantastic ball player—so good that he might make it to the majors. Maybe he'd be okay.

Darby flung herself across her bed and stared up at the ceiling. She still didn't like the idea of Jeb coming into her life and snaring his share of her dad's attention, but *maybe* in time she could get used to the idea.

"The little brat had the nerve to call me up and tell me that Cash was her dad and for me to stay away from him. Can you believe it?" Jeb said, pacing Belinda's bedroom while Whitney Houston crooned an aching melody in the background.

Belinda was polishing her long fingernails with agitated strokes. "She does sound like a brat," she said shortly, glancing up at him for a millisecond.

Jeb grinned. "I kinda like the idea that she had enough gumption to let me know how she felt. I'm not crazy about any of this, but I don't think I'd have the guts to call any of the Benedicts and tell them how I felt."

"Probably not."

Jeb stopped pacing and sat on the edge of the bed. "What's the matter?" he asked, taking the polish from her and setting it on the bedside table. "You've been out of it ever since I got here."

Belinda averted her gaze. "Nothing."

"You aren't fooling me. Look, I know this might be boring to you, but it's my life I'm talking about."

"And what about me?" Belinda asked, lifting a vexed gaze to his. "How do I fit in with your new family and your new life?"

"Nothing will change between us."

Belinda jerked her chin free of his grasp. "What if I told you I didn't want you to go to Lincoln?"

"I know you don't want me to go. We've talked the subject to death, but I thought we'd agreed that my going to school—at least for a while—was the best thing for our future. I thought we agreed that we weren't ready for marriage."

"You decided," Belinda said, her turbulent blue gaze meeting his. "I guess that means you aren't ready to be a father, either."

Jeb felt the blood drain from his head and then rush back in a painful, sickening wave. He knew now that what he'd heard about a person's past life flashing before their eyes at a moment of extreme stress was true. His past life flashed through his mind, and his future—a life filled with bills, a baby and Belinda—loomed before him. He felt dizzy and faint, though he'd never fainted in his life. He wondered how it had happened and asked her as much.

"How do you think it happened?" Belinda cried.

"But we were careful."

"There was that one time you didn't have anything and another when...it...broke—remember?"

Oh, yeah. He remembered. He remembered well. Despair washed over him in huge, drowning waves that sent what was left of his normal world crashing around his clay feet. Skye had been right all along. He and Belinda had been playing with fire. They'd danced, and now he had to pay the fiddler. The fickle finger of fate was pointed at him. There were no silver linings to his storm clouds. No brass ring. There'd be no baseball career, and probably no college. How could he have been so stupid?

He cast a bleak look at Belinda. "Are you sure?"

"I'm a week late," she said, her eyes filling with tears.

Though he felt like bawling himself, her tears were Jeb's undoing. This wasn't Belinda's fault any more than it was his. He was responsible, and he'd do whatever it took to

make things right. What he refused to do was let another
baby come into the world without a father to love it.

He reached out and pulled Belinda into a loose embrace.
She pressed nearer and dragged his head down so that she
could kiss him. Jeb knew she wanted him to make love to
her, that to Belinda, making love would prove he cared. But
he couldn't do that. Not now. Sex was the farthest thing
from his mind. He wondered if he'd ever feel those exciting
stirrings again and thought that maybe it would be best if he
didn't.

When he finally got Belinda calmed down, he drove
straight to Opa Herder's house. Like Skye, Opa was the first
person Jeb thought to go to when something in his life went
awry. He needed someone who would listen and not tell him
how he'd screwed up his life. Until he got a handle on the
situation, the last thing he needed was a confrontation with
Skye. Opa would be hurt by Jeb's careless actions, but he
tended to take life philosophically and was slow to anger and
pointing fingers.

Jeb found Harold eating a TV dinner and watching some
show about big cats on the Discovery channel. The old man
knew Jeb right off, so Jeb figured he was having a good
evening.

Harold invited Jeb to warm up a dinner, but Jeb declined, opting to pace the small living room. After a few
moments Opa pushed aside his TV tray. "You got ants in
your britches, boy?"

"No, sir."

"Then sit yourself down and tell me what's got you so
stirred up."

Jeb plunked himself down in a worn chair covered with a
brightly patterned afghan. He rested his elbows on his knees
and, locking his hands together between them, forced his

gaze to his grandfather's. "I've got a problem with Belinda."

"Pregnant, is she?"

Jeb couldn't hide his surprise. "How'd you know?"

"Not much else gets a young man so stirred up," he observed.

"What should I do?"

It was Opa's turn to look surprised. "You've got to tell your sister, that's what you should do. She has a right to know."

Jeb's heart sank. Obviously Opa wasn't having as good a day as he'd thought. "Opa, I don't have a sister."

Harold's face flushed with anger. "I told Susan she should have told the truth. Lies just beget more lies—ask your sister."

"Opa, I think you're a little confused."

Harold's face turned so red that Jeb knew his blood pressure was sky-high. Harold threw his hands up in the air, as if he wanted to wash himself of the whole conversation.

"I'm old, so I'm confused. Confused or eaten up with that funny disease that rots the mind. What's my name, boy?"

Surprised and a little scared by the depth of his grandfather's agitation, Jeb said, "Harold Herder."

"Have I ever lied to you?"

"No sir, not to my knowledge."

"And I never will." Harold sank back against the worn recliner back. "Lies," he muttered, almost to himself. "Nothing but lies and more lies. I've got to get this all straightened out before my mind does go rotten." He looked at Jeb. "Your Mama had her reasons for not telling the truth. She was trying to protect Jon."

Jeb felt as confused as he thought his grandfather was. Belinda was forgotten. All he wanted to do was get the old

guy settled down before he had a darned stroke or something. "The truth about what, Opa?" Jeb said in his most
soothing tone. "I already know that Cash is my father."

"Of course you do," he said, his ire on the rise again.
"Susan told you about him before she died. She should have
told the other child, too. Jon is dead. No use keeping it a
secret anymore." For long moments, he sat there staring at
a far wall, a blank look in his eyes. Then he scrubbed a
gnarled hand over his whiskery cheek and turned toward
Jeb. "Who are you?"

"Jeb, Opa."

"I don't know any Jeb," Harold Herder said, grabbing
the arms of the chair and levering himself to his feet. "I
know who you are. You're one of those kids on TV. The
ones who rob people."

"Settle down, Opa," Jeb said, getting up and trying to
force Harold back into the chair. "I'm not going to rob
you."

"I'm not scared of you, you punk!" Harold said, pushing at Jeb's hands.

"I'm going, Opa," Jeb said helplessly, unhanding the old
man and backing toward the front door. He pushed through
the screen door and paused. "What other child?" he asked,
trying one last time.

"Just get the hell out of here!" Harold cried. "Or I'll
shoot your damn fool head off."

Jeb gave up. He left his grandfather's place and headed
to Jimmy Bogart's house. Jimmy knew all about him and
Belinda—not because Jeb had said anything, but because
guys just had a way of knowing when something like that
was going on. Jimmy, who was the ripe old age of twenty
and whose family was on vacation, was a good listener who
could be counted on to keep his mouth shut. He never made
judgments and seldom offered advice, but when he did it

was usually good advice. Besides, Jimmy's dad had a well-stocked liquor cabinet, and Jeb felt the need to dull the edge of his pain.

Jeb called the Holiday Inn and told them he wouldn't be in to work—how could anyone work under this kind of stress?—while Jimmy picked the lock of his dad's liquor cabinet. After making them both some sort of rum concoction, Jimmy sat down and lent a sympathetic ear as Jeb told him not only about Belinda, but about his conversation with Opa. He gave them both equal time, uncertain which had him most upset—Belinda's possible pregnancy or the fact that his grandfather's mind was slipping farther and farther away.

Jeb wondered what Opa meant about him having a sister and Susan protecting Jon? He must mean Skye, Jimmy said. But, Jeb argued, if that were true, Susan had had two kids outside of marriage. And if she had, what role had Jon Herder, the man who'd died before he was born, played in the whole arrangement? How had Susan protected him—and from what?

Jimmy didn't know. Couldn't imagine. Several bottles of beer on top of the drink didn't clarify the matter for Jeb. All they did was muddle his head more. He left Jimmy's at 4:00 p.m., over his friend's objections and with the promise that he'd be careful.

With nowhere else to go, Jeb headed home, knowing that he risked incurring Skye's wrath by being tipsy. Maybe if he was asleep when she got home from the shop she'd think he was sick or something.

His mind was churning fuzzily over what Harold had told him and what he should do about Belinda when the doe ran out of the woods directly in front of the motorcycle. Though his reflexes were impaired by the alcohol, Jeb had enough presence of mind to know that hitting the deer would be deadly. He braked and wrenched the handlebars to the right.

As if he were experiencing the whole thing in slow motion, he felt the bike list to the side and go into a slow skid. He hit the shoulder and saw the ditch and the trees beyond, but he couldn't figure out what to do before he heard the sickening crunch of metal and felt an excruciating pain that clothed everything in darkness.

Chapter Eleven

Skye was taking the money from the cash register when the phone rang. Anxious to get home after a busy day, she considered not answering it, but grabbed it on the fourth ring on the off chance that it might be Cash.

"Herder's."

"May I speak with Skye Herder, please?" an unfamiliar masculine voice asked.

"This is she."

"Ms. Herder, this is Lieutenant Vickers, Marengo police."

Police! Skye's stomach took a nosedive. "Yes?"

"Are you related to Jeb Herder?"

"I'm his...sister," she said. Sweet heaven! What had Jeb gotten into now?

"I'm calling to inform you that your brother was in a collision just two miles from your house. A United Parcel Service driver reported the accident."

Tentacles of panic wrapped themselves around Skye's heart, while all sorts of horrible scenes flashed through her mind. "Is he okay?"

"We don't know the extent of his injuries yet. They took him to the hospital in Marengo."

Skye bit back a sob. "Do you know what happened?"

"It appears that he lost control of his motorcycle and hit a tree. We don't know the details, but it was obvious he'd been drinking."

"Drinking?"

"Yes."

Skye felt the weight of the policeman's words sink into her mind and her heart. Jeb. Drinking. An accident. Hospital.

"Are you all right, Ms. Herder?" the officer asked, the sound of his voice jolting her from the chaos of her thoughts.

"I'm fine," she said brusquely, even though she didn't feel fine at all. "I'll be there as soon as I can."

"Drive carefully," the policeman warned. "There's a storm brewing, and we don't need another accident on our hands."

Skye assured him she'd be careful and hung up. After locking the front doors, she hurried out the back, her heart thudding in apprehension and her mind filled with images of a broken, bleeding Jeb.

Drinking. She wasn't naive; she knew Jeb sneaked an occasional beer and an even rarer glass of wine. How many teenagers didn't? But it was hard to imagine Jeb drinking so much he lost control of his bike. He took his baseball seriously, and he was pretty health conscious, often working out at the Holiday Inn when he finished work. She'd never known him to abuse alcohol. Of course, there was always a first time, and the police didn't usually make that kind of mistake.

Skye had left the outskirts of Amana behind and was driving past Lily Lake when she was overtaken with a unaccountable feeling of fear that left her shaken. If Jeb's injuries were serious, or—God forbid—fatal, what would she do? Without Jeb, she'd truly be alone. Her stomach knotted, and she was struck by a sudden irrepressible longing to contact Cash.

She rejected the thought almost immediately. What was wrong with her? She was a nineties woman. Used to taking care of herself and Jeb. Hadn't Lee let her down both times she'd expected him to stand by her? Why did she think Cash was any different?

Because Jeb is his son. Because he said you could count on him.

She believed him. Her reluctance to call Cash originated in the fact that she'd stood on her own for so long and had gotten used to taking care of things herself. She didn't want to admit to the weakness of needing Cash—or anyone.

But you do.

Yes, she conceded, she did need him, whether she liked the idea or not. She was tired of being strong, tired of handling things, weary of smoothing out rough patches for other people. Just once, she'd like to turn over all the worries to someone else. Just once, she'd like to be on the receiving end of the consoling, instead of being the one offering comfort.

The needy part of her whispered that she should call Cash. He was used to dealing with major problems. Accustomed to crises. The bottom line was that he was Jeb's father, and if something terrible did happen to Jeb and she didn't let Cash know, he would never forgive her.

By the time Skye pulled into the hospital parking lot and turned off the engine, she'd come to a decision. She would find out about Jeb's condition, and then she'd call Cash.

Jeb was still in the operating room. She was told that he had a broken femur, and some broken ribs that had punctured a lung, which made breathing difficult.

The injuries were plenty serious, but because Jeb was young and healthy, the doctors were optimistic. Skye went to the pay phone and looked up the numbers Cash had made her write down in her address book. She'd never planned on using them.

Since it was approaching six, she figured that Benedict Periodicals had shut down for the day. She dialed Cash's town house and was taken aback when a young girl answered the phone.

"Is this Darby?" she asked.

"Yes. Who's this?"

Skye heard the wary note in Darby's voice. "Skye Herder. Is your dad there?"

"No, he's at a late meeting at the office." There was no disguising the chill that permeated Darby's voice.

"Can he be reached there?"

"No way," Darby said in an assured tone. "No one interrupts his meetings. But he said he'd be home by eight."

Skye's heart plummeted, and she felt tears of frustration gathering beneath her eyelids. She suspected that Darby could be more help if she wanted to be, but Skye didn't have the time or the energy to force the issue. If something happened and Cash didn't get here, he would have to deal with Darby in his own way.

"Look, this is an emergency. If you can't reach him, can you at least give him a message as soon as he gets home?"

"Sure."

"Tell him Skye called and that Jeb was in a motorcycle accident. He's hurt pretty badly, and they've taken him to the hospital in Marengo. Tell him...tell him..." Skye's voice broke and she choked back a sob. "Tell him that...I...tell him that Jeb needs him."

* * *

Even over the noise of her own pounding heart, Darby heard the unmistakable sound of tears in Skye Herder's voice. At Skye's insistence, Darby repeated the message, aware of the quaver in her own voice. Before she could say anything more, Skye thanked her and Darby was left holding the buzzing receiver.

She hung up the phone, sat on her father's sofa and chewed on a fingernail while she considered what to do about the news she'd just heard.

When Skye Herder identified herself, Darby had felt that familiar anxiety take hold of her. Her mom had cornered her dad about Jeb, and Cash told her that everything Darby had related was true. Yes, he had a son, and yes, he planned on making him a part of the family when he came to Lincoln to go to school. Even worse, according to her mother, her dad was romantically interested in Jeb's aunt Skye.

The last thing Darby wanted was for her dad to fall in love with another woman. He had told her there was no hope for him and her mom getting back together, but Darby didn't want to believe that. All she knew was that if he fell in love with this Skye person, there would be absolutely no hope. She didn't want a stepmother. Carrie Leyton had a stepmom, and she was a witch.

Darby looked at the information on the pad. She could call the number her dad had given her in case an emergency came up and it was absolutely necessary that his meeting be interrupted, but she'd never used it before. Besides, her violin recital, "Morning Moods," was tomorrow morning, followed by a brunch at an elegant hotel. Cash had promised her he'd be in town for that. If she told him about Jeb, he'd go to Iowa, there was no doubt about that. No doubt at all that he would choose Jeb over her.

Darby ripped the page from the notepad. She would tell him about Jeb, but it would be later, after she saw to it that he kept his promise.

* * *

The ringing of the phone interrupted Bart Blevins in midsentence. Cash glared at the offending instrument and lifted the receiver, prepared to lambaste whoever was intruding on the meeting.

"Cash!" Skye's low, breathless exclamation took him by surprise.

"Skye! What's wrong?" He intuitively knew something was wrong.

"Jeb's had an accident," she said. "He's in the hospital! I called Darby and she said you were in a meeting and couldn't be reached under any circumstances. Maybe I shouldn't have, but I called Ceil's house and got this number from her daughter. I'm sorry."

As Cash listened to the words gush from her in a torrent of despair, he felt the blood drain from his face. Every pair of eyes in the room was turned to him. "Slow down, Skye," Cash said. "Tell me exactly what happened."

He heard her take a deep breath. Then, more calmly, she said, "Jeb crashed his motorcycle an hour or so ago. They don't know the extent of his injuries yet, but he's in the operating room. I hated to interrupt your meeting, but I . . . I thought you'd want to know."

"Of course I want to know," Cash said. "Where are you now?"

"At the hospital in Marengo."

"Hang in there," he told her. "I'm going home to pack. I'll have to take Darby back to Liz, and then I'm catching the first available flight to Cedar Rapids. I'll be there as soon as I can."

"Okay," she said, her voice edged with tears. "Okay."

Cash told her goodbye and hung up. Ceil was looking at him, a cross between concern and question in her eyes. Bart looked irritated.

"What's going on?" he asked.

Cash got to his feet. "My son has been in an accident. I have to go back to Iowa."

As Cash's lawyer, Bart knew all about Jeb; he'd been working all week making adjustments in everything from deeds to Cash's will, assuring Cash that his son would get the part of Benedict Periodicals and the other Benedict holdings that were rightfully his. What with trying to save the magazine, Bart hadn't needed the extra work.

"You can't go to Iowa!" he said. "We've got to work through this proposal."

"Let Ceil take care of it," Cash said, striding toward the door.

"But I have no idea how you stand on some of those points," Ceil said, speaking for the first time.

"I trust your judgment. Do whatever you think is best."

"Cash, this is top priority. If you leave now, without getting some game plan worked out, *Hearth and Home* is as good as dead," Bart said. The angry statement sounded almost like a threat.

Cash jerked open the door and turned. "There's one thing you'd better get fixed firmly in your mind, Bart. From here on out, my family is my top priority. If my leaving is the kiss of death to *Hearth and Home,* then bury the damned thing and put us all out of our misery."

He gave Ceil a halfhearted smile. "Sorry to leave you in the lurch again, Sis, but I've got to go."

Ceil nodded, her eyes tormented with concern.

Without another word Cash closed the door behind him, Bart's curses ringing in his ears.

Thunder rumbled in the distance. Skye paced the waiting room floor, her hands clasped around a can of lukewarm cola. It was almost 10:00 p.m. Almost four hours since she'd called Cash, and he hadn't arrived yet.

The time she'd spent in the waiting room had given her ample time to pray for Jeb's recovery and to think. Time to put a lot of things in perspective. First, she'd been wrong in waiting to tell Jeb about being his sister. It was something they both could learn from, and something she should feel no shame for. She was proud to be his sister, because she loved him very much. She only hoped he felt the same about her.

She'd realized something else. The anger she'd felt for Cash all these years had been misdirected. It was Susan she'd been really mad at, but blaming Cash was easier because he wasn't there, and she'd needed her relationship with Susan to be everything it had been before Cash came into their lives and Susan had fallen from her pedestal.

She thought she'd made her peace with the past after reading Susan's account of what had happened between her and Cash, and maybe to some degree she had, until she read about Susan's affair with Larry Martin, her father. She'd been numb first, then hurt. Now she knew that she'd also experienced a resurgence of anger at Susan—not so much for the affair, but for not telling her about her real father once she'd grown old enough to understand.

Jeb's accident had made Skye realize that the reasons behind Susan's silence weren't really important. What was important was that she forgive her mother and learn from her mistakes. Life was too swift to harbor resentment. Too fragile to hold grudges. Too short not to hold on to what love you had.

Susan had made mistakes; so had Skye. Susan got caught; Skye hadn't. At least Susan had been strong enough to stand tall amid the censure around her and hold on to the men she loved by keeping the part of them they'd left behind.

Skye could only speculate about what had happened to change Susan's mind about marrying Jon Herder. Even though it was clear she'd felt no passionate love for him, the kind of security Jon could provide had probably looked good to seventeen-year-old Susan. No doubt the farm had looked like the haven it was.

Skye realized she would never know why Susan married Jon or why she chose to pass her off as her younger sister, but she knew one thing: Jon had been everything any child could ever want or need in a father. Even though times had often been tough, she'd loved living on the farm, learning the value of a day's work, an honest dollar and the very real meanings of love and faith. She'd missed him terribly when he died, and so had Susan.

Thinking of death made her think of Jeb in the Critical Care Unit and her selfish need to hold on to him, to begrudge him forging a relationship with Cash. She'd always known that her stance on the issue was wrong, but it had never seemed more so than at that moment.

She remembered Jon once telling her that if there was anything worse than a person's fear of not finding love, it was the fear of losing it once you had. He'd never spoken a truer statement. Her only consolation was that her fear of losing Jeb was a very human sentiment, one she hoped Cash would forgive her for.

Forgiveness. Such a small word. So hard to do. It had taken her almost twenty years to fully forgive Susan and Cash for what had happened that summer. As she well knew, that relationship colored the burgeoning feelings she had for Cash. No doubt he wasn't completely without doubts and fears, either. There was no simple answer to how they would deal with it. It all came down to whether or not they cared enough for each other and whether or not they ever reached a place they could truly forgive and forget. Skye felt as if she had finally reached that place tonight, waiting for word of Jeb's condition. She couldn't speak for Cash, but all indications were that he, too, had come to some sort of acceptance.

Skye glanced at her watch again. Where was Cash? She rubbed her throbbing temples and went to the window to stare out at the parking lot for the hundredth time that evening.

The storm the policeman had predicted had blown through almost two hours ago, growling and howling for the better part of an hour as it pelted the dry Iowa soil with a generous dousing of much-needed moisture. Light from the parking lot illuminated the darkness. Though its fury was spent, a gusting wind buffeted everything in sight with a stinging, persistent torrent.

Skye leaned her head against the cool glass of the window and stared without seeing at the shards of light glinting off the rain-slick surface of the cars. She wished she knew more about Jeb's condition. He'd come out of the operating room a couple of hours ago, and had been put in the Critical Care Unit for an indefinite period.

She drew a weary, troubled breath. Why couldn't she be with him? She'd feel better about everything if she could just be with him, but they had allowed her to see him for only a couple of minutes when they first brought him out of surgery.

Seeing him lying on the gurney so still and pale and unmoving had filled Skye with an unbearable fear and an intense sorrow. He was so young. His life was just beginning. To deny him the rest of his life, to even take a part of it, wasn't fair—but then, she'd learned the hard way that while life was many things, it was seldom fair.

She sniffed and brushed her fingertips over the moisture clinging to her eyelashes. Why wouldn't they let her see him? She just wanted to brush back his hair, kiss his cheek, hold on to his hand and tell him that she was there, and that in spite of all their misunderstandings she loved him....

* * *

When Cash entered the small waiting room he saw Skye standing at the window, her hands clutching a can of cola. Worry and fatigue had left their marks on her, from her slumped shoulders to her tousled hair to the downward droop of her mouth. Cash wanted to go to her, pull her into his arms and offer her whatever comfort he could, but he was still too uncertain of her feelings to risk her rejection.

"Skye," he said, instead.

She was so bogged down in her misery that it took a few seconds for the sound of his voice to penetrate her thoughts. She turned from the window slowly, a wary surprise in her eyes.

"You took so long," she said.

The simple statement sounded like an accusation. Cash stepped through the doorway and crossed the small room. He reached out and trailed a thumb over the dark circles beneath her eyes. Neither was aware that she turned her cheek into his caress.

"I'm sorry. I had a hard time finding Liz," he explained. His smile reflected his weariness. "I came straight here from the airport. How is he?"

The fingers of Skye's free hand circled his wrist; he caught her fingers with his and held tight.

"He's out of surgery. He has a broken leg, three fractured ribs and a punctured lung that they put a tube in," she explained. "Because all the broken ribs are close together, he has something they call 'flail chest.'"

"What does that mean?" Cash asked.

"He can't breathe spontaneously. The broken ribs make the chest wall unstable, and it compresses the lung when he tries to breathe in. They did a tracheotomy, and had to hook him up to a ventilator to help him breathe. He's in guarded condition—whatever that is," she told him, her eyes bright with tears. "They're keeping him in CCU at least over-night."

"Did you see him?"

She shook her head. "Just for a couple of minutes. They won't let anyone stay with him."

"I didn't think so. And how are you?"

"I'm fine," she said, too quickly. "The doctor told me to go home, that there was nothing I could do, but I couldn't leave...."

She swallowed hard, and the tears she'd fought to domi-nate for so long finally burst the dam of her control and trickled down her cheeks. She wiped at them with a tissue she pulled from her pocket. "I feel as if it's my fault this happened. It's as if God is punishing me."

"Why?" Cash asked, putting his arms around her. He drew her close, letting her lean on him, knowing she needed his nearness, but even knowing that, not mistaking that need for weakness.

The soft, feminine scent of roses and lavender wafted upward, and he breathed it in hungrily, wanting to press his lips to her warm skin and see if she tasted as good as she smelled.

"What can you possibly think you've done to deserve punishment?" he asked.

"I've done what Jon always told me the Bible says not to do," she said, her breath warm against his chest. "I've loved selfishly. I was jealous of you and Susan. And I've been jealous of your wanting to establish a relationship with Jeb."

She drew back and looked up at him. "Not that I didn't want the two of you to get closer," she hastened to add, "but I was afraid Jeb would...I don't know...love you more, or something. I was afraid that he'd go to Lincoln and get involved with his family there, and that you'd take him away from me."

"Why would I want to do that?" Cash asked in surprise. "He's my son. It's natural for me to want to be a part of his life and have him be a part of mine. That means that you'll be a part of my life, too. I'd never try to turn him against you or take his love away, if that's what you're worried about. I know how painful that is."

The tears fell harder, and she wiped them with the soggy tissue. "Everyone I've ever loved has died or left me. Jon. Susan. Lee. You. The Alzheimer's has taken the best part of Opa. Now it looks as if God might take Jeb away from me, too."

"That isn't going to happen," Cash assured her. "I know Jeb's injuries are serious, but he's young and he's strong, and he's a fighter." He smiled. "He gets that from you and Susan."

"And you."

"No," Cash said with a rueful shake of his head. "I've never been much of a fighter, but all that's going to change. I might not always win, but if I lose, I'll know I at least gave the battle all I had, and that includes fighting for Darby's and Jeb's love."

"It may take time, but he'll give it to you," Skye said. "He needs you, Cash, as much as you need him."

"I hope you're right." He smiled down at her and brushed aside the damp tendrils of honey-colored hair that clung to her wet cheek. "You're wrong about something else, too," he told her.

"What?" she asked, gazing up at him with wide, tear-spangled eyes.

Cash longed to kiss away the tears from her spiky eyelashes. Longed to kiss her trembling, naked lips. He tightened his hold on her and rubbed his hands up and down her back, loving the feel of her warm flesh beneath his touch.

"You said I'd left you along with everyone else. I was gone for a while, but I'm here now, and I'm not going anywhere—except back to the farm to put you to bed."

Confusion filled her eyes and sent a soft blush into her cheeks, but she didn't try to pull away. Cash knew she was no more used to teasing banter than Susan had been. The Herder women weren't the flighty, flirty kind of women he was accustomed to back in Lincoln. They were straightforward, plainspoken women, frank about their desires and harboring no qualms about setting out after whatever it was they wanted. They had no time for the silly games most men and women played.

"I can't leave Jeb."

"You can't do anything for him right now, except pray," Cash told her. "And you can do that at home. There's no sense in your wearing yourself out. He's going to need lots of care and attention when he's better."

"I know you're right," she said, "but—"

"No buts," Cash interrupted. "Now get your things. You're going home."

With a nod of acquiescence, she placed her palms against his chest to put some distance between them. "You're all wet," she said, as if she'd just noticed.

"I know. I didn't have an umbrella, and there weren't any parking places near the entrance, which means that you'll get soaked when we leave." As if on cue, a peal of thunder rolled halfheartedly in the distance.

"I won't melt."

"No," he told her with conviction, knowing that her inner core of strength enabled her to withstand more than a lot of women. "But I think I'll make you wait while I get the car, anyway."

She offered him a weary smile. "I'm too tired to argue."

"Good. Then let's go."

Minutes later they were ensconced in Cash's rental car, headed toward the farm. The lights of Marengo were soon left behind, and the car's powerful headlights cut a swath of brilliance through the rain-swept night. They illuminated the highway unfurling like a gray ribbon before them, and the corn that dipped in the wind, green arms reaching upward as if to thank the god of the harvest for the rain.

Cash didn't speak; he must have known how exhausted she was. The radio was tuned to a station that played soft instrumentals. The heady scent of a citrusy, masculine cologne pervaded the interior of the car. Combined with Skye's weariness and the comforting reality of Cash's nearness, the music worked its magic in a matter of minutes. She leaned her head against the seat, closed her eyes and let the tender melody take control of her.

She must have dozed, because the next thing she knew the music vanished along with the mesmerizing thrum of the car's engine. A comfortable mantle of warmth and silence wrapped her in a cocoon of contentment.

"We're here."

The sound of Cash's voice lifted the shroud of sleep that lay over her. Her eyelids drifted upward. Cash had half turned toward her, one arm along the back of the seat, the other gripping the top of the steering wheel. The glow of the pole light cast one side of his face in shadow; the other side was etched in tenderness.

He lifted his hand from the steering wheel. It trembled. Skye felt the gentleness of his touch as he threaded his fingers through her hair and leaned toward her, his gaze melded with hers, looking for the first hint of refusal. Her heart began to beat out a slow, heavy rhythm of anticipation.

He moved nearer, and nearer still. A familiar tingling tickled her breasts; her wanting femininity ached with need. She felt the soft rush of his breath against her lips, heard the

quiet suspiration of her own indrawn breath over the sound
of the heartbeats thundering in her ears. When his mouth
was a whisper away from hers, just after she saw his eyes
drift shut, she closed her own eyes, the better to savor the
moment.

His lips were soft; his kisses were hard and hungry. Unlike the kisses they'd shared in the apartment above the garage, it was as if the touching of their mouths finally
unleashed the passion they'd both held in check for so
long...the passion suppressed for twenty lonely, intermi-
nable years.

The fear that she was repeating the same mistake she'd
made with Lee was gone. Cash had banished it the moment
he'd stepped through the waiting room door. Regardless of
her past disappointments, she knew that he was a man who
kept his promises. Darby's potential disapproval was a
fleeting thought that vanished as Cash moved his hand up
her thigh.

The mating of their mouths, the age-old thrust and parry
of dueling tongues kindled a raging need inside her. She
pressed closer and moaned in frustration when that closeness was denied her by the cramped limitations of the front
seat.

Breathing as heavily as she, Cash ended the kiss. She felt
the curving of his mouth against her. He spoke against her
lips. "We're too old to be necking in the front seat of a car."

"Mmm," she agreed with a slight nod and a returning
smile. "Or back seats."

"Race you to the house."

Surprise lit her eyes. "You're on!" Without a word, she
reached for the door handle. She was out of the car in a
flash, slamming the door behind her and racing toward the
house. She heard Cash's door bang shut, heard his curse as
he chased her up the sidewalk.

The rain was cold and the night air held a chill, even though the temperature had hung near ninety all day. Instead of dampening her desire, the coolness fanned the flames of longing. For just this moment Jeb's accident was forgotten. Susan might never have been. Cash had no disapproving daughter, no ex-wife to cause him problems.

There was no one but her and Cash and the rainy night.

Skye felt young and carefree again. How long had it been since she'd run through the rain and found it enjoyable instead of cursing the inconvenience? How long since she'd felt this crazy urge to do something risqué and naughty?

Since the night you tried to seduce Cash when you were fourteen.

So long, she thought as she hurled herself up the steps and beneath the shelter of the porch. *Too long.* Laughing, though she wasn't certain at what, she pulled her wet knit shirt away from her body and watched Cash's long strides eat up the last few yards.

His shirt clung to his wide shoulders and a chest that looked muscular and hard. The longing to feel that musculature beneath her fingertips was a gnawing craving inside her. The sudden intensity of that hunger was frightening. To hide her sudden discomfort, she whirled and reached for the handle of the screen door.

She felt Cash's hands on her shoulders and froze. Her breathing stopped. So did her heart. His hands kneaded the tension in her shoulders and moved with languorous slowness down to her elbows and back again. She shivered. From the coolness. From the exquisite torture of his touch.

His hands moved to her neck, where they gathered her rain-wet hair and pushed it aside, baring her vulnerable nape. Skye felt the tips of her breasts contract, and her eyes closed of their own volition. She sensed movement and felt the heat of his breath against her neck before he touched the place behind her ear with a soft, openmouthed kiss. Her breath eased from her parted lips in a slow hiss.

Cash's hands moved from her shoulders down her back to her waist and then to her hipbones as one kiss followed another. He gathered double handfuls of her skirt, dragged it upward and pulled her back against him.

She was instantly, acutely aware of the physical differences in the male and female bodies. He wanted her. The knowledge was as exhilarating and as terrifying as jumping from the hayloft into a hay-laden wagon when she was a kid.

His hands moved. One upward to seize the fullness of her breast. The other past her bunched skirt to her silk-sheathed stomach and beyond. Caressing. Seeking. Threatening to destroy her last vestige of control and sanity.

She melted against him, throwing her head back and arching her neck to give him easier access to her throat, opening her body for his invasion. Somehow he'd worked his hand beneath her shirt. She gasped at the pleasure his caressing fingers brought. She felt boneless. Mindless with a yearning centered in the very essence of her womanhood.

Her passivity gave him permission to do with her what he wanted, and oh, she wanted! Wanted him to never stop. Wanted the fierce need building inside her so badly that she was ashamed of her lack of self-control.

Cash didn't disappoint her. Boldly, he broached the silken barricade and took possession of the uncharted territory beneath. He knew exactly how to elicit the desired response. For moments that seemed an eternity, they stood beneath the shelter of the porch, bathed in the muted light coming from the living room while Cash's clever fingers stroked her to a fever pitch.

Desire grew to untenable proportions; their breathing rasped in their throats. They craved the increasing sensations... savored the yearning that constrained their hearts to beat together as one while a keen passion—as fierce as the storm raging over the countryside—raged through Skye's needy body.

She felt the tremors of pleasure start deep inside her. Her teeth sank into her bottom lip to stifle a cry. The result was a gasp that mutated to a low groan.

"I love you."

Caught up in the intensity of the explosion rocking her body, Skye could only thrash her head from side to side in denial. This wasn't love. This was lust. Susan had taught her the difference well.

Rain sluiced down the rooftops, gathered in the gutters and rushed to the saturated ground. Tears pooled in her eyes. Lightning flashed halfheartedly, and the thunder rumbled sullenly in the distance, growing fainter and fainter along with the receding tremors of fulfillment racking Skye's body. She was filled to overflowing, yet curiously empty.

Cash's arms tightened around her. They were the only thing holding her upright. Keeping her close, he turned her to face him and backed her against the wall of the house. His hands cradled her face. His lips sipped the moisture from the corners of her eyes.

Skye raised a languid hand and let her fingertips trail lovingly over his face. There was a tender smile on his lips and a sheen of moisture in his own eyes.

"I love you," he said again, lifting her so that their bodies fit more intimately.

This time Skye didn't argue. She wanted so badly to believe.

Chapter Twelve

It was barely daylight when Cash woke up from the first deep sleep he'd enjoyed in months. His first fuzzy reflection was that he didn't recall the bed in the town house being so comfortable. That thought was supplanted by a sudden feeling that something was wrong. Opening his eyes, he pushed himself to his elbows and saw an unfamiliar floral painting across the room. That was when he remembered that he had flown to Iowa because Jeb had been hurt and realized that he was in Skye's house . . . in Skye's bed.

A slow, somewhat cocky smile of pleasure curved his lips. He rolled to his side and saw the outline of her tousled head, barely visible in the gray light of dawn. After they'd made love on the porch, she'd led him into the house, where they'd helped each other take off their wet, clinging clothes and fallen onto the bed to continue their exploration of each other. That pleasurable occupation had kept them busy far into the night.

It had been a long time since Cash had made love to a woman with such abandon. A long time since he'd given— or received—so much satisfaction from the act. He knew that part of the reason was that he'd finally fulfilled a long-dreamed-of fantasy. The other was that regardless of what Skye thought, he knew he was in love with her.

Whatever it was he'd felt for her in 1977—love, lust, a teenage crush—had lain dormant in his heart for almost twenty years. The moment he'd laid eyes on her that day almost three weeks ago, he'd known that even though she hadn't been part of his every thought the past several years, his heart hadn't forgotten her.

He knew Skye had had some bad experiences when it came to love, and she was hesitant to let herself care for him for that and many other reasons. He knew that because of Lee Ballard's shabby treatment, she worried that she was lacking somehow and feared all her relationships were doomed to failure.

He also knew she was concerned because there were other people's feelings to be considered, other lives that would be touched by their relationship. There were Jeb's feelings. And Darby's.

His lips tightened. He'd had a few choice words for Darby when he found out she'd refused to call him during the meeting and that she hadn't planned on telling him about Jeb until after her recital. She had cried, but the tears hadn't moved him. He knew he had a long way to go before she accepted the idea of Jeb; maybe even further before she accepted the idea of Skye.

He sighed. All he could do was take one day, one crisis at a time, and right now he needed to see about his son. Easing from the bed so he wouldn't wake Skye, he reached for his slacks and pulled them on over his nakedness before slipping from the room and going to the kitchen to start the coffee.

Once the fragrant brew started sending its enticing aroma throughout the cozy country kitchen, Cash rummaged around until he found the telephone book to look up the number of Marengo Memorial Hospital.

The nurse in charge of the night shift told him that Jeb was doing much better. They would probably be taking him off the ventilator at some time during the day, and chances were good that he'd be put into a private room by early the following morning. That burden lifted, Cash thanked the nurse and hung up. As he was putting the phone directory back into the shallow buffet drawer, he noticed several small books. On closer inspection, he saw that they were Susan's diaries.

Curiosity prompted him to gather up several of the journals and carry them into the kitchen, where he poured himself a cup of coffee. Feeling only slightly guilty, he sat down to see if Susan had written about their relationship that summer. He told himself it would be interesting to get her perspective, but he knew that he was looking for something more. He was looking for absolution.

Skye woke up to the sound of a blue jay's angry chatter. Her body felt different somehow. Relaxed, yet almost as if it contained a boundless source of energy. There was peace inside her heart and her mind, too, a peace produced by the night spent in Cash's arms.

She rolled to her back and saw that he was gone. Panic gripped her, and then she heard the back door slam shut. She relaxed against the pillows to consider what the night meant.

Though she'd denied that what Cash felt was love, she wondered if he knew that their making love was tantamount to a lifelong commitment for her. For once in her life, she had thrown caution to the wind and taken what she wanted with no thought of the consequences. She had pushed aside her fears that she wouldn't be as good a lover as Susan, had forgotten that Jeb and Darby and Lee were on the same planet, had refused to consider what letting Cash make love to her meant to the future, or even if they had a future considering all the strikes they had against them.

She couldn't deny that what she'd experienced in his arms was something rare and wonderful—a union not only of their bodies but of their minds and souls as well, an experience that shouldn't be taken apart and analyzed. Something that ranked up there with the Seven Wonders of the World. A rare and priceless gift to be cherished and remembered for a lifetime. That it had been so long coming made it more precious yet.

Skye closed her eyes and flung her forearm over her face, wondering how this would change things between her and Cash. Their making love hadn't resolved any of the real problems. The problems like Jeb and Darby and whether or not Darby would accept a woman in Cash's life. Skye sighed. The problem with throwing caution to the wind was that it always came back to smack you in the face.

Deciding that she'd play Scarlett and think about it all later, she drew back the sheet and reached for the satin robe that lay at the foot of her bed. She wanted to make the most of what time she had with Cash.

She found him sitting at the kitchen table. The battered oak surface was strewn with sunlight and Susan's diaries. His left hand was curled around a mug of coffee while his right clutched a small book.

Skye stood poised in the doorway, afraid to move, ready for flight. Her heart beat in her throat. It was all there for Cash to see. Everything about her and Susan and Larry Martin. Would Susan's confession raise questions and problems for him as they had for her, or would reading them be like closing a door to a past that was best forgotten?

As if he sensed her presence, Cash looked up. There was no doubting the pleasure in his eyes as his gaze moved over her with slow thoroughness. So far, so good, she thought with a tremulous sigh.

"Good morning," he said with a smile that brought the crow's-feet at the corners of his blue eyes into play.

"Good morning." She gestured toward the table. "I see you found the diaries."

Guilt stole into Cash's eyes. "Yeah. I wasn't really prying. I was looking for the phone book so I could call and check on Jeb and saw them in the drawer."

"How is he?" Skye asked, a concerned expression crossing her face.

"Much better. The nurse thinks they might take him off the ventilator today."

Skye's relief was obvious. "Thank God," she said, going to the coffeemaker and pouring herself a cup.

"Yes. Thank God." She felt Cash's eyes on her as she sat down across from him at the oak table. He indicated the journals. "I hope you don't mind my reading these."

"I suppose not," Skye told him. "But I should warn you that there are some earth-moving things in there."

"I don't think anything Susan ever did could be that shocking."

"No?" Skye said, forcing her gaze back to his. "What if I told you that Susan was my mother, not my sister?"

Cash grew very still. "You're serious, aren't you?" he asked in a hushed tone.

"Very."

"And you didn't know?"

"I had no idea until a few days ago."

"I guess it took you off guard."

"More than you can imagine." Her voice held a cautious neutrality; her gaze was fixed on his face. "My real father was killed in a car accident. Susan saw the whole thing."

"Dear God!" Cash mulled over that scenario for a few minutes and then said, "Why did she tell everyone you were her sister?"

"I have no idea, and last night I realized that it didn't really matter. Susan had her reasons, and whatever they were, she did what she thought was right. Being angry about it doesn't make much sense after all this time."

"No," Cash agreed. "Did you find out anything else?"

"I think so," Skye said with a nod. "I gained a new insight to her as a person, and I think her comments about her mistakes and learning more about her early life have helped me get some perspective on the past."

"I guess that's what I hoped for," Cash said.

"And?"

"I think I've found it." He smiled, albeit sadly. "I've carried around a fair amount of remorse over what I did— probably because deep in my heart I knew I'd rather it were you than Susan. That caused me to feel more guilt than I might have otherwise."

Skye felt the heat as a blush of pleasure rushed into her face. "And last night?" she queried, meeting his gaze with a steady one of her own. "Do you feel guilty about that?"

Cash's grin was wide and extremely beautiful to Skye. He reached across the table and traced his finger across the knuckles gripping her coffee mug.

"No," he told her. "Last night was the culmination of a lifelong dream. No. Not the culmination. Maybe it was just a beginning, because now I want that fantasy to last forever. Do you think that's possible?"

"I don't know," she told him honestly. "There are a lot of things we have to work out. A lot of things we all have to come to terms with, like how you feel about having made love to a mother and her daughter."

"Honestly?" he asked with a wry smile. "You might not like this answer, but I feel grateful. Not many men get lucky enough to love two women like you and Susan. What's more to the point, how do you feel about it?''

"At first I was furious at Susan for lying for all those years and not telling me the truth. And then I saw it as just one more obstacle for you and me to overcome if there was something growing between us. Right now I can truly say that I came to terms with it all while I sat in that little room at the hospital waiting for news about Jeb. No matter what happened in the past, we have to make what peace we can with it and move on. We don't have any guarantees about tomorrow. We live in the now, the present, and I don't want to waste a minute of it on resentment and misplaced anger.''

"Then we just go on from here, one day at a time, and see what happens?''

"That's all we can do.''

The phone shrilled, breaking the silence that had fallen. Skye answered the telephone and, after a couple of noncommittal remarks, hung up.

"That was the hospital,'' she told Cash as she recradled the receiver. Joy glowed in her eyes. "The doctor just finished making his rounds, and he took Jeb off the ventilator. The nurse said he's been asking for me.''

"I guess we'd better get our behinds in gear and get over there,'' Cash said, his smile matching hers.

"You can use the downstairs bathroom,'' Skye said, not yet comfortable with the idea of the intimacy of sharing a bathroom with him.

"Fine.'' Obviously unaffected by her comment, Cash stood and stretched in a purely masculine way. Mesmerized by the electrifying sight of his bare chest and the hard flatness of his abdomen, Skye had the sudden wish to recant her offer.

He saw the look in her eyes, crossed the room and took her in his arms. Hers went around his waist. "I may as well tell you that I'm a pushover for blondes, just in case you decide to change your mind and join me."

Skye opened her mouth to come back with a saucy reply, but Cash stopped it with a kiss. After several long, satisfying kisses, she pushed him away reluctantly. "Go," she said in a husky voice. "We don't have time for this."

Cash went, but he went grumbling.

Skye was putting together an omelet when she heard a knock at the door. She wiped her hands on a dish towel and went to see who could be there at such an ungodly hour of the morning.

When she opened the door, her heart took a nosedive. Standing on the porch, looking out toward the driveway where two people sat in a new Honda, stood a tall young woman with dark hair. Even before the girl turned, Skye knew exactly who she was.

"Hello, Darby," she said, while inside her heart began to mourn a loss she couldn't put into words.

Darby lifted her chin a fraction. "Hello," she said with complete composure. "You must be Skye."

Skye wondered if that kind of aplomb was part of the gene makeup of the wealthy, or if it was a learned art. Whatever, she found it disconcerting coming from a twelve-year-old. "Yes. Would you and your friends like to come in?"

"They don't want to," Darby said. "But I will. I came to see my father. He is here, isn't he?"

Skye nodded. "He's in the shower."

That ruffled Darby's poise. Darby's embarrassment made Skye feel more awkward than she already did. Kids today weren't stupid, and Darby was smarter than most. After taking one look at Skye in her nightgown and hearing that her dad was in the shower, she knew exactly what had transpired the night before.

"Would you like some breakfast?" Skye asked.

"No, thank you," Darby replied in her best finishing-school voice.

"Well, then, would you like to join me in the kitchen? I'm making us something before we go to the hospital." Skye waited for Darby to ask about Jeb, and when she didn't, Skye said, "Jeb is doing better, thank you."

Her not-so-subtle hint that Darby's manners were amiss brought a blush to the child's thin cheeks. Skye felt about two inches tall for taking out her frustrations on Cash's daughter, but it was obvious that the child needed taking down a peg or two.

With a sigh of futility, she went back into the kitchen. Darby followed and seated herself at the table while Skye went about finishing breakfast. She watched Cash's daughter from the corner of her eye and saw the younger woman looking around curiously.

"How old is this house, anyway?"

"Over seventy-five years," Skye said, hoping that Darby was going to loosen up.

"Mom and Dad's house is only two years old," Darby said. "We have a huge wood-covered refrigerator that cost fifteen thousand dollars."

So much for hopes. Darby didn't want to have a nice conversation. She wanted to point out the differences between her life-style and Skye's.

"I thought Cash and your mother were divorced. He has a town house, doesn't he?" Skye asked, turning to face Darby.

Darby looked disconcerted for a moment. "Yes. For now." She eyed Skye's hair thoughtfully. "Is your hair real?"

"It was the last time I looked."

"I mean, are you a natural blonde?"

"Yes, why?"

"My mom's hair is a lot lighter than yours. And her eyes are the biggest, bluest eyes I've ever seen. She was runner-up in the Miss Nebraska contest one year."

Skye's heart ached. She understood fully where the conversation was headed. She'd been down this road before with Lee's girls. "She sounds beautiful. You must be very proud of her."

The unexpected comment silenced Darby for a moment. Finally, she said, "I play violin."

"That's wonderful. My grandfather plays the fiddle. He's very good."

Darby wrinkled her nose at the word *fiddle*. "Mom says I'm a veritable virtuoso. Does Jeb play anything?"

"Pool," Skye said, breaking eggs into a bowl. "And pinball machines."

"I *meant* a musical instrument," Darby said with exaggerated patience.

Skye wanted to tell Darby that the only thing musical Jeb played was the CD player, but she didn't. "No. He doesn't play any musical instruments. He plays baseball, though."

"Oh, sports," Darby said with a dismissive wave of her hand. "I take fencing lessons, and golf and tennis," Darby told her. "And ballet," she tacked on as an afterthought.

Skye wanted to ask her when she got a chance to let her hair down and just be a twelve-year-old kid, but again she held her tongue.

Darby's agenda was obvious. She'd come to point out the differences between herself and Jeb and between her mother and the woman who'd caught her father's eye. Not only was she jealous of Jeb, she was jealous of his sister. She didn't want Jeb Herder for a brother, and she certainly didn't want Skye Herder for a stepmother. What she wanted was what most kids of divorces wanted—for her parents to get back together.

Skye wondered how Darby had found out about Cash's feelings, and decided that it didn't matter. She knew and, as Lee's girls had, she objected to the liaison. That was that as far as Skye was concerned. She wasn't into taking candy away from babies or coming between fathers and daughters.

As she'd told Jeb, kids needed the love of their parents—both of them if they should be that lucky. She hadn't known her own father, hadn't known that Susan was her mother, but she'd had Susan to guide her every day of her life, and she'd had Jon, and that had been the same thing. She thought about all Jon had taught her about the history of the area, about the plants, and the animals on the farm. She remembered the good example he'd set for her, and the way he'd loved her like his own.

As much as Skye was beginning to believe she needed Cash, her heart told her that Darby needed him more. She needed him as much, if not more, than Jeb did. Without Cash to keep her feet on the ground, she'd grow up into another snobby rich kid. Without Cash's love, she would become a shallow person who was content with the superficialities of life.

How could she come between Darby and the things so vital to learning to be a loving, responsible person? As much heartache as it was bound to bring, Skye would give up Cash and the tentative beginnings of their love, if it meant Darby's happiness. She couldn't do anything else and be happy herself.

She heard a noise and turned toward the doorway. Darby heard it, too. Cash stood there, a large white towel wrapped around his lean waist, his hair eel slick from his shower, a supremely happy smile on his face. Skye knew she would always remember that smile, that moment.

When Cash saw Darby sitting at the table, the expression on his face vacillated somewhere between pain and anger.

Shadowed with a piercing sorrow, the sadness in his eyes reflected the loss of Skye's hope and the remnants of their shattered dreams.

While Skye went upstairs to get ready, Cash read Darby the riot act. She could hear his third degree through the vents.

How the hell had she gotten there?

She'd given Kevin Parker two hundred dollars of her birthday money to drive her from Lincoln to Marengo. Leslie had come along for the ride. They'd gotten directions to the farm from a gas station attendant in town.

Why had she come? Cash asked.

To keep Cash from making a big mistake in marrying Skye Herder, that's why.

How had she found out about that?

From her mother.

Skye heard a blistering curse from Cash. Did Liz know where she was? he asked Darby.

No.

Then go call her, and let him talk to Liz when she was finished.

When the dust settled, Cash told Liz that he would drive the kids home in Kevin's car once he was certain Jeb was out of danger. And when he got home, they were having a serious talk about their future.

Cash confiscated the keys to Kevin's car, and with instructions to eat what they wanted and to stay put or else, he left the kids at the farm while he and Skye drove to the hospital to visit Jeb. Neither had much to say during the short drive. Darby's surprise visit spoke for itself.

When they reached the hospital, Skye was able to rouse Jeb long enough that he realized she was there. Long enough for him to offer her a smile that looked more like a grimace of pain and tell her he had a hell of a hangover.

With tears streaming down her cheeks, Skye pressed a kiss to his forehead. Then Cash stepped to Jeb's side. Incredulity flickered in his drug-glazed eyes.

"What're you . . . doing here?" he asked in a faltering voice.

Cash felt his throat tighten, and he couldn't stop the two tears that slipped down his cheeks. Maybe it was the unmanly thing to do, but Jeb was so out of it, he'd never remember. And even if he did, Cash didn't care if Jeb thought his tears showed weakness. It was frightening to think that he'd come so close to never knowing about Jeb's existence. Even more so to think of losing him, now that he had found him. There had to be some way to make Darby understand . . . some way to make her care about her brother.

"I came to make sure you're okay."

"I'm okay. . . . Think I . . . trashed the Harley, though."

"It doesn't matter," Cash said. "You just get better." He tried to smile at Jeb. "I've got to go back to Lincoln in a little while, Jeb," he said in an unsteady voice. "But I'll keep in touch with Skye, and I'll be back as soon as I can."

Jeb gave a single nod.

"We'd better go and let you rest," Skye said.

Cash started to turn away.

"Dad."

The single word paralyzed Cash. Jeb had never called him dad before. He searched Jeb's face for a sign of what he was feeling. Jeb didn't say a word, but he held out his hand. Cash took it. Jeb squeezed his hand with surprising strength, considering the ordeal he'd just come through. Fighting the urge to break down and sob, Cash held Jeb's hand until he fell asleep. He held on to it as though it were a lifeline.

Maybe it was.

* * *

They were driving back to the farm when Skye finally voiced the refrain that had been running through her head. "It won't work, Cash. We have too many strikes against us."

He cut his angry gaze from the highway to her momentarily. "It'll work," he said, determination in his voice. "I'm going to make it work."

"I've been through this once with Lee," Skye said in a reasonable tone. "It's a no-win situation, and you and I are better equipped to deal with the loss than Darby. You told her you couldn't choose between her and Jeb. Well, I'd never be able to look at myself in the mirror if I thought I'd made you choose between Darby and me. If you lose her, I don't want it to be my fault. I can't grab my own happiness at the expense of someone else's. I won't."

"It sounds as if you've made up your mind." His voice was heavy with resignation.

"I have."

"Does this mean you don't want me to call?"

"No," she said, trying to keep the tremor out of her voice. "Jeb needs to know you care. He needs to hear from you."

"If that's the way you want it, that's the way it'll be," he told her stiltedly.

"That isn't necessarily the way I want it," she said, "but that's the way it has to be...."

Cash drove back to Lincoln barely aware of the three kids in the car. His thoughts were focused on Skye and Jeb and how he could make the people in his life come to some middle ground of compromise. It was hard to believe that he and Skye had overcome so much—twenty years, Jeb's animosity and his affair with Susan—just to be done in by a twelve-year-old.

He had no idea how to help Darby understand the many faces of love. He knew that time might help her come to terms with the divorce, but how could he make her understand that Jeb and Skye posed no threat to her? His single greatest fear was that the problem would prove too formidable for her, and he would have to spend the rest of his life without Skye....

Jeb was home in a week's time. Skye turned over the shop to Margie so that she could be at home to nurse Jeb back to health. During the week Jeb was in the hospital, Cash called at least once a day, if not more often, to check on Jeb's progress. He hadn't made any plans to come back, citing the necessity of getting *Hearth and Home* back on its feet as well as twice-a-week counseling sessions with Darby.

The prognosis for the magazine's future looked somewhat better. Liz's resignation had paved the way for Ceil and Cash to hire a new managing editor, and the woman they chose had some definite ideas for the direction the magazine should take to pull it up from its downward slide.

As for Cash returning to Iowa to see Jeb and Skye, the counselor thought it unwise at this point. Darby's tender emotions had reached overload. Reading between the lines, Skye knew the bottom line was that he wouldn't be coming back to the farm for a while—if ever.

Skye told him Jeb understood. She understood, too. All too well. She tried not to dwell on what might have been and worked on improving her relationship with Jeb.

By the time Jeb had been home a week, he was driving Skye up the wall. Television was boring, he'd read every magazine in the house and everyone was at work so there was no one to talk to on the telephone. There wasn't much to do but think, and he spent a lot of time doing just that.

He gave Belinda's pregnancy a lot of thought and considered ways to break the news to Skye... who would then, no doubt, tell Cash. He decided to wait. He wasn't up to a shouting match, or their disappointment.

He had come to one realization, though, and that was how easy it was to fall into the sexual trap. Cash had been his age when he'd slept with Susan, and from the way his own hormones had been howling Jeb could honestly say that he'd have done the same thing if he'd been in Cash's shoes. He *was* doing it. The only difference was that Belinda wasn't almost twice his age.

He cursed. He should have listened to Skye. She'd tried to warn him that he was thumbing his nose at destiny, and he, in his youthful arrogance, had thought he was too smart to get caught.

Jeb thought about the television message that showed a young man doing things with his little boy. The final line said something about anybody being able to make a baby, but it taking a real man to be a father. The public service announcement showed beyond doubt that a baby changed lives . . . forever. Whenever Jeb thought about becoming a parent, he wanted to cry. He wasn't sure he was ready to be a real man. He wasn't sure if he could be.

Whenever Jeb got tired of thinking about his own problems, he thought about Skye. The change in her after her fateful conversation with Cash was dramatic. It didn't take a rocket scientist to figure out that both she and Cash were miserable. When he'd asked Cash what was wrong, Cash had told him. It pleased Jeb to think his dad considered him mature enough to confide in.

He tried talking to Skye, to no avail. She was like the way he remembered his mom: stubborn as a Missouri mule. She informed him that she didn't want to talk about it, and that was that. Jeb knew better than to push.

He was lying on his bed pondering the tangle of their lives when Skye announced that Belinda had come to visit. Jeb was a little surprised. Though he'd talked to her every day since he'd been able to stay awake for longer than ten seconds, she'd never come to see him.

He had to admit that she looked good in her shorts and sandals and her sleeveless cotton shirt. Really good. He thought he might live after all.

"Hi," he said, smiling.

"Hi." Belinda looked definitely uncomfortable.

"Uh...how are you—you know—feeling?" he asked, unable to formulate the words that would add substance to his nebulous fears.

"Fine," she said, twisting her fingers together.

Fine. What does that mean? "Sit down," Jeb said, indicating the straight-back chair that sat at his desk.

"I can't stay but a minute," Belinda said, ducking her head to avoid his gaze. "I just came to tell you that I'm okay."

"Okay?" he echoed.

She nodded. "I'm not pregnant."

Relief left Jeb light-headed. He leaned back against the pillows propped against the headboard.

"There was never really any doubt," Belinda said. Tears filled her eyes and she shifted her gaze back to his. "I was just...afraid of losing you, and I thought that if I told you I was going to have your baby, you wouldn't go to Lincoln."

The harsh sob that ripped its way up her throat melted the fear that had held him in its grip for more than two weeks.

"It was wrong of me," she said. "And selfish. When I heard about the accident and that you'd been drinking, I knew it was my fault. The thought of me having your baby made you so miserable that you went off and..." Her voice trailed away and she swiped the back of her hand across her eyes. "You could have died because of me."

"Come here," Jeb said, holding out his hand. Hesitantly, Belinda went to sit on the edge of the bed. Jeb took her hand in both of his.

"I won't deny that I was upset that day, but it wasn't because you were going to have my baby. I already had a lot going on in my life with Cash and everything, and that was just the straw that broke the camel's back, you know?"

She nodded.

"I don't want you blaming yourself. You didn't hold my mouth open and pour that beer down my throat. I made that decision." His lips lifted in a half smile. "I hope I have better judgment in the future."

"But I lied to you."

"Yeah, that was wrong, but you're making up for it now."

"You aren't mad?" she asked with a sniff.

"No," Jeb said, "I'm not mad. I do think we need to give some serious thought to breaking up for a while, though."

Belinda looked as if she might start sobbing again, but she nodded.

"You know as well as I do that we're playing a dangerous game, Belinda. You might not be pregnant now, but who can say for sure about next month? Or the next? This accident has given me a lot of time to think, and what I've come to realize is that we have to be willing to take responsibility for our actions. If that means marriage and a family when we'd rather go to school or become a fashion model, then that's just the way it is. And I've realized that I'm not ready for that kind of responsibility. I don't think you are, either."

"You're right," she said in a trembling voice. "I'm not."

"We can still date sometimes," he told her.

"That might not be a good idea," she said. "I'm not sure either of us is strong enough to stand up to your new ideals."

She had a point. "We can still be friends, then."

Belinda shook her head. "I doubt it, Jeb. I don't think we can go back to that now."

Somehow, Jeb doubted it, too. And something about that made him sad.

Jeb's temperament improved somewhat after Belinda's visit, but he was still bored. Still concerned with how Susan's and Cash's actions had affected his life and were still affecting it, he began to read Susan's diaries that he discovered by accident while looking for a pencil. Like Cash and Skye, he wanted to get to know his mother better. And like Cash, he was looking for some sort of vindication for his actions.

He kept his discovery a secret until he stumbled onto a piece of shocking information. Skye was scrubbing potatoes for dinner when he limped into the kitchen, one of the books clutched against his chest. "Is it true?" he asked.

Skye turned from the sink. When she saw that he was holding a diary, her heart skipped a beat. "Where did you get that?" she asked.

"Out of the buffet drawer," he said. "I was looking for a pencil to work on a crossword puzzle. Is it true?"

"What?" she asked, but she knew.

"That you're my sister, not my aunt."

Skye nodded wearily, glad it was out in the open at last.

"Why didn't you tell me?" he asked, sitting down at the table with the heaviness of an old man.

"I didn't find out until after Cash came and Opa gave me Susan's diaries, and by then you and Cash had clashed." She shrugged. "I thought you had enough to deal with without that, and then you had the accident."

"She wasn't married when she had either of us."

"No," Skye said. "Don't be too hard on her, Jeb. We all make mistakes."

Jeb smiled grimly. "Don't I know it." He looked at Skye, a question in his eyes. "She told me about Cash. I wonder why she never told you about Larry?"

"Why didn't she ever contact Cash and tell him about you?" Skye countered. "Who knows? Susan was secretive in a lot of ways."

Jeb rested his elbow on the table and pinched the bridge of his nose in a way that made Skye think of Cash. The similarities between the two of them were amazing, considering they'd never set eyes on each other until a few weeks before.

"Wait a minute," he said, looking over at her with a gleam of understanding germinating in his eyes. "I went to Opa's the day of the accident and he got to raving about my sister. I know now that he meant you, but at the time I thought he was just off that day, you know?"

Skye nodded, thinking of the many times she'd misconstrued Opa's statements for the ramblings of a deteriorating mind.

"He kept saying that Mom should have told the truth, that she was trying to protect someone. I didn't have any idea what he was talking about, but now that I've read about Larry and you and Susan marrying Jon, it makes sense."

"What makes sense?" Skye asked, not following him at all.

"Susan lied about your being her child because she cared for Jon."

"Of course she cared for Jon. So?"

"She didn't think she was good enough for Jon."

"How do you know that?"

"Look how long it took him to talk her into marrying him. And when she did agree, what did she do? She passed you off as her sister."

"Okaaay..." Skye said, drawing out the word. "I know all that, but why?"

"Because, just like Opa said, she wanted to protect Jon. She knew how much Jon's religion meant to him, and how well liked and respected he was in the community. Susan knew he was making a big sacrifice by marrying her."

"It was no sacrifice. He adored her."

"I know that. But from Susan's point of view, it was above the call of duty. She respected him a lot. I think she chose not to claim you as her daughter because she was afraid that the people in Amana might think less of him for marrying a *tainted* woman."

Skye pursed her lips thoughtfully. She'd read the diaries, too, and what Jeb said made a lot of sense when she thought about it in the context he suggested.

"You could be right," she said. "Knowing Susan, the lie would seem like little enough for all he gave her through the years."

"Makes sense to me," Jeb said. "But why didn't she tell Cash about me?"

"Because she knew Cash was young, with his whole life and a promising future ahead of him. She didn't want to have him tied down to a woman almost twice his age. She didn't want him to come to resent her—maybe to hate her."

Jeb thought about that for a few minutes. "Being an adult isn't easy, is it?"

"Nope," Skye said with a smile. "But it happens to the best of us, whether we're ready or not. Usually life drags us kicking and screaming into adulthood."

Jeb smiled back. "I broke up with Belinda yesterday."

Skye couldn't hide her surprise. "You did?"

"I told her I thought we were getting too serious."

"And how did she take that?"

"Better than I expected." He cast Skye a penetrating look. "Better than Cash took your turning him down."

Skye's face flamed with color.

"Why'd you tell him you two were a no go?" he asked. "I don't have a problem with it if it doesn't bother you about him and Mom."

"That was a part of it at first, but almost losing you made me realize that we should be more forgiving of the people we care about. Our time here is too short, too tenuous to hold grudges."

Jeb nodded. "So if it isn't Mom and Cash, what is the problem?"

"Darby," Skye said simply. "Darby is a confused little girl who's being used by her mother as a pawn in the game of life. Darby is having a hard enough time coming to terms with the fact that she has to share her father with you. She isn't ready for a new brother *and* a new stepmother, and I care too much about Cash and her to make him choose between us."

"It must run in the family."

"What?"

"That noble streak. You sound like Susan."

Skye only smiled.

"Do you love him?" Jeb asked.

"I think on some level I must have always loved him," Skye admitted. "I know I never completely forgot him."

"He cried in the hospital." Jeb made the announcement in a voice filled with the slightest bit of awe.

"He was worried about you," Skye said. "He loves you, Jeb."

"I know that." Jeb looked as if he might cry himself. He cleared his throat. "You're right. Who knows what's going to happen with baseball. I need an education if I decide to stay here and work on a farm."

"I'm glad you see that."

"I want to get to know him. I'm going to spend the weekends with him—if that's okay with you," Jeb tacked on hurriedly.

Skye put down the forgotten vegetable brush and crossed the kitchen. She cradled Jeb's face between her palms and planted a motherly kiss to his forehead.

Jeb pulled away and looked up at her with his familiar devilish grin. "Does that mean yes?"

"That means yes," she said.

Jeb's smile faded; the look in his eyes grew serious. "I love you, Skye. Nothing will ever change that."

A great weight seemed to lift from Skye's shoulders. The old saying really was true. If you gave something its freedom and it came back to you, it really was yours all the time.

Chapter Thirteen

The days passed. Jeb's recovery was nothing short of miraculous. Skye put him on a plane to Lincoln in mid-August. The corn ripened and was picked; the stalks turned sere in the late-summer heat.

She visited Opa daily, going to and from work to see that he was bathed and had clean clothes and food to eat. Maybe it was her imagination, but it seemed to Skye that his good days were growing fewer and farther between. He called her Susan sometimes and had total recall of things that had happened in the past, even though he couldn't remember where he put the remote control. It was easier to go along than to confuse him more by trying to make him understand he was wrong.

Jeb called frequently. He'd met Darby, Ceil and her two kids, Samantha and Seth. He had joined Cash and Darby at the counselor's. It was okay.

August dwindled to its last lonely days. September brought cooler nights, but no peace of mind.

Jeb's letters and calls were the only bright spots in Skye's life. Seth and Sam were a trip. It was almost like having siblings. Samantha had taken him to a party with all her friends and he'd had a blast. Seth was teaching him how to play golf. Jeb had finally met Ceil's ex-husband, Gage, who seemed like a nice enough guy even though he'd had an affair.

Benedict Periodicals was an awesome place. Jeb couldn't believe it would all be partly his some day. He and Cash were getting along okay. School was fine. He liked history class and hated English. Darby seemed to be coming around little by little. Liz was a witch who should be burned at the stake. How were things going at the shop?

October came. Skye awakened one morning to a ground covered with frost. Autumn was definitely in residence; winter was not far away.

For Halloween, Skye decorated the yard with hay bales and a scarecrow surrounded by pumpkins that Opa had grown. It broke her heart to think that by next year he might not be able to remember enough to plant and tend his garden.

On Halloween night Skye passed out candy to the few trick-or-treaters who lived down the road, but the most frightening thing about the holiday was the dark circles that had taken up residence beneath her eyes.

Early November brought a light dusting of snow. Skye decorated the store for Thanksgiving and started thinking about what to buy Jeb for Christmas, even though her heart was in neither project.

She missed Jeb, and she missed Cash. It was amazing to her that her sorrow was so acute when they'd had so little interaction with each other, so little time together.

Skye was contacted by someone from *Hearth and Home* who wanted to do a feature article about the shop and her pressed flower art. She saw Cash's hand in the overture, but was neither too proud nor too stupid to refuse. The exposure to the magazine's readership was tantamount to free advertising and worth its weight in gold.

The only other bright spot in Skye's life was that Jeb was coming home for a long Thanksgiving weekend. She threw herself into her plans for their turkey dinner with all the careful consideration she might have used if she'd been expecting the President. She bought a turkey so big she would be eating frozen leftovers for months. She didn't care. Jeb's homecoming was nothing short of a celebration.

Darby lay on her bed and stared at the ceiling, her heart as heavy as the pound cake she'd had for dessert an hour earlier. Jeb was going home to Iowa for Thanksgiving the next day, and her dad wished he was going, too. Darby could see it in the expression that came into his eyes whenever Jeb talked about going home.

Her dad was miserable.

She had known it for months, but she was too stubborn to admit it, just as she'd been too stubborn to admit that he was in love with Skye Herder, and too stubborn to admit that Jeb wasn't the ogre she'd painted him. Seth and Samantha had accepted him with no problems, and the trio often did things together. Sam, who was having boyfriend problems, thought he was wonderful and "thanked God" for bringing him into her life. Seth thought Jeb was cool.

Secretly, Darby did, too. She wasn't sure when her feelings about Jeb had changed. It had happened so gradually she couldn't pinpoint the exact moment she'd stopped seeing him as a usurper to her position as Cash Benedict's only heir and begun to see him as someone who made her life more fun—fuller, somehow.

From the moment Jeb had come to Lincoln to start college, Cash and Ceil made it a point to bring all of them together whenever possible. Martyrlike, Darby had kept herself apart from their fun and games, but finally, when Seth called her an uppity little snot, she'd started joining them. At first she just went along, but gradually, she began to join in and have fun.

They played miniature golf; she and Seth whipped the pants off Sam and Jeb, and Jeb treated them all to pizza afterward. They went bowling. They went to movies. Jeb taught them how to play poker—but her mom didn't know. When they played cards or went to the park to play ball it was Jeb's turn to shine. And through it all, Darby began to learn something: it wasn't fair to make a person choose who he loved most. There was plenty of room in a person's heart to love more than one person. She'd always been crazy about Seth and Sam, and she'd never imagined that she could feel that same depth of emotion for Jeb.

But she did.

Jeb didn't treat her like a baby. He gave as good as he got, but he took up for her when he needed to. He listened to her when she gave an opinion. Really listened. He was funny. He was smart. He was good-looking. He had a mean fastball. And he'd never once made her feel guilty for coming between her dad and his sister.

It was that, more than anything, that finally won her over, but still, she'd refused to make the move that would set things right. She was a lot like her dad when it came to admitting she was wrong. Apologizing to Jeb would mean apologizing to her dad and ultimately to Skye. She'd behaved terribly, but her dad had never said a word, which only made her feel more guilty, a condition that worsened every day.

Darby sighed, pushed herself to her elbow and reached for the telephone. Thanksgiving was two short days away. She wanted her dad to be thankful she was his daughter. Not sorry.

A barely suppressed excitement simmered inside Skye, the closest thing to happiness she'd felt in months. Jeb was coming home that evening, catching a ride with someone he'd met at school, and she had taken the afternoon off from the shop so that she could bake her pies.

She took the last pie from the oven at eight o'clock, just as she heard the sound of a car pulling into the driveway. She untied her apron and flung it onto the countertop, eagerness in her steps, a smile wreathing her face.

Through the lace curtains at the front door, she saw the silhouettes of three people getting out of the car, a familiar champagne-hued Lexus. Her smile faded. Was the car Cash's? If so, why on earth had he brought Jeb home?

Trembling like a leaf in a brisk autumn wind, she cast a glance at her image in the mottled mirror of the antique hall tree gracing the entryway. Her makeup was gone and the hair that she'd snatched up into a haphazard ponytail earlier was straggling around her face. She was scrubbing at a flour smudge that streaked her cheek when the glass doorknob turned and the door swung wide.

In the mirror, she saw Jeb filling the doorway, a wide, silly smile on his face. Cash and Darby stood behind him. Both faces wore looks of apprehension, the same apprehension that made Skye's heart pound painfully inside her chest.

Only Jeb seemed natural... only Jeb looked happy. Slowly, Skye pivoted to face them, her heart thudding with painful beats, a dozen questions tumbling through her mind. Before she could voice any of them, Jeb grabbed her in a big bear hug and planted a smacking kiss on her cheek.

He released her and glanced around at the Thanksgiving decorations. "The house looks great, as usual," he said.

"Thanks," she replied automatically, her eyes going to Cash. His face wore a look of dead seriousness...and an emotion that looked startlingly like apprehension. What did he have to fear? she wondered.

"What are you doing here?" she asked him, her confused gaze moving from his face to Darby's and back again.

"Jeb needed a ride home," Cash answered, as if the simple statement was all the explanation she needed.

"I thought you were catching a ride with Mike," Skye said to Jeb.

"His plans changed. Dad said he didn't mind bringing me. I told him you wouldn't mind them joining us tomorrow." Twin slashes appeared between his dark eyebrows. "It is okay, isn't it? You always fix enough for an army, and we have plenty of extra room."

Skye didn't answer immediately. Darby wrung her hands.

"If it's a problem, we can—"

"No!"

"Skye!"

Both Skye and Darby spoke at once.

"Excuse me," Darby said in her most polite manner.

"It's all right," Skye responded. "It's no trouble. Really. I just never expected..." Her voice trailed away. After the way she'd sent him away, she'd never expected to entertain both Cash and his daughter on her doorstep, much less entertain them in her home for a holiday.

"Hey, Darb," Jeb said, "come on into the living room. I want to show you the Christmas ornaments Opa carved for me when I was a kid."

"Sure." Darby started to follow Jeb, but paused in front of Skye. "I asked Daddy to bring me because I wanted to tell you I'm sorry for all the terrible things I said that day," she blurted out, her eyes brimming with tears. "It was very rude of me. And unfair."

Skye knew what the confession must have cost the child. "Oh, Darby," she said, fighting the sting of tears, "there are times we all say and do things we know we shouldn't."

Darby's smile was sweet and fleeting. "Jeb said you'd understand. Thanks."

"Sure."

Skye watched as Darby followed Jeb into the living room. "She was scared to death to come and apologize to you."

The sound of Cash's voice drew Skye's gaze back. Her wry smile and accompanying laughter were reminiscent of Susan's. "Am I such an ogre?"

"You're not an ogre at all," he declared, moving nearer. He reached out and brushed his knuckles across her cheek in a gesture that was achingly familiar. His eyes held determination and an undeniable sincerity. "You're beautiful and smart and clever, which is why I love you so much."

She gasped and tilted her head back, away from his touch. "Don't say that!"

"Why not? It's true."

"I thought we agreed in July that how we felt made no difference, that it was Darby's feelings that mattered."

"We did. And they still do. But her feelings about Jeb and you have changed."

Disbelief widened Skye's eyes.

Cash took her hand. "Darby and I have been through some pretty intense counseling sessions. Liz has even joined us a few times. While I don't think my ex-wife and I will ever be bosom buddies, I think we've come to an agreement about our daughter. Liz understands how close she came to causing permanent damage to Darby, and Darby has learned about the different kinds of love." He smiled. "She and Jeb have grown pretty close the past few weeks."

"I'm glad," Skye said, giving his fingers a slight squeeze. "What about you? What did you learn?"

His eyes bore an earnestness that held her spellbound. "That I had to forgive myself for all the mistakes I'd made, that I couldn't go back and change any of it. All I can do is move forward, which is why I'm here. I can't change what happened between me and Susan." His sigh was harsh, ragged. "I can't even say I'm sorry. I have Jeb because of that summer, and I can't imagine my life without him. Can you understand that?"

Skye's throat grew tight with unshed tears. She nodded. "Better than you think."

"Can you accept it?"

She nodded.

"I want you to know that what happened between me and Susan has nothing to do with how I feel about you. Not now. Not then. That feeling might have been a teenage crush, but whatever it was, I never forgot it, or you, and whatever it was has grown into something I know for sure is love. Darby knows how I feel, and she accepts the love I feel for you."

Skye wondered if something was wrong with her hearing. Had Cash just said that Darby had really accepted his feelings for her?

She felt his arms go around her, felt the solidity of his body against hers as he pulled her close. He tipped her chin upward, forcing her eyes to meet his.

"Are you serious?" she asked.

"Very. All I need to know is whether or not you love me."

"You know I do," Skye said in a tremulous voice.

"Then marry me."

With her heart beating out a raptured cadence, Skye gave a single, brief nod. And then Cash's lips were on hers and the room went into a slow, crazy spin. Miraculously, Skye knew that her world had never been more grounded.

The kiss ended, and, for long moments, she and Cash were content to just hold each other, knowing that they'd come so close to missing each other completely. If not for Susan, Cash might never have come back this way.

Behind her closed eyelids, Skye saw an unmistakable image of Susan. Susan was smiling that wry, taunting smile of hers, as if to say that she'd known all along that things would come out all right. Susan—her very best friend, the mother she'd always longed for, beloved sister.

* * * * *

COMING NEXT MONTH

#1021 MOLLY DARLING—Laurie Paige
That's My Baby!
Rancher Sam Frazier needed a mommy for his little Lass—and a wife in the bargain. He proposed a marriage of convenience to Molly Clelland—but he never dreamed he'd long to call the instant mother his Molly darling....

#1022 THE FALL OF SHANE MACKADE—Nora Roberts
The MacKade Brothers
Footloose and fancy-free, Shane MacKade had a reputation as a ladies' man to uphold, and he took his job seriously. Who would have thought a brainy beauty like Dr. Rebecca Knight would cause this irrepressible bachelor to take the fall...?

#1023 EXPECTING: BABY—Jennifer Mikels
An urgent knock at the door introduced Rick Sloan to his neighbor—Mara Vincetti, who was about to give birth. Next thing Rick Sloan knew he was a father figure for the new single mom and her baby!

#1024 A BRIDE FOR LUKE—Trisha Alexander
Three Brides and a Baby
When sister-of-the-bride Clem Bennelli met brother-of-the-groom Luke Taylor, it was a case of opposites attract. They agreed theirs would be a passionate, no-strings-attached relationship—but neither one expected to want much, much more....

#1025 THE FATHER OF HER CHILD—Joan Elliott Pickart
The Baby Bet
Honorary MacAllister family member Ted Sharpe was carefree and single. But secretly he yearned to be a husband and a father. And when the very pregnant divorcée Hannah Johnson moved in next door—he lost his heart, but found his dreams.

#1026 A WILL AND A WEDDING—Judith Yates
Commitment and marriage were two words Amy Riordan never believed would apply to her. After meeting similarly minded Paul Hanley, however, she began to think otherwise—and now the word "wedding" was definitely in her future!

MILLION DOLLAR SWEEPSTAKES

As seen on TV!
Free Gift Offer

With a Free Gift proof-of-purchase from any Silhouette® book, you can receive a beautiful cubic zirconia pendant.

This gorgeous marquise-shaped stone is a genuine cubic zirconia—accented by an 18" gold tone necklace.

(Approximate retail value $19.95)

Send for yours today...

compliments of ▼ *Silhouette*®

To receive your free gift, a cubic zirconia pendant, send us one original proof-of-purchase, photocopies not accepted, from the back of any Silhouette Romance™, Silhouette Desire®, Silhouette Special Edition®, Silhouette Intimate Moments® or Silhouette Shadows™ title available in February, March or April at your favorite retail outlet, together with the Free Gift Certificate, plus a check or money order for $1.75 U.S./$2.25 CAN. (do not send cash) to cover postage and handling, payable to Silhouette Free Gift Offer. We will send you the specified gift. Allow 6 to 8 weeks for delivery. Offer good until April 30, 1996 or while quantities last. Offer valid in the U.S. and Canada only.

Free Gift Certificate

Name: _____

Address: _____

City: _____ State/Province: _____ Zip/Postal Code: _____

Mail this certificate, one proof-of-purchase and a check or money order for postage and handling to: SILHOUETTE FREE GIFT OFFER 1996. In the U.S.: 3010 Walden Avenue, P.O. Box 9057, Buffalo NY 14269-9057. In Canada: P.O. Box 622, Fort Erie,

---

FREE GIFT OFFER   079-KBZ-R

ONE PROOF-OF-PURCHASE

To collect your fabulous FREE GIFT, a cubic zirconia pendant, you must include this original proof-of-purchase for each gift with the properly completed Free Gift Certificate.

079-KBZ-R

Silhouette SPECIAL EDITION™

THE MACKADE BROTHERS

the exciting series by

Nora Roberts

Coming this April

THE FALL OF SHANE MACKADE
(Special Edition #1022)

Footloose and fancy-free, Shane MacKade had a reputation as a ladies' man to uphold. Who would have thought a brainy beauty like Dr. Rebecca Knight would cause this irrepressible bachelor to take the fall?

If you liked the first three books,
THE RETURN OF RAFE MACKADE (SIM #631),
THE PRIDE OF JARED MACKADE (SSE #1000), and
THE HEART OF DEVIN MACKADE (SIM #697)
you'll love Shane's story!

 These sexy, trouble-loving men have been heading your way in alternating months from Silhouette Intimate Moments and Silhouette Special Edition. Watch out for them!

You're About to Become a

Privileged Woman

Reap the rewards of fabulous free gifts and
benefits with proofs-of-purchase from
Silhouette and Harlequin books

Pages & Privileges™

It's our way of thanking you for
buying our books at your
favorite retail stores.

**Harlequin and Silhouette—
the most privileged readers in the world!**

For more information about Harlequin and
Silhouette's PAGES & PRIVILEGES program call the
Pages & Privileges Benefits Desk: **1-503-794-2499**

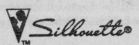